D1527732

Another Chance

A Christian Romance

A Series of Chances #1

Diane Lil Adams

Copyright 2011 Diane L. Adams
All rights reserved.

This is a work of fiction.
All the characters and events are
the result of the author's imagination
Any resemblance to actual persons,
living or dead,
is purely coincidental.

All Scripture taken from the HOLY BIBLE,
NEW INTERNATIONAL VERSION (trademark)
Copyright 1973, 1978, 1984
by International Bible Society
Used by permission of Zondervan
All rights reserved

♥ ♥ ♥

♥ ♥ ♥

Cover images adapted from Bigstock Photo
©Life On White, ©Coisax

♥ ♥ ♥

All the glory to God
and all my thanks to Tank

♥ ♥ ♥

Brigadoon is a romantic musical written by
Alan Jay Lerner & Frederick Loewe. It opened on Broadway
in 1947 and premiered as a film in 1954. Two Americans happen
on a village called Brigadoon while touring Scotland. One of the
men falls in love with a woman from the village, then learns that
Brigadoon only wakes from its mysterious slumber for one day,
every hundred years.

♥ ♥ ♥

If you, O Lord, kept a record of sins,
O Lord, who could stand?
But with you there is forgiveness ...
- Psalm 130: 3,4

♥ Chapter 1 ♥

Anna Brown turned her car onto an asphalt road and leaned forward to peer through the windshield. A tall security fence indicated she might have found her destination, but she couldn't see whether there were buildings beyond the dense woods. Since she had already tried every other road that intersected the state highway, she shifted her old Volkswagen into first gear and forced it to crawl up a steep hill. At the top, a stone entryway bore a regal sign: John B. Casey's Institute.

Anna sighed with relief and drove on, wondering if a deer might cross her path, or a raccoon, or even a bear. When she came to a gray stone house with a manicured lawn, the vista was so incredible, she had to stop for a moment to enjoy it. Lucky was the person who lived in *that* house, she thought enviously, imagining the view from their windows. The blue hills of southern Missouri rolled off into the horizon, beckoning to her soul.

" 'Surely God is in this place,' " she said with awe. She could only hope that she was meant to be in this place too.

The engine coughed and died, but Anna didn't bother to restart it. Shifting into neutral, she allowed gravity to take her downhill onto the campus, into a parking slot designated for visitors. The ivy-covered buildings made her think of an English boarding school, but she didn't expect to hear the strident voices of children at play. Casey's Institute was a prison, a correctional facility for children, but one that catered to the offspring of the wealthy. No child was sentenced to Casey's unless they had the recommendation of influential people, *and* their family could make a sizable "donation." The school was officially labeled an experiment, even though twenty-five years had passed since its conception.

Anna could see that there was no lack of funds. The bricks were neatly tuck-pointed, the trim was freshly painted, the grounds were spotted with trees that would soon flower. Anything that required maintenance obviously received more than adequate attention. It was a beautiful, peaceful setting and there was little evidence that anyone was incarcerated within its boundaries.

Reminding herself that she was already late, Anna climbed from the car. The pungent smell of country air was pleasing, but the sharp bite of the March wind was not. She gazed at the heavy gray clouds and uttered a quick prayer that it wouldn't snow. Then she hurried to the double doors of the administration building and presented her papers to a uniformed guard. After finding her name on his list, he examined the items in her small purse and motioned her through an archway with a metal detector. A second officer asked that she read and sign a legal form for his records. Anna noted that they both wore holstered guns, which she should have anticipated but hadn't.

"You're late," the man said, attaching a copy of the signed form to a visitor's pass and clipping it to her collar.

"I drove up and down the state highway four times, looking for a sign," she said in apology.

"Don't waste your excuses on me," he laughed. He escorted her up a flight of stairs and down a wide hallway to the outer office of the administrator.

The waiting room was crowded with people, and Anna hoped it meant her tardiness hadn't been noticed. "Anna Brown," she told the secretary. "I have an appointment with Michael Grant?"

"You were scheduled at two," the woman said, tilting her head at the large clock mounted on the wall behind her desk.

It was now closer to three.

"I'm not familiar with the area and I couldn't find the turn,"

Anna apologized. "There are no signs, or at least I didn't see any."

"Please be seated," the secretary instructed.

Anna turned to comply, but every chair was taken and a dozen people stood. She searched for a friendly smile, but no one even glanced in her direction. Finally she turned to a group of teenagers, shuffling nervously before a wall of filing cabinets.

"Hello!" she said, putting out her hand as she approached them. "I'm Mrs. Brown."

The girls giggled and the boys snickered.

"We're not allowed to make physical contact," one girl explained, staring pointedly at Anna's outstretched hand.

Anna let it drop, struck by the harshness of the rule.

"We're dangerous," one of the boys warned, causing the girls to giggle further.

Anna took a deliberate step backward as though she believed it, but smiled to let them know she didn't.

"Are you a shrink?" the prettier of the girls asked.

"No, but I look as if I've been to one." She put her hand on top of her head and made a silly face. Anna was just over five feet tall and her size was usually the first thing people commented about.

They laughed, then the tall boy took a step closer. "Are you a teacher?" he asked.

"Not yet, but maybe you could put in a good word for me?"

"Like they listen to us," the pretty girl complained. "What do you teach?"

"I'm applying for a position as a substitute, but if I had my druthers, I'd teach American History."

"What are 'druthers?' " another girl asked.

"Oh, you know. I have to do my homework, but I *druther* watch TV."

"Are you *really* a teacher?" the girl asked doubtfully.

Anna decided it was time to be serious. "It's a Catch-22. No one will hire you because you have no experience but you can't get any experience because no one will hire you."

"Yeah, I know," the second boy agreed. "I couldn't even get a job flipping burgers."

3

"Who makes up these rules?" Anna asked them collectively.

"Probably my mom," the boy said.

All five children suddenly stiffened and Anna turned to see what had frightened them. Slowly her chin tilted upward, until she was staring into eyes the color of toast, just before it burned. Even in her highest heels, with her hair fastened into a knot on the top of her head, the man towered over her. He wore a navy pinstriped suit and a blue tie. His white shirt was crisp with starch; his dark hair was neatly trimmed.

Anna wondered at the way he was looking at her. She was certain they hadn't met before, yet he seemed familiar. It wasn't likely that she would have forgotten the acquaintance of a man so tall and good looking, with such a commanding presence.

"How do you do," she said, extending her hand. "My name is Anna Brown."

♥ ♥ ♥

Dr. Michael Grant rarely made physical contact either, especially with the women who worked on Casey's campus. This time though, something made him capture her delicate fingers between both of his hands. He looked into her smoky green eyes and suffered the eerie sensation that he knew her, that he had known her for a very long time. He nodded his head, almost imperceptibly, and the five students filed silently past him. "Ms. Brown," he said with marked reserve.

Anna Brown. He had just attached a post-it note to her file, labeling her "NS." His secretary knew it meant "not suitable" and she would know why. Anna had arrived nearly an hour late, and hadn't called ahead to explain her tardiness. Michael had dropped the file on Tina Peterson's desk even as Anna greeted him, her smile so earnest and sincere, he almost smiled back. As soon as he returned to his office, Tina would explain that the position had already been filled. Normally a stickler for honesty, Michael overlooked his secretary's white lies to spare her the ire and agony of disappointed job applicants.

He wished he could rewind the entire scene and make an exception this time, but he knew he could not. Reluctantly, Michael released Anna's hand and followed the students into his office, closing the door behind him.

"Sit down," he ordered, gesturing at the couch and chairs that faced his desk.

"She's really nice," one of the girls said boldly.

"I hope you hire her," said one of the boys.

He ignored their remarks, though he wanted to ask what Anna Brown had done to make herself so appealing. Perhaps it would help him understand his own desire to know her better. "You know why you're here," he said sternly, eying each of the children in turn. "I'm waiting to hear an explanation for your behavior in the cafeteria."

Michael had a remarkable memory. If he had met Anna before, he would recall where and when. In spite of fastening her dark hair into a bun, and wearing dangerously high heels, she wasn't much more than five feet tall. He would have remembered her size, if nothing else.

By now, Tina would have informed her that the interview had been canceled. He wondered how she had reacted – with anger or with tears?

He trained his eyes on one of the girls and crossed his arms, aware that it was an intimidating gesture. As she stammered a feeble excuse for her behavior, he moved to the window and stared down at the parking lot. It had started to snow, and it was coming down thick and fast.

Before long, Anna appeared. She slipped twice on the icy sidewalk, but managed to regain her balance without a fall. She got into an ancient yellow Volkswagen, a '69 or '70, but soon climbed back out, wearing a silly red hat with a white pompon. Much to Michael's amazement, she went to the rear of the car, lifted the hood, and began to tinker with the engine. After a moment, she returned to the driver's door and slid into the seat again. He watched for gray exhaust to rise from the tailpipe, but it didn't look as if she were going anywhere.

Under normal circumstances, he would've called downstairs and asked the security guards to help a stranded motorist. Instead, he lifted his hand to silence the students, then instructed them to remain seated until he returned.

"Keep an eye on them," he advised his secretary, and without

5

a word of explanation, headed down the stairs, past the security guards, into the wintry day.

♥ ♥ ♥

Anna had already turned the key a dozen times, in spite of her son's frequent reproach – *Do not grind the starter!* Andy had tried to persuade her to rent a car for today's journey, but she had declined. Now here she was, a hundred miles from home, stuck in a spring snowstorm with less than fifty dollars in her wallet and no credit card. If she called Andy, he might be able to talk her through a repair that would get her as far as a service station. But she couldn't call him unless she returned to the building and how much help could he be if she wasn't standing near the car as they talked? Both of her children had offered their cell phones, but she had adamantly refused. *Why am I so stubborn?* she asked herself. It was a question she had been asked multiple times by every member of her family and most of her friends.

She shivered and pulled her hat over her ears. "Eighty percent of your body heat escapes through the top of your head," she recited, turning the key again.

Someone knocked on the windshield – the tall man with the brown eyes. The window on the driver's side had jammed long ago, so Anna opened the door and stepped out.

"You shouldn't grind the starter," Michael lectured, trying to slide the seat back so he could sit down.

"It's bolted in place," Anna explained.

He grimaced and somehow managed to pry his large body behind the steering wheel. He turned the key, leaning his head to one side as he listened. "Is the gas gauge functional?"

"Yes it is," Anna said, raising her chin. She didn't like it when people made fun of her old Volkswagen.

"It's on empty," he told her. He struggled out of the car and slammed the door, handing her the keys and her purse. "Where's your coat?" Michael had raised his voice, to be heard over the wind.

"At home." She lifted her shoulders to her ears, wishing for a better answer.

"I may have another opening on campus. If you're qualified, would you be interested in interviewing for that position instead?"

Anna knew she should ask for details, but given the circumstances – his hair was quickly turning white – she chose to act impulsively. "Yes I would!"

He took her arm with one hand and rested the other on the small of her back. Anna was grateful since her shoes had leather soles and the sidewalk was slick.

Once they stepped inside the door, Michael gently brushed the snow from her shoulders. "She won't need a badge," he told the guards, who were gaping with shocked expressions.

Anna saw their curious looks and remembered the hat. She tried to snatch it from her head, but it snagged on her hair pins and wouldn't come loose.

"Let me help," Michael offered, leaning over her, as though he did this sort of thing every day.

Maybe he does, Anna thought, standing as tall as she could, focusing on his blue silk tie. She breathed in his scent – something fresh and clean that made her think of a cabin in the woods.

"Sorry," he said, when her long, dark hair tumbled over her shoulders.

Anna handed him her purse and quickly fished the hair pins from the tangles, inserting them between her lips. Using her fingers with practiced ease, she combed the unruly tresses into one long strand and fastened it into a bun. Then she plucked her purse and hat from Michael's hands, feeling more than a little foolish.

He studied her with an expression of delight, then escorted her up the stairs. "Have a seat," he said, once they arrived in the administrator's offices. "I'll be with you as quickly as I can."

There were no seats, so Anna stood before the filing cabinets, out of the way. Though she hoped she appeared poised, her inner self was leaping and dancing with joy. *Praise the Lord!* she worshiped silently. She might not have a job yet, but at least she had been given a second chance!

Her mind raced in a dozen directions. An opening elsewhere

on campus … What sort of job did he mean? What if he was looking for another security guard? Anna tried to imagine telling Paula and Andy that her new occupation meant wearing a gun. Not that she would actually consider that! She wondered how she would get her gas tank filled. Perhaps the tall man had a gas can stowed in the trunk of his car? What if he advised her to call the nearest service station and have the car towed? Anna didn't want to contemplate what *that* might cost! More than the fifty dollars she had, no doubt. And if she spent all of her money on a tow, she wouldn't have enough to fill the tank and drive home, let alone buy something to eat. He would think she was a complete ninny, and rightfully so.

He must be Michael Grant, the administrator, she realized with a touch of awe. *Doctor* Michael Grant, she corrected herself. Was he married? Surely he was! She realized that the secretary was watching her and stepped closer to the desk.

"I'm sorry if I made a mistake, about the position being filled," the young woman said politely.

"You didn't," Anna said. "He mentioned another opening? He didn't say what it was. I don't suppose you'd know?"

The woman shook her head. "No, I definitely wouldn't."

Anna extended her hand across the desk. "Anna Brown. It's nice to meet you."

"Tina Peterson. Likewise." She gave Anna's hand a hearty shake.

The door to the inner office opened and the five students exited, wearing solemn expressions.

"It was nice chatting with you," Anna told them as they filed past.

They didn't answer, but one of the girls waved her hand.

"Are there no seats in the waiting room?" Michael canvassed the crowded room. "I'm sure Miss Peterson wouldn't mind if you sat in her spare chair."

"Will I be in your way?" Anna asked, even as she circled the secretary's desk.

"Not at all," Tina said, staring wide-eyed at her boss.

The administrator ushered a scowling young man into his office and closed the door.

Dr. Michael Grant, Administrator, Anna read the brass plate. Michael, archangel, field commander of the Army of God. It seemed a fitting name for the administrator of a juvenile correctional center.

Anna sat down and watched Tina try to juggle phone duties and paperwork. "Could I help in some way?" she offered. "I've just come from being a secretary."

"Thanks, but nearly everything I do is confidential."

Dr. Grant opened his door, prodding the young man ahead of him. He dropped a folder on Tina's desk, then turned to Anna. "Are you in a hurry? Should I work you in ahead of everyone?"

"I can wait," Anna said, unwilling to become an inconvenience. In her excitement, she had forgotten the snow.

He pointed his finger into the waiting room and a young woman hastened toward him, her eyes filled with unconcealed devotion.

She probably suffers a crush on the man, Anna mused, unaware that she had already begun to suffer one of her own.

"I do appreciate the gesture," Tina said. "You're the first person who has ever offered."

"Most people probably realize that you'd have to say 'no,' " Anna said graciously.

The next time the administrator came out of his office, he stooped beside Anna with a handful of forms. He paged through them while she watched, pointing out questions that would need special attention. When he retreated behind his door again, Anna found Tina staring at her with amazement. "What's wrong?" she asked with concern.

"Were you and Dr. Grant already acquainted?" the secretary asked.

"No, why?" Anna said.

Tina shook her head, as if to dismiss the subject.

Anna found a pen in her purse and turned her chair to the table. She almost groaned aloud as she scanned the questions – working with juvenile delinquents presented stricter requirements than teaching at a regular high school. Many of the forms were psychological evaluations, to ensure that potential teachers weren't unstable. Though Anna had no mental deficiencies that she was aware of, she suffered an uncomfortable feeling that she was revealing them.

She was still working on the first page when Michael reappeared.

"I'm not going to be able to see all of these people today," he told Tina. "Put some of them off until Monday and cancel everything after four o'clock." He pointed to a man with a briefcase and went back into his office.

Though Tina didn't comment, Anna could see that she was surprised by her boss's behavior. She hoped Tina wouldn't instruct *her* to return on Monday.

At 4:30, Dr. Grant ushered a well-dressed couple into the hallway and closed and locked the door behind them. He reached over Tina's head and pressed a button in a box affixed to the wall, smiling at her exclamation of surprise. "Why don't you go?" he said, pointing to the window. "They're calling for eight inches." He paused at Anna's chair, resting his hand on her shoulder. "I'll be with you in a minute," he promised.

Tina was watching, as she hurried into her coat. "I'll look forward to seeing you again," she told Anna.

"I may not be qualified for the job he has in mind," Anna said realistically.

"I have a very good feeling about it," Tina said with a wink.

Anna felt as if the secretary was giving her some sort of signal. "Is something wrong, besides the weather?" she asked.

"No, actually, it looks as if something might be very right," Tina said. Then she hurried out the door.

Anna wasn't vain enough to suspect that she could be the cause of the day's oddities. She just hoped the break in routine wouldn't cause Michael Grant to forget her empty gas tank and leave her stranded.

"Ms. Brown?" He stood in the doorway to his office. "I'm sorry, was that *Mrs.* Brown?" He nodded at the diamond ring on her left hand.

"Either is fine," Anna assured him.

"Are you married?" he asked more directly.

"I'm a widow."

"I'm sorry," he said, with appropriate reserve. "Do you have

10

children?"

"Two. Which reminds me, may I use your secretary's phone to call them? They'll be worried, with the bad weather."

"Of course. Are they with someone who'll keep them all night?"

Anna laughed. "The youngest is nineteen." She went to Miss Peterson's desk and reached for the phone before turning back with a look of dismay. "All night?"

He gestured at the window in the waiting room. "Surely you're not planning to drive home in this."

She contemplated her circumstances. "Volkswagens are very good in the snow," she said, to bolster her confidence.

"That may be true, but the tread on your tires is worn dangerously thin."

Anna stared out the window, determined to remain calm. "Do you know of an inexpensive motel nearby?"

"You can stay in the women's dormitory for free. Why don't you come and use my phone," he offered.

His office was located on the front corner of the main building, and several large windows overlooked the campus. Anna commented on the beauty of the winter scene, then turned to note the details of his domain. A long sofa was upholstered in a soft plaid, facing two blue arm chairs. An oversized desk and matching credenza were arranged so that the administrator had a breathtaking view whenever he raised his eyes. An adjoining room contained a conference table, surrounded by a dozen chairs.

"Did he paint that one especially for you?" Anna asked, pointing to the Norman Rockwell print of the black-eyed girl, waiting to see the principal. Its familiarity made it the friendliest item in the room.

He chuckled in answer, and patted the leather chair behind his desk.

Anna sat down, lifting the receiver when he slid the telephone within reach. "I feel a little guilty. I talked them into coming home for the weekend before I found out about the interview."

"They don't live with you?"

"They're in college."

Anna hoped Andy would be the one to answer, especially if

the administrator planned to eavesdrop.

"Andy? Don't tell Paula it's me. Um ... I don't know yet. Listen, I'm going to stay the night, on account of the snow. I'll call you tomorrow, before I head home." She made a face. "I'll try to be back before you have to leave. Love you!" She hung up, shaking her head. "Poor Andy. Paula will be mad at him for not calling her to the phone."

"Which one is nineteen?"

"Paula. Andy will turn twenty-two this summer."

Michael settled on the edge of his desk. "Where do they go to school?"

"Paula is at Mizzou and Andy is at Harvard, studying law. He graduated early, from both high school and college." She hoped it didn't sound as if she were bragging.

"Like mother, like son?" He lifted a yellow folder from the top of his desk. "Yours is an impressive transcript, especially given the fact that you were working full time and raising two children."

Anna shrugged, uncertain how to respond to such praise.

"Why Casey's?" he asked, tapping the folder against his thigh.

Though he had uttered the question in a casual manner, Anna could tell that he was studying her body language. She tried not to squirm.

"It's all right to admit we were last on your list," he said. "I won't penalize you for being honest."

"Only because it's so far from home," she said earnestly. "Casey's is exactly the sort of school I had in mind when I decided to become a teacher. I want to work with kids who are special."

"Special?" He tipped his head back and laughed. "You're the first person to describe my kids that way!"

Anna's heart gave a little lurch. "I like that you refer to them as *your* kids."

"That's the way I think of them," Michael said without embarrassment. He tossed her folder to his otherwise empty desk and studied her for a moment. "Do you like animals?" he finally asked.

Anna couldn't conceal her surprise. "Animals?"

12

"You know, furry little creatures with four legs?"

She tried to smile, but couldn't quite carry it off. "Why do you ask?"

He crossed his arms. "A number of prisons have established a program where inmates work with pets as part of their rehabilitation. It's been very successful. Have you heard about it?"

Anna shook her head. *Animals! Hadn't she just told him how she longed to work with kids who had special needs?*

"While it's more of a challenge to implement such a program in a juvenile facility, I'm considering it on an experimental basis. Theoretically, the local humane society will bring us homeless dogs and the students will care for them and train them. I'm looking for someone to oversee the process."

"It sounds very interesting, but ..."

"I want the kids to be present when the animals arrive," he went on, as though she hadn't spoken. "They should see them at their worst – dirty, infested with fleas, malnourished. They'll help clean them up and nurse them back to health, then they'll teach them to become companions to the elderly or assistance dogs for the disabled. It's a win-win situation. The kids benefit when they see the dogs become useful to society and the dogs are given a fresh start, rather than being euthanized."

"I need to be honest with you," Anna said. She scooted to the edge of the chair, as if she might need to make a quick getaway. "I've never had a pet."

"That's not a prerequisite."

"I'm actually a little afraid of them."

"Dogs?"

"Dogs, cats, guinea pigs, hamsters."

He smiled. "Don't you know that you should face your fears, Mrs. Brown?"

She smiled too. He couldn't *force* her to take the job, after all. "I *do* know that, and I'm sure it's a worthwhile project, but you need someone who believes in it. Someone who has a lot of enthusiasm and a love of animals."

"You must be hungry," he said. "Let me make a few calls and then we'll get you something to eat."

Anna thought she should sigh with relief, but instead, she

feared she might cry. "Is it all right if I stay at the women's dorm, even if I'm not interested in the position?"

Michael laughed. "I intend to spend the dinner hour trying to change your mind. Will you give me a fair hearing before you make a final decision?"

Anna brought her hands together and raised them to her face, touching her fingertips to her chin. She recalled the moment when the handsome administrator had taken her hand in the waiting room. A delicious sensation had settled over her soul, leaving her to feel as if she had finally come home. It had been such a shock, a moment later, when the secretary informed her that the job had already been filled.

God sent the snow today, Anna. God wanted you marooned at Casey's. Don't be afraid; just believe.

"I guess there's no harm in discussing it," she said.

"Why don't you wait for me in the outer office then. I promise I won't be long."

"Yes, of course." She jumped up and hurried out the door, closing it quietly behind her.

The moment she had gone, Michael jammed his hands into his pockets and strode to the window. Staring into the woods, now blanketed in white, he struggled to make sense of his behavior. He had seen the startled looks on the faces of the security guards when he escorted Anna Brown back into the building. He had broken his own "no exceptions" rule when he said she might return upstairs without a badge. He could scarcely believe he had offered to help remove her hat.

Her hair had smelled like something tropical and felt like silk as it slipped through his fingers.

He had never offered an applicant a different position than the one they were applying for. He had never invited anyone to sit in his chair and use his telephone and would refuse such a request. He didn't cancel appointments, even if it meant remaining in his office until midnight.

All his life, he had been drawn to tall, willowy blonds –

sophisticated women with natural style and presence. He had never dated a woman who wasn't well-educated, quick-witted and possessing a certain arrogance. There was no logical explanation for his attraction to this tiny woman who was anything *but* sophisticated. She drove a car held together with paper clips, wore a silly hat but no coat, and spoke from the heart, even if she must realize that the answers she gave were not what he would wish to hear.

He did not socialize with the faculty or staff at Casey's. He couldn't, if he wanted to maintain their respect. Before long, people would start calling him "Mike," dropping in on his residence, asking for favors. He had seen men in similar positions of power make that mistake.

Technically, Anna was about to become a member of Casey's staff, but the job would only last ten weeks. It was probably all she wanted – enough experience to dress up her résumé. At the close of the school year, he would explain that pet therapy wasn't a viable option at Casey's, as was sure to be the case. He couldn't see how spending a few hours with a temp would jeopardize his standing as administrator.

Without further deliberation, he pulled his cell phone from his pocket and dialed the number for his private club. He reserved a table for dinner, confident that Anna would be impressed by the classy restaurant that served gourmet food.

When he stepped into the waiting room, she stood at the window, her hands clasped behind her back as she gazed over the campus. She wore a navy suit with a straight skirt, and a plain white blouse.

"Anna?" he said. "If I may I call you 'Anna'? " He noted that her teeth were very white, if a little crooked.

She turned and smiled. "Please do," she said.

Her green eyes sparkled and her cheeks were flushed with a healthy glow that wasn't artificial.

"Our cafeteria fare isn't much to offer on a Friday night. I'd like to take you somewhere a little nicer for dinner."

"That's not necessary," she protested. "I'll be perfectly satisfied with peanut butter crackers from a vending machine."

"I'm afraid I've already made a reservation."

15

"Oh! Then sure, that would be nice."

He had expected her to be thrilled, not reluctant. But her reticence only increased his interest in getting to know her.

♥ Chapter 2 ♥

Anna slipped into the restroom and studied her appearance with dismay. Her bun was off-center, there were dark circles under her eyes, and she had somehow acquired a run in her stocking. She felt tired and upset and sorry to have come to Casey's. She was even sorrier that she hadn't been able to avoid the administrator's dinner invitation.

She didn't have the social finesse to make casual conversation with someone like Michael Grant. Once he realized that she could not be talked into the job he was offering, what would they talk about? She didn't play golf or tennis and she doubted whether he liked to go bowling. He probably read the Wall Street Journal in his leisure time, while she liked to curl up with a Christian romance novel.

She wished again that she had carried one of her children's cell phones. If only she could call home and describe her predicament and ask her kids for advice! But didn't she already know what they would say? Andy would tell her to go to dinner with the administrator, hear him out and promise an answer in the morning. Paula would wonder if he was good looking and fuss because her mother hadn't asked what the job would pay.

I'll take Andy's advice, she decided, searching her purse, though she knew she wouldn't find a comb. She bent at the waist and finger-combed her hair again, fastening her bun so tightly, it brought tears to her eyes. She would encourage Dr. Grant to do the talking while she proved herself a good listener. And she would eat fast, so that the dinner came to a quick end and she could retire to the women's dormitory.

Michael was waiting for her in the hallway, holding a black topcoat. He insisted on draping it across her shoulders, chuckling when it fell to her ankles. When they reached the bottom of the stairs, the security guards had gone. Michael held the door, then slipped an arm around her shoulders. Anna didn't protest, since the sidewalk was slick.

Casey's campus was well lit, especially against the white landscape. "Listen," Anna said. "It's so quiet!"

"And cold," he complained. "It's supposed to dip into the twenties."

Anna shivered, as her shoes filled with snow. "Is it a '62?" she asked, when he stopped before a cherry red Corvette, sheltered in a covered alcove.

"I'm impressed," he said, helping her in.

"I have four brothers," she explained, once he was seated beside her. "Cars were always the main topic of conversation at our dinner table."

Michael backed from his parking space and accelerated with caution. "Were you the only girl?"

"Three girls. Always outnumbered when it came to a vote."

"What did your father do for a living?"

Anna smiled at the way a man's mind works. "He was a janitor at the elementary school, and my mom was a cook in the cafeteria. Do you have siblings?"

"Just one – an older brother." He adjusted the heater, though it wasn't yet blowing warm air. "Did you grow up in St. Louis?"

"Arlington, Virginia. I lived there until I married. Where did you spend your childhood?" It suddenly occurred to Anna that this wasn't meant to be a conversation. He probably intended it to serve as an extension of her interview, where he asked all the questions.

"I was born and raised in Kansas City," he said. "How did you end up in St. Louis?"

Anna stared out her window at the gathering darkness. She hoped he wasn't going very far, given the accumulation of snow. "My husband's job was there."

He pumped the brakes as they descended the hill, and turned onto the state highway. Then he turned his head to look at her. "Is there a good reason why you've never had a pet?"

She wished he would keep his eyes on the road, but she could hardly say so. "One of my sisters was highly allergic, so it was out of the question while I lived at home. After I got married, my husband felt animals belong in the zoo, or on a farm. And once Paul died, it didn't seem fair. Since I worked and the kids either went to school or to a sitter, the dog would've been locked up all the time."

"Your husband didn't die recently then?"

"Paula was still a toddler." Anna studied the snow-packed highway with apprehension. She hated traveling during winter storms, no matter who was driving. "Where are we going?" she asked, hoping he wouldn't think it a rude question.

"I belong to a private club and they have an excellent chef. You'll enjoy it, I promise."

Anna wasn't the type to appreciate expensive restaurants or gourmet food. She would be just as satisfied with a hamburger or a chicken sandwich. She rubbed her empty stomach.

"Have you ever had a bad experience with an animal?" Michael asked.

Anna turned in her seat, both to avoid looking at the snowy roads and so that she could study him while they talked. She was struck anew by how handsome he was, and suspected he had sent her out of his office so he could alert his wife that he wouldn't be home for dinner. "Not really, no," she answered his question. "I think some people are natural animal lovers and some are not. I had friends who talked about their pets as if they were family members, and even allowed them to sleep in their bed. I had nothing against them, really, but I didn't especially like sharing sleeping quarters with a dog or cat when I stayed over."

"You don't think a person can develop an affection for animals?"

"Possibly, but I doubt whether I'm that person."

19

He had raised both hands to the steering wheel and Anna noted that he didn't wear a wedding band. Even if he didn't have a wife, she warned herself, it was likely that he had a serious girlfriend.

"Given my lack of enthusiasm, not to mention my ignorance of the subject, I can't understand why you'd want me to accept the job," she said honestly.

"In part, for that very reason. Any real animal lover will be more interested in the animals than the children. My first priority is always the students."

Anna hadn't thought of that aspect. "How much of the job would be working with pets and how much of it working with kids?" For the first time, the position began to have some appeal.

"Your job would be to oversee the students as they work with the animals. How many credits are you short of an Associate's degree in Psychology?"

"I don't know," Anna admitted.

"We may be able to get you qualified as a licensed counselor. I'll have to look into it."

A licensed counselor … It had almost as much appeal as being a teacher.

"Animal activists were opposed to the idea at first," he said. "They assumed that incarcerated criminals would be cruel to animals, but they were wrong. Statistically, those dogs trained in a prison make better service animals than those trained by regular volunteers. Dogs offer prisoners the unconditional love they've been craving, and the inmates are naturally willing to return the favor."

"It makes sense," Anna said thoughtfully.

"It makes perfect sense, yet it never occurred to me," he confessed. "Of course, there will be exceptions to every rule. You'd want to keep a close watch over the animals to be sure none of them were being abused by the students."

"How would I know whether someone was taking proper care of an animal?" Anna wondered. "I don't know anything about them. How often do they eat? How often do they go outside? How do you know if an animal is sick? Would I even recognize abuse?"

"Animals display the same sort of symptoms people do, if they're injured or sick. If a dog cowers whenever a particular student comes near, you'll want to keep a close eye on the situation. The students will have to apply and be interviewed before being accepted into the program. I'll probably require six months prior without any written discipline issues."

"What if an animal should harm a child?" Anna couldn't pretend she wasn't afraid of being harmed herself.

"We'll disqualify any animals that are aggressive."

"Even so, mixing animals with children ... Aren't you inviting law suits?"

Michael shrugged. "We have a whole nest of vipers standing by, should the need arise."

"A nest of vipers?"

"I am not particularly fond of attorneys," he said dryly.

Anna thought of Andy, studying law at Harvard. She wouldn't want anyone to describe him as a "viper."

"I would have guessed you studied law yourself, in order to hold your position," she said.

"I did."

"I see." Anna wondered at his tone.

"I'm sorry," he said, and reached across the console to rest his hand over hers. "I didn't think of your son. I meant no offence."

"None taken," Anna said politely, though it wasn't entirely true. Andy, a viper? She knew it was the way most people felt about lawyers, and she realized that a good many lawyers deserved it, but ... "Not all lawyers are vipers, you know."

"I'm sure that's true. It's been my misfortune to deal with the ones that are."

She looked at their hands, and began to wonder about his intentions. Before she could decide whether to pull away, he did. Shifting to a lower gear, he carefully changed lanes and drove up the exit ramp. She looked around, but there was nothing to see, other than woods and fields.

"Where is your club?" she asked.

"Not much farther," he answered vaguely.

He turned onto a two lane road that hadn't been plowed. Anna sat forward in her seat, the muscles in her shoulders tight with

21

tension.

"Have you applied to a lot of schools?" Michael asked.

"I've been rejected so many times, I'm developing a complex." Anna laughed, so he would know that she wasn't serious.

"Do you mind sharing the names of some of the schools you were considering?"

She named a few in St. Louis and the outlying areas. "I returned for a second interview several times, but in the end, the position always went to someone with more experience. It's hard starting a career at my age."

Michael reached over and squeezed her hand, releasing it quickly this time. "At Casey's, I'm far more interested in a mature applicant who is aware that she has a lot to learn than in one who thinks she already knows it all. He or she, I should say."

Anna was beginning to relax in his company. If not for the bad weather, she might be able to enjoy herself. "Did I remember to say 'Thank you' after you came out and tried to start my car?"

"I'm sure you did."

For the first time, Anna realized how unlikely it was that the administrator would come to the parking lot to offer assistance while his waiting room was filled with people. "Did you come after me because you had decided to offer me this other position?"

"I looked out the window and saw you working over the engine and thought maybe you could use some help."

"May I say 'Thank you' now, in case I neglected to say it then?"

He smiled. "You're welcome."

"So you didn't actually intend to offer me the position when you came outside?"

"Does it matter?"

She thought it *did* matter, but she wasn't sure why it should. "I was about to ask the security guards to call a gas station. It was lucky for me that you chose that moment to look out the window."

"And for me. If your gas tank hadn't been empty, you would have driven off and forgotten all about Casey's, leaving me with no one to oversee the pet program."

Anna laughed. "Trust me, I would *not* have forgotten about Casey's! It was a very brave and daring thing I did today, driving a hundred miles on my own, being interviewed by a whole roomful of people at once. And then, getting lost in the wilds of Missouri! I took every exit off the state highway and some of those roads are *not* well maintained."

"Didn't you see the signs?"

"I didn't see any signs at all, once I left Briarton."

"There are several on the right hand side of the highway," Michael said with confidence.

Anna decided she would ask him to point them out on the way back. "So much of our destiny relies on chance," she mused. "Sometimes it seems as if we have no control over our own fate."

"With very few exceptions, I believe we create our own fate," Michael disagreed. "Our destiny is created by the choices we make."

"I didn't *choose* to run out of gas," she protested.

"In a sense you did. You said the gas gauge operates properly, so why didn't you stop for gas before driving out into the country?"

The board members had only allowed her thirty minutes to reach Casey's campus, though they warned her it was a good half hour away. She hadn't had time to stop for gas, or for lunch. "I didn't realize how 'out in the country' it was." She would have had plenty of gas if she hadn't gotten lost. "We can't always anticipate what will happen, and even if we could, we can't always prevent it." Anna enjoyed a friendly debate on such issues. She had forgotten that she was being interviewed for a job.

Michael chuckled. "This reminds me of my college years. We used to stay up all night and argue about things that can't be proven, one way or the other. It's the oldest debate on record, I imagine. Does a man have any real power? If so, will he be penalized by the universe, should he misuse it?"

"Will he? What do you think?"

"I think our power is very limited, given 'chance,' as you called it." He glanced at her. "Now you're going to accuse me of contradicting myself, aren't you."

"It all depends on the timing," Anna decided. "Whether we made the choice before the random event occurred."

"You're not a Christian, Anna?"

"Yes, I am!" she said, pressing both hands over her heart. "I hope I'm a Christian before I'm anything else!"

"Then how does God's will fit into your theory?"

Anna thought about it for a moment. "I guess I'd call 'destiny' God's will and those random events … maybe they're Satan's doing."

"Satan?" he said with amusement. "Does he have horns and a forked tail?"

Anna tried not to feel offended. "He could look like that, but I think he more often resembles us."

"Us?" Michael said with surprise.

"You or me. Anyone. We all have the capacity for evil." She clenched her hands together, chilly, in spite of the fact that the heater was set at its highest position. "The snow. Now there's a perfect example of something we didn't choose."

"Our choice lay in how we reacted to it," he insisted.

"If it hadn't been for the snow, you wouldn't have invited me to dinner." She hadn't thought of that before, but suspected it was true.

"I'd hate to think my decisions regarding Casey's are influenced by something as incidental as the weather," he objected. "What about you? If it hadn't been snowing, would you have accepted the invitation?"

Anna decided she had taken the discussion too far. She didn't want to be backed into a corner where she might inadvertently admit to a romantic interest in the handsome administrator. "This whole day is so far out of the ordinary for me, it's impossible to guess what I would've done." She leaned her head on the back of the seat and exhaled noisily. "I feel as though I stumbled into Brigadoon."

Michael's laugh seemed genuine. "I hope not! I don't want to wake up tomorrow and find myself a hundred years back in the past."

Anna was glad that he was familiar with the imaginary village in Scotland. "Casey's seems like a different world, if you know what I mean."

"I guess I don't. What makes Casey's so different?"

Anna couldn't say that he was a large part of the reason. "It's not Casey's per se, I guess. Just that sometimes life carries you along until, one day, you wake up and realize – this isn't who I meant to be! But you can't just change into that ideal image you once had of yourself. There are too many people who expect you to behave as you did the day before."

"Your life at Casey's won't be filled with people who have those expectations," he followed her thoughts. "No one knows you."

"It would be a lot easier to change, to become someone else."

"Given the opportunity, who would you like to become?"

"I don't know," she said, waving her hand in the air. "If I'd always been meek, I could become assertive, or vice versa. I could choose my political party based on a new set of criteria. I could turn into a health nut, or a hypochondriac."

"Are you intentionally wording this so that I won't have any clue about who you are?" he seemed to tease.

"What would you like to know?" Anna offered. "I'll share anything except the number of my Swiss bank account."

Michael laughed again, and Anna was pleased that she had amused him. "Everyone wants a second chance in life, don't you think?" she persisted. "An opportunity to start over and get it right?"

"There are no second chances," Michael said, suddenly very serious. "You can change, but you can't start over."

Anna knew this to be tragically true. There were some choices that set a person's life on a course that could never be undone. "Even so, I feel as if I've been given a clean slate," she said. "My future is suddenly filled with unlimited possibilities."

"Unlimited possibilities." Michael repeated the phrase as he turned into a long driveway, recently cleared, and drove to the door of what looked to be an antebellum mansion.

Leaving the car to be parked by an attendant, he took Anna's arm and escorted her inside, where the maître d' greeted him by name. They were taken through a dimly lit room to a table in a corner, where their conversation would be very private. Anna gazed around with an uneasy feeling. The furnishings were overdone, to her taste, with deep burgundy carpeting, velvet-backed chairs, and elaborate tableware. She hoped she wouldn't make a fool of herself.

"Would you care for a cocktail?" Michael asked.

"Thank you, no," she said politely, opening her menu.

"Not even a glass of champagne? This is a celebration of sorts, isn't it?"

"I don't drink." She hoped he wouldn't either, so he would have his wits about him during the drive back to Casey's.

"You never drink? No exceptions?"

She shook her head. "Just water," she told the waiter. She hoped he would bring a basket of rolls or some crackers. She hadn't had anything to eat since breakfast.

"How about an appetizer? Do you like oysters?"

"I've never tasted them, but I'm not much for seafood, in spite of being raised on the coast."

"Why don't you bring us an order of six," Michael instructed the waiter.

Anna didn't want to taste an oyster, or scallops or clams or sushi. "The chicken sounds good." There were no prices on the menu, which was somewhat alarming. She wanted to offer to pay for her own dinner, but what if he accepted? She would need her money tomorrow, to buy something to eat and put gas in her car.

The waiter arrived with their drinks and a basket of warm rolls.

Michael closed his menu and set it aside. "The lobster comes with steak. How does that sound?"

She sighed. "I don't think I'd care much for lobster either."

"But you do like steak?"

"Yes, but … I don't want you to feel I'm taking it for granted that you'll pay for my dinner. I'm afraid I didn't anticipate an overnight stay and I didn't bring a lot of cash with me."

"It's my treat," he assured her. "May I order for you?"

Since he was going to pay, she didn't think she should refuse. "That's fine, thank you." She handed him her menu and reached for a roll. "May I help myself?" she asked, as her hand hovered over the basket.

"Of course," he said, pushing the butter dish closer to her plate.

She tore the roll in half and took a large bite before carefully buttering the other half.

"So, what was it like to grow up with six siblings?"

"Four of them boys," she reminded him.

"Never a dull moment?"

She rolled her eyes as she devoured the roll.

"Were your parents strict?"

"They were. Very loving, but also very strict."

The appetizer arrived and while Michael ordered the rest of their meal, Anna studied the oysters.

"Why do they bring them in seashells?" she wondered, once the waiter had gone away.

"Maybe because it makes it look like more?" He lifted one to her plate, and handed her a tiny fork. "They're very good for you."

"So I've heard." Anna watched him, to learn the procedure, before stabbing an oyster and wrenching it from the shell. Closing her eyes and praying she wouldn't gag, she shoved it far back on her tongue and washed it down with a great gulp of water. "Delicious," she lied, while tears stung her eyes.

"Are your parents still living?" he asked, ladling two more oysters onto her plate.

"No!" Anna protested.

"I'm sorry," he said soberly.

"What? My parents? They're yes, still alive. Happily retired." She knew she must sound as ridiculous as she felt.

He gestured to her plate. "Eat your oysters."

Anna didn't want another oyster, but she wanted less to admit that she had lied about liking the first one. With remorse, she removed one from the shell and poked it down her throat. She took another long drink of water and imagined the oysters swimming gaily about in her stomach. "Here, you have the last one," she said, and shoveled it back to his plate.

He nodded, but said nothing.

"What do your parents do?" Anna asked, wishing he would take a turn to talk. She sat back so the waiter could serve her salad.

"My father is an attorney. The viper variety. My mother does charity work, or at least that's what she calls it."

Anna was shocked by this disclosure, and the tone of his voice. She hadn't imagined that he would confide in her about something so personal, and she didn't know how to respond. "I'm sorry," she said. "I didn't mean to pry into your personal affairs."

For a long moment, neither of them spoke.

"It must have been very difficult for you when your husband died," Michael finally said. "Being left on your own with two small children?"

"I was lucky to have a wonderful neighbor," Anna explained, relieved by the change in subject. "Her own children were grown and she said she was glad to be needed. She's already offered to watch over things while I'm away. That is, if you decide I'm suited for the job."

"The job is yours for the next ten weeks, if you want it," he assured her. "I'm sorry. I thought you understood that."

Anna *did* want it, very much. "Thank you," she said, barely resisting the urge to cry.

He smiled at her. "Does that mean 'yes'?"

"Yes," she said happily. "Yes, yes, yes."

He sat back in his chair. "Will I order that bottle of champagne after all?"

Anna pursed her lips. "Feel free to order some for yourself, but I'm not a drinker." She hoped he wouldn't keep asking.

"How much notice will you need to give your current employer?" Michael asked.

"None. The kids felt … Well, it was my daughter, not my son. She convinced me that I should quit so I'd be available whenever I got called for an interview."

"Are you in desperate straits then?"

Anna balanced her knife on the edge of her plate. "I haven't reached the stage I'd call 'desperate.' " Though she was fast approaching it …

"But willing to venture a little further from home?"

Anna could tell that he thought Casey's was a last resort. "Please don't think I'm not sincere in wanting to work at Casey's.

28

I can't tell you how excited I was when I got the call to set up the interview. Other than the distance, Casey's would have been my first choice. I'm hoping that if I ..." She hesitated.

"If you what?" he pressed.

Anna took a deep breath. "If I make a good impression, is there any possibility I might be hired to teach next year?"

"I didn't think you'd be interested. Ten weeks experience and a letter of recommendation should spruce up your résumé well enough to get you a job closer to home."

Anna began to explore her salad, so he wouldn't see the disappointment in her eyes.

"What's wrong?" he asked.

"Nothing!" she said. There were pale green chunks of something mixed with the lettuce. Anchovies, she decided, pushing them aside with her fork.

"Would you consider moving to Casey's on a permanent basis?" Michael asked.

She sighed and set her fork beside her plate. "It's hard to explain, but I feel as if I'm meant to be at Casey's."

"*Meant* to be?" He sat back in his chair. "You would relocate permanently because it happened to snow one night?"

"I'm not saying I *would*," she replied defensively. "But if I *did*, it would be because I felt I was doing God's will."

Michael took a long drink of sparkling Perrier, studying her over the rim of the glass. "Perhaps we should let some time elapse before we discuss the future. These kids are nothing like your children or their friends. It may turn out to be beyond your comfort level."

Anna thought she understood what he was trying to say. Given her physical size, he probably assumed she wouldn't be able to handle the students. She took another roll and began to butter it. She would have ten weeks to prove herself. If only the job didn't include animals ...

The maître d' appeared at their table, wearing a worried expression. "Excuse me, Dr. Grant, but I thought I should apprise you of the weather conditions. The roads are quickly becoming impassable."

"Thank you," Michael dismissed him.

"Did he say 'impassable'?" Anna asked with concern.

"I'm sure it's an exaggeration. People who aren't accustomed to this sort of weather have a tendency to panic."

"Yes, but don't you think you should see for yourself?" Anna had been raised where deep snows were not unusual, but that had only given her a healthy respect for slick streets. "I've always heard that Corvettes aren't good in the snow."

"We didn't have any trouble on the way here, did we? I have excellent tread on my tires and many years of experience driving during winter conditions."

Anna folded her napkin and placed it beside her plate. "I think you should take a look outside. It would be very awkward, should we be stuck here for the night."

"They do have rooms," Michael said.

Anna felt her face grow hot as she suspected she had been too gullible. Had Michael Grant already reserved a room? *One* room? "I wouldn't be comfortable with that," she said firmly. "If the weather forces us to remain overnight, I'll sit right here at this table until morning."

Michael rose from his chair. "Please go ahead and start eating if the waiter arrives with our food."

Maybe he hadn't meant that they should share a room, she tried to tell herself. "Yes he did," she murmured aloud. She had so wanted to believe that Michael Grant was different than other men, but why should he be? She was suddenly exhausted, and desperate to go home. If only they didn't have to drive all the way back to Casey's first!

"I spoke to a few people who have just arrived," Michael said, standing behind his chair. "They don't feel there's any immediate danger, but they do recommend we leave soon. Our meal should be coming any moment. Do you want to eat before we go?"

Without answering, Anna stood and tucked her purse beneath her arm. She followed him to the exit, reluctantly allowing him to place his coat across her shoulders. As they stepped outside, an icy wind stung her face with sleet.

"Are you sure it's safe to drive?" she worried, once they were seated in the car.

"If I wasn't, we wouldn't be leaving," he said with a touch of authority. He accelerated slowly, offering no comment when the front of the car slid to one side.

Anna wondered if he was doing it intentionally, before it was too late to change her mind. She set her jaw. As badly as she wanted the job, she wasn't willing to sacrifice her reputation. While she was no one of interest to the media, Dr. Michael Grant was. If she spent the night at his club, and a scandal erupted one day ... She hadn't even asked if he was married!

Neither of them spoke as he drove slowly along the outer road. Regardless of his assurances, Anna could see that he was tense.

"I'm sorry," he said, as they approached the interstate, where traffic was moving slowly in one lane. "I've shown very poor judgment this evening."

"No apology necessary," Anna said politely, though she felt it was her due.

"I should've taken the weather prediction seriously and I shouldn't have gone so far from Casey's."

Anna wished he would apologize for inviting her to spend the night at his club. As far as she was concerned, the rest was forgivable, but *that* was not. "Who thinks we'll get a massive snowstorm in March?" she said generously.

"You've lived in the Midwest long enough to know that we often get our worst winter storms in March," he chided.

Anna couldn't think of anything else to say. He was right – they shouldn't have left Casey's campus.

"I'm afraid we aren't likely to get back to Casey's until after midnight," he said. "Most of the faculty women will be asleep."

"Are you saying I can't stay in the dormitory?" Anna asked with alarm.

The car began to skid, and only Michael's quick reflexes kept them from sliding off the road.

"Anna ... I think it might be best if I turn around at the next exit and take you home, rather than try to make it back to Casey's."

"Home?" she repeated with surprise. "You mean to St. Louis?"

He eased the car up an exit ramp and sighed aloud when he reached the stop sign. "I'm very sorry," he said. "You have every excuse to be furious."

31

"I'm too frightened to be angry," she said honestly. She could feel her heart racing. "What if we get stuck? We could freeze to death."

"I can't promise we won't get stuck, but we're not likely to freeze. And if we head to St. Louis, we'll be driving out of the storm."

Anna no longer felt confident that she was in God's will. "I'll keep quiet so you can focus on your driving," she said in a small voice. She would also begin to pray, which is what she should have been doing all along. If she had asked her Heavenly Father's advice, they probably wouldn't have left Casey's campus and she would now be snug in a bed at the women's dormitory.

Michael accelerated to a crawl, crossing the bridge and turning down the entrance ramp. Then he eased the tires into the deep tracks left on the highway from previous vehicles. After a few moments, he glanced at Anna. "Are you being quiet for my sake, or because you're less frightened and therefore angry?"

Anna shook her head, though he had already turned his face back to the windshield. "I'm not angry," she said, surprised that she wasn't. "I'm upset, but with myself, not with you."

"May I ask why?"

"I'd rather you didn't." She had no desire to try to explain her complicated thoughts, since she had yet to decipher them for herself.

"It's something of an adventure, anyway. Somewhat in keeping with Brigadoon." He lifted first one hand, then the other, stretching his fingers before taking a tight hold on the steering wheel again.

Anna inhaled deeply, to calm her nerves. She understood that he was changing the subject to try to put her at ease. "According to my daughter, my life is far too dull. She'd probably say a little danger is good for me."

"What would she have you do to change your boring existence? Apply at Casey's?"

"Actually, she didn't like the idea. Apparently there's a limit to how much danger she would prescribe."

He chuckled. "If Casey's isn't the sort of excitement she has in mind, what is? Would she like you to travel? Rob banks? Sing in public?"

Anna laughed, and turned to look at him. It was late in the day and his five o'clock shadow had darkened. He looked tired, but no less handsome. She knew exactly what Paula would say, and it suddenly occurred to her that he and Paula might meet. She would rather warn him than try to stutter out an explanation *after* Paula managed to embarrass her. "She wants me to date. She'll probably ask whether you're single, hoping she can fix me up with you." She laughed again, so he wouldn't think she was hinting. She didn't care how eligible he was, she wouldn't want to go out with him again.

"Why don't you date?" Michael asked, ignoring the question of his marital status.

Anna had no intention of discussing *that* subject. "Even if this were part of my interview, that question wouldn't be appropriate."

"Point taken," Michael said, sounding contrite. "Though I'm sure it can't be for want of invitation."

Anna made a face in the darkness.

"I don't want you to be afraid of me," he said quietly.

"I'm not afraid of you. I was concerned for my reputation, not for my safety."

"Did you see someone you knew?"

"That's hardly the point." She was beginning to feel angry again. "I generally heed my own conscience and ignore the opinion of others, except when it comes to my children. I try to set a good example for them at all times, even if they're a hundred miles away. If we had been forced to spend the night at your club, and they found out about it later, they might rightfully ask why I went there with you on a snowy night."

"I tend to go there because it's restricted to members," Michael explained. "There's little risk I'll run into anyone from Casey's and be forced to spend my evening acting as administrator."

"I hadn't thought of that," Anna said. "But in any case, I'm not questioning your behavior, only my own."

"Under other circumstances …"

"We can only deal with the circumstances of the moment," she interrupted. She glanced at him, certain he must regret giving her that second chance at a job. "Please don't misunderstand. The restaurant was very nice."

"Did you enjoy the oysters?"

Before Anna could determine whether he was inviting a confession, the car swiveled to the right, then slid from the shoulder onto the grassy space beside the road. There was a crunching sound as the tires glided across the snow, then the engine died, creating a deafening silence.

Michael gasped, still clutching the steering wheel with both hands. "Are you all right?" he asked anxiously.

"I'm fine," Anna assured him, though she was terrified. "What about you?"

"I'm fine. Overdosed on adrenaline, but otherwise fine."

"Do you think the car is damaged?"

He turned the key and the engine revived.

Anna sat back with relief, then covered her mouth with both hands, to stifle a scream.

Michael turned and found a face pressed against the glass. Without hesitation, he put the window down.

"You folks okay?" a man asked. "Anybody hurt?"

"We're okay. Just trying to catch our breath."

"I'll wait until you get back on the road, in case you have trouble."

"Thanks," Michael said. "I appreciate it very much."

"No problem," the man said, touching his hat with his gloved hand before disappearing into the night.

"At least we're headed in the right direction," Michael said, easing the car into first gear. "Anna, are you sure you're all right?"

"I'm positive," she said, taking a firm hold on the dashboard as they bumped across the grass.

The road was only yards away when the car lurched and the tires began to spin. "I've hit something," Michael guessed, shifting between reverse and first gear. "I'll have to get out and take a look."

"Wait!" Anna said, reaching for his hand. "I'm scared you'll lose your way in the snow."

"I'm not going more than three feet from the car," he said, twining his fingers with hers.

"I know, but it's easy to get disoriented in this kind of weather."

"If I'm not back in two minutes, open your window and call to me, so I'll know which direction to go."

"Be careful," Anna cautioned, as he stepped out. "Don't slip and fall."

He closed the door and stooped beside it. The problem was easily discerned – the car was lodged on a discarded railroad tie. He waved to the driver in the other car. "I'm stuck!" he called.

"Want me to get a local tow truck?" the man hollered back.

"Yes! Thanks!" Michael waved one hand, as the man raised a phone to his ear.

"Are you all right?" Anna asked, leaning across his seat to open his door. "I heard you shouting."

"Our friend is going to call a tow service from the area," he explained, slipping back into the driver's seat, brushing the snow from his hair. "Twenty minutes or so, we'll probably be on our way." He turned to look at her, his face a study in regret. "Let me say again how sorry I am. I'm sure you wish you had driven home on your own, in spite of the forecast and your bald tires."

"Think of the excitement you're adding to my otherwise dull and boring existence," Anna said. She could tell that his apology was sincere and she had no desire to make him feel worse.

"Are you cold?" He reached over and tucked his coat more securely around her.

"I'm fine," Anna said, though her teeth were chattering. She wished for her hat, but she had left it on the table behind Tina Peterson's desk. *Eighty percent of your body heat escapes through the top of your head* … it seemed she had recited the adage weeks ago.

"Are you always so agreeable?" Michael asked.

It was a shocking compliment, since she felt as if she had been extremely difficult. "I was thinking I owe you an apology for being stubborn about staying at your club," she admitted reluctantly. "It was foolish to insist on coming out in this storm."

"Not at all. You made some valid points."

Anna turned to look at him. "Is there someone you should call, so they won't worry?"

"Are you asking if I'm married?"

Anna was grateful for the cover of darkness.

"Don't you have a cell phone?" he asked. "You're welcome to use mine, if you'd like to call your kids."

Anna noticed that he had again left the question of his marital status unanswered. "Thanks, but it isn't necessary," she said quietly. Even if he was currently unmarried, surely he was attached to a woman who didn't know where he was and wouldn't approve if she did. It made Anna feel cheap.

"Is this something you've always wanted to do?" Michael asked. "Teach school?"

Anna turned her head to stare out the window, but all she could see was a blinding curtain of snow. "Please, couldn't we talk about something besides me for a while?" She was suddenly so tired, she didn't care if she offended him.

Michael turned off the engine. "We don't want to get asphyxiated," he said, drumming his fingers on the dashboard.

"You don't like to talk about yourself either," Anna guessed.

"No, I don't," he admitted. "I've always been a very private person."

"So have I. All these interviews …"

"I can't imagine why you weren't hired," Michael said, turning in his seat to study her. "You present yourself very well, and your record is impeccable. I'm sure your former employer wouldn't have anything unfavorable to say."

"I can't imagine that he would," Anna agreed. "I've never given him any trouble."

He turned the key and started the car again, switching on the windshield wipers, so that they could see what was happening outside. "How did you first hear of Casey's?" he asked. "I'm just making conversation now, if that's all right."

"I read an article in a magazine. Then Andy called and mentioned that they had discussed Casey's in one of his classes. A few days later, I saw a note on an online bulletin board, about the position for a substitute." Anna watched the faint red circles from the taillights of passing cars. "Someone at church mentioned it too. It kept popping up everywhere." She could hardly talk, her teeth were chattering so hard.

Michael began to rummage behind her seat. "I used to keep a blanket in the car, in case something like this should happen." He pulled out an unyielding length of wool, folded into a stiff square. Working together, they managed to open it, and Anna didn't argue when he tucked it around her. "The heater isn't working right either." He began fiddling with the controls. "I am so sorry," he apologized again.

"May I ask you one thing," she said, keeping her eyes trained on the floor of the car. "Are you married or not?"

"Not," he said.

Anna felt a huge surge of relief. She glanced over at him, and wondered what it would be like to work with him after such a disastrous beginning.

"Anna, if it isn't asking too much, once we have all this behind us, do you think you might …"

"Forget it ever happened?"

"No, not forget. Just …"

"I won't mention it," she anticipated his request.

"I've made it a personal rule not to socialize with anyone from Casey's."

Why had he made an exception in her case? She wasn't sure whether to be flattered or insulted. "You're as cold as I am," she noted, when she saw his hands shaking. "Couldn't we share the blanket?"

Michael didn't argue. He pulled the blanket over his knees and stretched his arm across her shoulders.

Anna yawned, and covered her mouth with embarrassment.

"You've had a long day," Michael said with understanding.

"I have," Anna agreed. "I can't believe I finally got a job! I've been applying for months."

"And then you landed in Brigadoon."

"Yes!" Anna said with a sleepy giggle. She wasn't aware that she was snuggling against him. "Do you know the story?"

"I used to. Something about a man who's willing to give up everything to be with the woman he loves?"

"Yes," she said, though she wouldn't have summarized the musical in quite the same way. "Yes, that's it. He's willing to give up everything to be with the woman he loves." She yawned again, and finally gave in and closed her eyes.

♥ Chapter 3 ♥

Michael Grant sat up and looked around. He had obviously spent the night in someone's guest bedroom.

Anna Brown. She had fallen asleep while they were waiting to be rescued. He woke her and helped her into the cab of the tow truck, then woke her again so she could return to his car. She had promptly curled up like a pretzel and gone back to sleep.

He glanced at her frequently while he was driving, resting his hand on her shoulder, smoothing wisps of hair away from her face. *Who are you?* he wondered. *Why am I so intrigued by you?*

He tried to wake her when he reached the city limits, but she was unable to mutter anything more than gibberish. Finally he pulled over and searched her purse for an ID with a phone number and called to ask her son for directions. Half an hour later, Paula opened the door and helped her mother up the stairs to her bedroom.

It seemed polite to accept when Andy offered him a cup of coffee. For several hours, he sat on a comfortable chair in Anna's cheery yellow kitchen and grew acquainted with her children. He had enjoyed their company.

He swung his legs over the side of the bed, and gathered his clothing from a chair. It had sounded perfectly feasible when Paula suggested he should sleep for a few hours before driving back to Casey's. Perhaps he was undergoing a mid-life crisis.

He took a quick shower in the adjoining bath, dressed and

exited to the living room. There were plants everywhere, dressing up the inexpensive and tattered furnishings. A thick wooden mantle was mounted over a brick fireplace, covered with childish renditions of candlesticks and candy dishes. On either side, two bookcases were stuffed with worn paperbacks. On the wall hung the Rockwell print of the girl with a black eye, waiting to see the principal – the same print he had chosen for his office at Casey's. He wondered if the girl was meant to represent Anna or her daughter. He ran his fingers through his hair and went to the kitchen.

After a moment of silent debate, he searched for what he needed and prepped the coffee maker. He sat at the table and watched the liquid drip through, rehearsing the words of apology he would recite for Anna. It wasn't his practice to coddle people, but he was deeply ashamed of the way the evening had ended.

"Morning," Paula said from the doorway. "You started the coffee pot? Great! I am badly in need of a jolt of java."

He smiled at her. She had dark brown hair and green eyes, like her mother, but she was taller and her personality was altogether different.

She placed two mugs on the counter. "Did you find everything you needed? I'm afraid Andy and I weren't very good hosts."

"You were exceptionally gracious, given the circumstances."

Paula looked pleased. "What do you take in your coffee?"

"Black is fine."

She brought the steaming mugs to the table and sat down. "So, how'd you wind up at a place like Casey's?" she asked.

"It's a long story," Michael said evasively, "and I'd far rather hear about you. I don't recall that you mentioned your major last night?"

"I'm in nursing school."

"She's hoping to hook a rich doctor," Andy said, as he entered the kitchen.

"Better than a poor lawyer," Paula said drolly.

"There's no such thing," Michael quipped.

"That's an *honest* lawyer," Paula corrected him.

Andy poured himself a cup of coffee and sat down. "So how'd you wind up at Casey's?" he asked. "Did you plan to do something like that after you got your degree?"

Michael glanced at Paula and they both began to laugh.

♥ ♥ ♥

Anna sat up and clutched her hands over her heart. How had she come to be in her own bed? The last thing she remembered was jumping down from the tow truck and climbing back into Dr. Grant's car.

Someone knocked on the door, and Anna realized it wasn't the first time. "Who is it?" she called uneasily.

"Who do you think?" her daughter said, pushing the door open. "I didn't think you were ever going to wake up!" She dropped onto the foot of the bed and smiled at her mother.

"I wish I hadn't." Anna leaned against the headboard, rubbing her fingertips against her temples. "I fell asleep in the car and I don't remember what happened after that."

"He couldn't wake you so he looked in your purse and found your emergency card. Then he called and got directions, and brought you home."

Anna cringed and closed her eyes. "What a disaster!" She threw the covers back and planted her feet on the floor. She was still dressed in her skirt and blouse and her bun rested over her ear. "It's almost a two hour drive – who's going to take me to get the car? I'm sure there isn't a bus that runs anywhere near the place. It's in the middle of the woods, miles from the nearest town. It'll be days before all that snow melts."

"He's going to give you a ride back," Paula assured her.

"No thank you," Anna said with a shiver. She couldn't imagine ever facing Michael Grant again.

"Why not? He said he'll wait till you get packed."

"I'm not going. I've decided not to take the job."

"What do you mean!" Paula snapped, rising and stomping around the room. "You finally got an offer and you're going to blow it off?"

"It wasn't the right job for me," Anna explained patiently.

"How do you know?"

"It's not a teaching position. That job was already filled when I

41

arrived."

"Not really." Paula smirked. "You were an hour late, and he never hires anyone who doesn't make it to their interview on time. He said this is the first time he's ever made an exception to the rule."

Anna unfastened her bun and allowed her hair to fall over her shoulders. "What did you do, stay up talking with him all night?"

Paula giggled. "Just about!"

"He lied to me then," Anna said. It was one more offense against him. "He didn't even give me a chance to explain *why* I was late."

"It's policy, Mom. A school is like a hospital. There are certain rules that have to be ..."

"Do not lecture me!" Anna warned, feeling her temper rise too near the surface.

Paula lifted both hands in apology.

"You didn't want me to apply at Casey's," Anna reminded her.

"That was before I met Michael," Paula said, going to the window. "He convinced me you won't be in any danger."

"That's interesting, since he admitted to me that there might be considerable danger." Anna got up and began making the bed, trying to organize her thoughts as well. "It involves animals." If she didn't convince her headstrong daughter that her decision was justified, Paula was likely to carry a grudge for months. "You know I'm not good with dogs."

"You're not too old to learn something new," Paula said. "At least that's what you kept saying while you were attending college."

Anna sighed. Nothing Paula said would change her mind. Michael Grant was handsome and intelligent ... and terrifying.

"He got up and made breakfast for Andy and me. It was supposed to be for you too, but you slept through it."

Anna froze, imagining the administrator of Casey's rummaging around in her kitchen. "He *got up*?" she repeated. "He spent the night here?" *He'll wait till you get packed ...* The words finally registered.

"He only slept a couple of hours and now he needs to get back, so I told him I'd wake you."

Anna slumped down on the side of the bed. She was going to have to face him, to tell him she had decided not to accept the job. She would apologize for wasting his time. No! She would *not* apologize!

"Want me to bring you a cup of coffee?" Paula offered.

Anna stared at her daughter with confusion. Paula's sudden show of compassion probably had more to do with the good looking man waiting downstairs than any softening of her heart. For some reason, her daughter was determined to secure her mother's future before she left home for good.

"I'll be down in less than ten minutes," Anna said firmly.

"Give him a chance!" Paula said, touching her shoulder. "He seems like a really nice person."

"Well, he's not," Anna said brusquely. "You're blinded by his good looks."

Paula sighed with disappointment. "What did he do, to make you dislike him so much?"

Anna wasn't about to explain and receive another lecture. Without answering, she went to her dresser for clean clothes. She would take a shower, and mentally make use of the time to find the words that would allow her to gracefully sever all ties to the school and to Michael Grant.

Moments later, as Anna stood beneath the spray of hot water and began to relax, she found herself reflecting on her reasons for applying at Casey's. When she began the quest to put her degree to use, she first researched special schools throughout the metropolitan area. Gradually, she broadened her search to include schools an hour from home, but it was due more to curiosity than any serious intention to actually apply.

Until she heard about Casey's, a unique experiment based on a Christian philosophy. A high percentage of Casey's students returned to their lives and became exemplary citizens, serving their communities in noteworthy fashion. When asked the secret of the school's success, John Casey attributed it to old-fashioned Christian principles taught by example. Reading those words, Anna had immediately longed to become part of Casey's success story.

Did John Casey realize what sort of man served his school as administrator? Their good reputation might soon be tarnished if Michael Grant remained in charge. Perhaps this was the reason God wanted her at Casey's – to expose the administrator so that he could be replaced.

Anna stepped out of the shower and shivered, as much from the temperature as from her thoughts. Move to Casey's? Move to a desolate spot where she knew no one? Work with animals? If God wanted her there to right wrongs, the job itself didn't matter, but ... She tried to dismiss the idea, but the still, small voice urged her to pursue it.

She remembered getting up in the darkness the day before, smiling while she dressed and ate breakfast. She had sung hymns all the way to Briarton – praise hymns. She had been positive that she was in God's will, even while she sat through the long interview with Casey's board members.

She had become stressed while driving up and down the state highway, searching for the school. But once she found it, she had been *so* excited. She remembered loitering in the waiting room, chatting with the students, enjoying a warm feeling that suggested she had "come home."

No, that wasn't right. The warm feeling had not occurred until Michael Grant came out of his office and shook her hand. She had known, right then, that she had finally come to the right place. She had understood, with total clarity, that all those months applying at other schools had been a waste, because God wanted her at Casey's.

"Now what?" she asked in a whisper, drying her hair, growing anxious as the confrontation approached. "Give me some help!" she pleaded with the Almighty, dressing in gray wool slacks and a white sweater. *What do you want me to do?*

She felt no wiser as she finished twisting her hair into a knot on top of her head, but her fear began to dissolve. This wouldn't be the first time she went into a situation without any idea what the outcome would be, or even what she *wanted* it to be. "Give me the right words to say and the courage or humility to say them," she prayed. Then she put the outcome in the Lord's hands and let go of it.

Michael was seated at the kitchen table with her children,

sketching something on a pad of paper. His clothes were rumpled, but it looked as if he had shaved.

He was as handsome as she remembered. Her heart began to race, though she told herself she was not attracted to Michael Grant, in spite of his good looks.

She studied Andy's face for some indication of his opinion, since he never pushed her to find a mate. He smiled at her, in a way that said she had accomplished something wonderful.

"Good morning, or should I say 'Good afternoon'?" she greeted them.

She could almost hear their collective sigh of relief.

"Sorry to have to wake you," Michael apologized.

"Sorry to have slept so late," Anna apologized in return.

"We saved you some breakfast." Andy jumped up and retrieved a plate from the refrigerator, neatly covered with plastic wrap. "Mike makes great pancakes."

"I'm not sure how good they'll be warmed up," Michael said modestly. "I'd be happy to mix a fresh batch."

"These will be fine," Anna assured him, tucking the plate into the microwave. She poured a cup of coffee and sipped at it, hoping the caffeine would ease an oncoming headache.

"I told him," Paula said glumly.

"Told him what?" Anna asked with a sinking feeling.

"That you changed your mind. That you don't want the job."

"*Paula*," Anna said with annoyance.

"Would you like a few days to think it over?" Michael offered.

"It's just that …" They were all three looking at her.

The microwave beeped, and Anna removed her plate and doctored the pancakes with butter and maple syrup. She hoped the food would settle her stomach.

After a moment of silence, Andy seemed to pick up on her need to be ignored. "So," he said, tapping his forefinger against the paper. "What you're saying is that the attorney draws a diagram on the chalkboard, and the defendant, caught off guard, will generally correct him?"

"I wouldn't say 'generally,' but I've seen it happen more than once. It's a cheap trick, and doesn't prove a thing, but the jury can't help forming conclusions."

"It's clever, if it works," Paula said, smiling at Michael.

"I dunno," Andy said thoughtfully. "It seems sort of ..."

"Dishonest?" Anna volunteered. After last night, it was exactly the sort of thing she would expect Michael Grant to recommend.

"How's it dishonest?" Paula asked.

"The attorney has to pretend he misinterpreted something," Michael explained. "Your mother's right, it *is* dishonest."

"It seems justified though, if it makes a guilty person admit their crime," Andy argued with uncertainty.

"You promised me you would never sacrifice your principles to win a case," Anna reminded him.

Andy crumpled the paper and held it up as evidence of his intentions. "Speaking of ethics, I need to squeeze in some study time before my ride gets here." He looked pointedly at his sister. "Bet you've got studying to do too."

"Not really," Paula said with nonchalance. "Of course, I'm just learning to save people's lives, which isn't nearly as important as winning a frivolous lawsuit."

"I think Andy is trying to provide an opportunity for your mother and I to talk," Michael said.

"I should think you'd want us to stay, in that case," Paula retorted, but she rose and carried Anna's plate to the sink. "May I say one thing?" she asked her mother.

"No," Anna said firmly.

Paula sighed and followed her brother from the room.

"I'm sorry," Michael said, before she could say anything. "For speaking out of turn and for spending the night in your home without permission. It seems the list of my sins is too long to be enumerated."

Anna wasn't sure what to say. She wouldn't label most of the things he did as "sins" but ...

Michael waited patiently, his hands folded on the table, his eyes meeting hers with a steady gaze.

How many times must I forgive my brother? the still, small voice whispered inside Anna's head. Michael had apologized last night too. Numerous times. It wasn't as if he had tried to force her to do anything. He had only provided the circumstances, in case she might say "yes."

Given the weather, she had almost been *forced* to say "yes." If she had realized how bad the roads were, she probably would've succumbed without an argument.

Anna, she rebuked herself. *You knew it was possible that you were going to get stranded at his club. Didn't you hear him tell his secretary that the forecast was for eight inches?*

This realization so shocked her, she couldn't get past it for a moment.

"I assure you, last night's behavior will not be repeated," Michael said quietly. "I truly hope you won't let it prevent you from accepting the job."

Anna didn't look at him, for fear he was somehow privy to her thoughts. How could she condemn him when some part of her mind had subconsciously agreed to the plot? Oh, she wouldn't have shared a room with him, whether or not that was his intent. But hadn't she been willing to take a foolish chance so that she could spend a little more time in his company?

Only because I wanted the job, she tried to convince herself. "Would you like to take a walk?" she asked. She could scarcely believe the words had come from her mouth.

He started to speak, then cleared his throat. "That would be fine."

"Just let me tell the kids we're going."

She ran up the stairs, to Andy's room. "How soon are you leaving?" she asked. She never allowed herself to confide her troubles to her son, for fear of becoming dependent on his counsel.

Andy glanced at the clock on his dresser. "Any minute, why? Do you need me to do something?"

Anna shook her head. "We're going for a walk, so I'll tell you good-bye now, in case you're not here when we get back."

He jumped up and gave her a hug. "You'll be great as a counselor, Mom. I think you'll like it more than teaching, truth be told. I remember how you always listened to my friends and tried to help them figure out a good solution to their problems."

Anna stepped back and studied his expression. He wasn't just trying to make her feel better.

"Just one thing," he added. "Please don't drive back and forth any more than you have to. That bug hasn't got many miles left and the tires are almost threadbare."

Anna smiled. It was an argument they had repeated countless times. "I'll call you as soon as I know for sure what I'm doing."

"And make sure you have a number where I can call you. Should I go down and tell Mike good-bye?"

Anna shook her head. "I'll tell him for you." She waggled her fingers at him and hurried down the hall to Paula's bedroom. She found her lying on the bed, staring up at the ceiling.

"Is he gone?" Paula asked with a long face.

"No, he's waiting for me to go for a walk."

"A walk?"

"Andy's leaving any minute. What about you?"

"I'm waiting to hear from a sorority sister, but she probably won't remember to call until she pulls in the driveway."

"Then we'd better say good-bye now."

Paula got up and gave her a hug. "He really did seem nice. Andy thought so too."

"We're going to try to talk it out."

"I hope you can." Paula stepped away and tipped her head to one side. "You look different."

"Different how?" Anna automatically checked to see if her bun was centered.

"I'm not sure. Something is just different."

"I'll call you tonight," Anna promised.

"Don't forget," Paula said, resting her hands on her hips.

"I'm not the one who forgets to call," Anna laughed.

She found Michael in the living room, standing at the mantel, studying a vase made from a milk carton. Crepe paper flowers rose from pipe cleaner stems – a child's expression of love.

"Are you going to wear a coat this time?" he tried to tease.

Anna went to the closet and took out her winter jacket, a deep burgundy with wooden buttons. Michael held it for her, before he retrieved his own coat from the couch. She wrapped a striped scarf around her head and pulled on a pair of black gloves. "Would you like to borrow a scarf or a hat?" she offered.

"Thanks, but … It's warmed up some."

As soon as they stepped outside, Anna discovered that he was right. The sun was shining and the temperature was probably in the fifties. She unfastened the scarf and allowed the ends to dangle free. "This is probably the last thing you feel like doing."

He thrust his hands into his coat pockets. "I'd like to mend fences with you."

She drew a deep breath. "Then I need to ask some questions." Now that the opportunity was before her, she knew she couldn't speak as bluntly as she wanted to. What if she accused him of planning her seduction and he laughed and said she wasn't his type? "What sort of living arrangements will I find in the women's dorm?" Once more, the words had spilled from her lips without permission. She clapped her hand over her mouth, wishing she could call them back.

She heard him sigh with relief and knew it was too late to change her mind.

"You'll have a living room and bedroom, but no kitchen. The restroom is communal."

"Is the apartment furnished?"

"Yes, but not lavishly."

They had reached the end of the street, and she headed down a foot path to a park where Andy and Paula had played as children. "Are you a Christian?" She felt foolish, but she looked up at him expectantly.

"I must be the most backslidden Christian on God's earth," he said, shaking his head with a smile. "In light of my sinfulness, I doubt there's anyone more grateful for God's grace than I am."

It was an impressive confession. "Are you referring to last night?" She held her breath.

"To many nights, and many days," he said ruefully.

Anna wasn't satisfied. She wanted him to confess his evil plan and apologize and beg her forgiveness. She knew it was wrong, but she wanted it all the same. "I'm still wondering why you followed me to my car and offered me a different job."

"You made a good impression. Casey's needs people like you."

"I showed up an hour late, with an empty gas tank, no coat, and very little money. I don't know how I could've made a *worse* impression."

"I liked the way you were with the kids, while you were waiting in the outer office."

"How could you know about that?" She didn't think it was likely that his secretary had interrupted his conference with a whispered phone call.

"One of the girls commented that you were nice. One of the boys said he hoped I was going to hire you. You didn't treat them like criminals, as so many of the teachers do."

Anna was pleased by his observations, though it didn't seem reason enough to chase her down and offer her another job. "Paula told me that the substitute's position hadn't actually been filled. She said you eliminated me as a prospect because I was late."

"I've always believed that a serious applicant will allow ample time to cover any but the most dire emergency."

"The first interview ended half an hour before my appointment with you. Even if I hadn't gotten lost, I don't think I could've made it in time."

"I'll speak to the board members about that," he promised.

"I wasn't trying to get them in trouble," she said meekly.

"They're my bosses. You can hardly get them in trouble." He stopped, so she stopped too. "I wasn't aware of the unusual circumstances or I would have made an exception. Normally, the board members send the interviewee home before they discuss their suitability. If a majority is in favor of hiring, they send the file to me and Miss Peterson calls to set up a second interview. I'm not sure why they asked her to fit you into my schedule yesterday. Perhaps because of the weather forecast and the distance you had come."

"So you resented me before ..."

"Not at all," he said firmly. "It wasn't personal. It's just policy. You were late and you didn't call to explain why."

"I don't carry a phone and there wasn't anywhere I could stop to call, once I left Briarton."

He shrugged his shoulders. "I'm sorry. Is that what you want me to say?"

"You don't sound sorry."

He raised his hands in a gesture of helplessness. "Punctuality is one of the most important issues at an institution like Casey's. When people are late, it almost always results in a crisis. If I were the administrator of a regular public school, I wouldn't be in the position of holding so strictly to the rules, but Casey's is a school for convicted criminals who happen to be under the age of eighteen. Discipline, including punctuality, is essential."

His speech made Anna feel like a naughty child. She picked up the pace and walked as far as the ball fields, uncertain whether he was following her. After a moment, she felt his hand on her shoulder, but she moved away before she turned to look at him. "I don't appreciate the fact that you tried to make my children take sides."

He met her eyes, but said nothing.

Anna knew she must stand up to him if she wanted to earn his respect. "They were both pushing me to take the job."

"They were friendly and curious about Casey's and the concept of pet therapy. I merely answered their questions."

"Why did you tell Paula that you didn't hire me because I was late?"

He chewed his lower lip for a moment. "The questions she asked forced me to either tell her that, or tell her a lie."

"And you chose to tell the truth for a change?" She couldn't remember another occasion in her life when she had been so rude to anyone, let along the man who might very well become her new boss.

"If you've changed your mind and you'd rather not work at Casey's, please do us both a favor and just say so," he said, with what seemed deliberate calm. "I felt I owed you additional leniency, but there has to be a limit to my tolerance."

Anna was embarrassed and ashamed, in spite of the fact that it was true – he *had* lied to her and he *had* encouraged Andy to lie.

Without warning, she burst into tears, hiding her face in her gloved hands. "I'm sorry," she sobbed. "I'm just confused and upset."

He stepped forward and gently put his arms around her. She fell against him, weeping copiously into his black coat. He pulled her close and pressed her cheek over his heart. She sighed and slipped her arms around his waist, wishing she didn't have to try to explain something she didn't understand. Finally she drew back to look up at him. "I'm really sorry," she told him. "I was so rude! It was inexcusable."

"Understandable," he said softly.

She gazed up at him and wondered if he was going to kiss her, though it was a preposterous notion. And then he lowered his head, so quickly, she didn't have time to decide how she should react. She found herself rising onto her toes, turning her face up, kissing him back.

He held her tightly for another moment before he pulled away. "That wasn't meant to happen," he said, while he kept a firm hold on her shoulders. He looked as surprised as she felt. "Not if you're still considering the job at Casey's."

She held perfectly still, afraid that once he let her go, he would never touch her again. "Is it still on offer?"

He smiled, then dropped his hands to his sides. "Shall we go back to the house so you can pack?"

Anna suddenly felt exhilarated. She wanted to run and leap in the air, clicking her heels together. She wanted to slip her hand through the bend of his arm or ask him to push her on the swings. She laughed, but when he asked what was funny, she wouldn't answer.

♥ Chapter 4 ♥

"What can I do to help?" Michael asked, as soon as they had returned to the house.

"Help me think," Anna said. "There must be a million things I should do, but I have no idea what they are. Paula! Andy!" she called up the stairs. No one answered and she turned to him with a stunned expression. "I guess they're both gone."

"Should you contact that wonderful neighbor?" Michael suggested.

"Yes! I'll ask her to water my plants."

"And maybe she'd get the mail, until you can have it rerouted? Will you give her the perishable food items?"

"Ten weeks … Yes. Whatever would spoil."

"I can bag those things while you pack," he offered.

"How will I decide what to take?" She ran up the stairs, sat down on her bed and tried to catch her emotional breath. Was she really going to do this? Go away for ten weeks? Work with dogs? Live in close proximity to Michael Grant?

She touched her fingers to her lips, finding it hard to believe that he had kissed her, that she had *wanted* him to kiss her, that she had kissed him back. Shouldn't she have been offended and angry? She hardly knew him! They had met only the day before, less than twenty-four hours ago.

Anna had quit dating, after too many bad experiences. Each time she shared her belief that a physical relationship should only take place between a married couple, her date voiced approval of her old-fashioned morals. But once the actual date commenced, he spent the entire evening trying to become the one exception to her rule.

Was Michael Grant any different? Hadn't he taken her to his club with those same intentions?

Maybe not. Maybe it was a misunderstanding. He had explained why he liked to go to his club, and his explanation made good sense. But he had kissed her! Just as she was trying to explain her rude behavior, he had silenced her with a kiss.

Unlike the unhappy experiences with other men though, she had wanted him to kiss her. She had wrapped her arms around him and enjoyed every second of their embrace.

"Do you want me to put the bread in the freezer, or give it away?" he called up the stairs.

Anna jumped up and went to the door. "Whatever you decide will be fine!" she called back. Then she began opening drawers and tossing shirts and socks and nightgowns onto the bed.

She filled a suitcase and several trash bags, and insisted on lugging it all down the stairs herself. She chose a few small plants to take and set them beside a Tupperware container filled with homemade cookies. She returned upstairs several more times, and went to the basement twice, for no particular reason.

Michael accompanied her next door, carrying two bags of groceries that wouldn't keep for ten weeks. Finally, there was nothing left to do but lock the front door.

"There's just one more thing," she told Michael, as he was loading the car. "It will only take a minute, I promise."

It wasn't as if she were permanently leaving home but, other than vacations, she hadn't lived anywhere else for over twenty years. She ran upstairs and stood at her bedroom window, thinking of the many nights she had kept vigil here, praying over her sick husband, her troubled or disobedient children. She could only hope the room in the women's dormitory would provide a likely spot where she could continue her habit. Right or wrong, she found it easier to pray when she had a view of the sky. Satisfied that God had taken note of her forwarding address, she hurried down the stairs, locked the door, and pocketed the key.

♥ ♥ ♥

During the drive, Michael carefully refrained from asking Anna for personal information. He felt as confused as a teenager, and didn't know where to begin sorting it out. Why should this be happening now? After so many years of standing fast in his vow, why did it suddenly seem ridiculous and unnecessary? It wasn't as if he had been sentenced to the life he led. He had chosen his penance and still believed it was just.

He wondered what Anna would say if he told her the story of his past. There were so many questions he wanted to ask! Why didn't she date? Why hadn't she remarried? But he couldn't pry into her history unless he was willing to describe his own. Twenty-four hours ago, Michael would have laughed at the notion of sharing his feelings with *anyone*. Now it seemed urgent that he confide everything to Anna.

He thought back to the night before, when he made comments so critical of his parents. What had he hoped Anna might say? He certainly hadn't expected her to be unwilling to pursue the topic. She didn't react to anything the way he expected. He thought she would be thrilled when he invited her to dinner, and flattered when he chose to speak to her of personal things. She didn't seem attracted to him in a romantic way yet, when he kissed her, she had kissed him back.

That he should not have kissed her was obvious.

Michael teased himself that none of it would have happened if he had refused to shake her hand when she introduced herself. If he hadn't looked out the window, would she have found another way to get her gas tank filled? Would she have driven away, out of his life forever? Or would he have made an excuse to call her, and offer her a different job ...

Even if he *had* felt compelled to spend a little more time with her, why didn't he take her to dinner in nearby Briarton? He knew the forecast was for eight inches! Had he secretly hoped they would be marooned at his club? There would've been little to do but talk, as they had done in the car. He could've asked her to explain her beliefs in depth, and shared more about his own life

55

philosophy. He could've been something other than lonely for the first time in years.

It was obvious that Anna wasn't eager for that sort of relationship, at least not with him. She was only interested in beginning her new career and she had every right to expect him to act as a professional. And so he would.

It was far too quiet in the car. Michael began reciting facts from Casey's brochures, and quoting favorable statistics. He recited a familiar litany of Casey's success stories, and saw that she was spellbound by the information. "Do you have any questions?" he asked.

"Only about a million of them," she said with enthusiasm.

Anna quizzed him about the facilities and the faculty, the security guards and the grounds. She asked what hours school was in session and what sort of things the students were allowed to do on weekends. Were they made to wear uniforms? Were they allowed to go home for the holidays? Were there bars on the windows of the classrooms and dormitories?

"What do you think happens to a child to make them end up someplace like Casey's?" she asked.

"I don't believe there's any one answer to that," Michael told her. "There are probably as many reasons as there are kids."

"Why do you think the kids from Casey's are more likely to be rehabilitated than the kids who are sent to traditional juvenile detention?"

Michael appeared to think it over before he answered. "When I first heard about Casey's, I wrote it off as a way for the rich to avoid consequences. I understood the hardships for kids of privilege, that they're often given 'things' to make up for an absence of love and attention. But I thought they ought to pay their debt to society, the same as a child who grew up in poverty. Why should they be sent off to some posh boarding school?"

"I wondered about that too," Anna admitted. She also wondered whether Michael was describing his own childhood. "Given human nature, it seems like the kids at Casey's would feel like they managed to get away with their crimes."

"Some of them do. But fortunately, most of them don't."

"What do you think would happen if you brought kids from poor families to Casey's too?"

He glanced at her with a morose expression. "We tried it with disastrous results. The children of the rich teamed up against the children of the poor, and vice versa. It was an impossible situation."

"That's sad," Anna sighed.

"It's tragic. Ideally, underprivileged kids should have an equally nice environment that encourages true rehabilitation, but it would have to be an expensive private school in order to have a Christian curriculum. We live in an age where Christians are being demonized and blamed for every evil event in recorded history. Those with deep pockets prefer to attach their donations to organizations with no religious affiliation."

"Do you think it's the Christian curriculum that makes the difference in whether the kids change their attitude?" Anna asked.

"I think that's the major reason, but in part, it's our general approach. When kids get into trouble, the first thing most professionals want to do is figure out 'why.' They want to look at the student's background – family, environment, and significant life-altering events. Sometimes that's helpful, but if you're looking at it from a Christian perspective, you can't dwell on the causes. We try to teach them to consider the past, but focus on the future. It's important for them to believe that once they've confessed and expressed genuine remorse for the poor choices they made, God forgives them and they should forgive themselves. The Bible doesn't encourage us to sit around discussing the cause of our sins, or describing them to one another in detail. Confess and repent and move on."

"I never thought about it that way," Anna said, wondering why his theory couldn't be applied to adults as well as children.

"Their crime was an error in judgment, not a measure of who they are. God forgives them, we forgive them, and they must forgive themselves. Once the slate is wiped clean, they can begin to explore their options. By time they leave Casey's, hopefully they're ready to discover their calling and pursue it."

"Sort of like a second chance?" Anna teased.

He glanced at her and smiled. "It's just a matter of semantics."

"Should I call it *another* chance then?"

"Another chance," Michael repeated. "All right. I can live with that."

They were both quiet for a moment, while Anna thought about the things he had said. "Why did you call yourself a backslidden Christian?" she wondered. He sounded like a far better Christian than most other people she knew. She couldn't seem to make up her mind – was he a good guy or a bad guy? Maybe she needed to label him as a bad person in order to keep from falling in love with him?

"I don't attend church regularly anymore, or read my Bible as avidly as I once did. But I've never stopped believing," he added, reaching across the console.

Anna sandwiched his hand between both of hers. She understood about straying from the faith. She had done it herself a time or two, but she hoped she had better sense now.

The roads were clear and the conversation made the time pass quickly. Michael parked beside her Volkswagen and turned to regard her with a serious expression. "As ridiculous as it might seem, I'm going to suggest we repack everything in your car. It would be best for both of us if no one is aware that we were together outside the school grounds."

"Okay," Anna agreed.

She agreed, but it rankled. So long as no one actually asked whether she had ever been with the administrator away from Casey's campus, it wasn't a lie. But it *felt* like a lie.

While he went in search of a gas can, Anna quickly transferred her things from his car to hers. Then she slid behind the steering wheel and gripped it with tension. Had it only been twenty-four hours since she rolled down the hill and parked in this space? She shivered, though the day had warmed considerably. How would she feel when the time came to repack her car and head home? Disappointed or relieved?

How do you feel now? she asked herself. Disappointed that Michael didn't want anyone to know they had become friends? Or relieved that he apparently planned to treat her the same as everyone else … It was as though the kiss had never taken place.

Michael appeared at the window. "You're headed for that building," he said, pointing his finger. "I called Gayle Summers before we left St. Louis and she said she'd be around all day. She's the president of the women's dormitory and will assign you to a room. Ask anyone you see and they'll help you find her." He knocked once on the roof of the car and backed away.

She turned the key a time or two, mindful of grinding the starter. When the engine began its distinctive chugging noise, she turned her head to back from the parking space. She pretended not to notice that Michael stood watching until her car turned at the bend in the road.

Anna parked in front of the dormitory and took a moment to calm herself. She should pray, but God suddenly seemed so far away. Had she left Him behind in St. Louis?

She got out of the car and went to the door, knocking with confidence she didn't feel.

A plump, smiling woman greeted her. "You a new angle on Avon?" she teased.

Anna held a briefcase in one hand and a plant in the other. "I'm Anna Brown, a new employee. Dr. Grant said to ask for Gayle Summers?"

The woman giggled and opened the door. "You don't have to knock. Nobody does. I'm Doris Michaels, home ec. C'mon in. Gayle's sorta tied up, but I can give you a tour, if you want."

"That would be great. Will my room be on the first floor?"

"Dunno. But the kitchen's on the first floor. And the den." She stepped through a doorway and extended her arm. "Ta da! The den." A worn carpet covered a hardwood floor, and four tattered couches made a square around it.

"It's comfortable looking." Its worn look made Anna think of home.

"No one ever uses it. No TV."

"Ah," Anna said. "Is that the kitchen?"

"Sort of." There was a freezer and refrigerator, a small

Formica table and four chairs. "No cooking facilities, except the microwave," Doris explained. "Not a good idea to miss meals." She paused and stared briefly over Anna's shoulder, then resumed speaking in a lowered voice. "Some people have …"

"It's against the rules," a voice said sternly.

Anna turned to find a tall, gray-haired woman. She started to smile, but the woman's disapproving frown was so severe, she hastily changed her mind.

"I'm Gayle Summers, president of the women's dormitory and I will explain how we operate." She glared at Doris.

"Nice meeting you," Doris said, and quickly disappeared.

"Are you Anna Brown?" Gayle growled. "I expected you earlier. It's nearly dinner time."

"I'm sorry," Anna said. "It's the first time I …"

Gayle raised her hand, to indicate that she wasn't interested in hearing Anna's excuse. "This is the kitchen. You must store your snacks in this room. No food is permitted outside of this room, on account of a problem with bugs."

"All right," Anna agreed, thinking of the box of homemade cookies in her car.

"I have the right to inspect your room if I suspect you're hiding food," Gayle said emphatically. "Label items clearly. Do not help yourself to someone else's snacks."

Gayle moved along quickly, reciting a multitude of rules as they were documented in the Dormitory Regulations Handbook. "Any questions?" she asked, standing at the foot of the stairs.

"None," Anna told her. Whatever questions she might have, she would ask them of Doris, or perhaps one of the other women she hoped to meet.

They climbed two flights of stairs before Gayle unlocked the door to apartment #307. Anna followed her into the room, pleased with what she found. There was a faded red couch and sagging arm chair, a coffee table resting on a blue rug, and a desk flanked by two bookcases. A small television was mounted on a shelf across from the couch. A closet formed a wall and behind it, a bed and dresser filled the tiny bedroom. Both rooms profited from a large window, meagerly covered by ruffled curtains.

"It's much more than I expected," Anna said.

Gayle looked pleased, then her expression turned sour again. "This is a government project, even if it is privately subsidized." She opened a desk drawer and removed a stapled pamphlet, slapping it down. "The dorm rules. Read it. Avoid the troublemakers, as I will not hesitate to write you up for an infraction."

"I will read it," Anna promised.

"You don't look as if you have an infirmity," Gayle said crossly, studying Anna's small frame.

"Excuse me?" Anna said with confusion.

"Dr. Grant suggested I give you a room on the first floor. I wondered if you told him you had a disability."

"I didn't. I don't. I have a two story home."

"It's unusual," Gayle said, mostly to herself. "I'll tell him you requested third." She went to the door and stood with her hand on the knob. "Were you acquainted with Dr. Grant before coming to Casey's?"

"No," Anna said, recalling that Tina Peterson had asked the same question.

Gayle squinted as she studied Anna for a moment. "Your key is in the desk drawer," she said, and pulled the door closed behind her.

Anna exhaled with relief and went to the window, pushing the curtain aside to reveal the view. There was the winding drive that led to the school itself, and the narrow road heading back toward the gates. She could see the stone house, and beyond it, the Missouri hills, still shrouded in white. She turned back to her apartment and decided it only needed personalization to become a sanctuary.

She took a quick bounce on the mattress, found her key, and started downstairs, wondering how many trips it would take to carry everything up to her room. She hadn't gone far before someone called out. When she looked up, she found five faces looking down.

"Want some help?" a pretty blond offered.

Another woman was already headed in her direction. She had dark curly hair and a friendly smile. "I'm Marianne Faraday, your next door neighbor."

"We'll want to be compensated," a tall woman warned, following behind Marianne.

"How about homemade cookies?" Anna suggested.

"Shhh!" they warned simultaneously, raising their fingers to their lips.

"Do you want to get written up before you're even moved in?" an older woman whispered.

Within moments, their arms were filled with trash bags and plants and Tupperware. They trooped noisily upstairs again, talking and laughing, making Anna feel included and welcome.

"This is Susie and Sally and Tonya and Rea." Marianne made the introductions, once they had united in Anna's room.

"Anna Brown. And thank you all very much for your help."

"Thanking us is not enough. You mentioned cookies?"

"Just be careful," Marianne said, casting a wary glance over her shoulder. "Gayle is obsessed with edibles being removed from the kitchen."

"She's scared of bugs," Susie explained.

Anna pried the lid off the Tupperware container and set it within easy reach.

"Oh, these are wonderful!" Rea said, holding one hand beneath the other to catch crumbs. "They really are homemade!"

"I thought she had that look," Tonya said, grabbing a cookie for each hand.

"You make your bed every day, don't you," Sally accused.

"She probably washes the dishes before she runs out of clean ones," Susie said with disgust.

"She may even vacuum," Marianne said with horror.

"I'm not as bad as that," Anna insisted. "Sometimes I don't dust for two days in a row."

They laughed, and helped themselves to cookies until the container was empty.

"You need to be forewarned," Sally said, settling on Anna's couch. "We're the black sheep of Casey's."

"Thanks to the twins."

"Cindy and Melody. They're identically horrible."

"They spy and eavesdrop and report back to Grant."

"And he believes everything they say."

"They told Susie's fiancé she was cheatin' on him."

"Did he believe them?" Anna asked Susie.

She shrugged and looked away.

"So if you want to make brownie points with Dr. Grant and Gayle, you'll avoid our company," Marianne said unhappily.

"Tell us about you," Tonya urged, settling on the floor. "How come you left, then Grant went after you?"

Anna didn't know how to answer, without breaking her promise to Michael.

"I heard your car wouldn't start."

"And Grant tried to fix it."

"I was just out of gas," Anna said sheepishly.

"Dr. Grant doesn't do car trouble," Tonya informed her. "If he saw me broke down on the side of the road, he'd keep right on going."

"Next thing, Grant has you sitting in Tina's area, which is strictly forbidden," Rea continued the inquisition.

Anna raised her shoulders. She recalled the way Tina had seemed surprised when Michael offered her extra chair.

"Then he tells her to cancel the rest of his appointments and sends her home early. Last winter, she had a temperature of 104 and he wouldn't let her go home."

"That's terrible!" Anna said.

"Her temp was only 101," Tonya chastised. "And he made her wait till her mom could pick her up 'cause he didn't think she ought to drive."

"But he really doesn't bend the rules for anybody," Marianne said seriously.

"Except you," Sally seemed to accuse.

"Did Tina say *that*?" Anna asked.

"You kidding?" Susie laughed. "She wouldn't tell us the building was on fire unless Dr. Grant gave her permission."

"Rea was one of the appointments that got cancelled," Marianne explained.

"What did you think of him?" Sally asked.

"He was polite and intelligent," Anna said, as if she didn't realize what they were asking.

Susie hooted. "She didn't notice he's handsome as the devil."

"As the devil?" Anna said, raising an eyebrow.

"As your favorite movie star, how's that?"

"Okay," Anna laughed. "Maybe I *did* notice."

"He's not the only good looking guy at Casey's," Rea said. "Wait'll you get a look at Bruce Carlisle."

"He might *look* good, but speakin' of the devil ..."

"What does he teach?" Anna asked.

"He's a counselor," Sally explained.

"A counselor?" Anna repeated with dismay. "I thought they're all meant to be Christians."

"We're *all* meant to be Christians," Sally said. "But that doesn't mean any of us is perfect."

"Brian Mason," Susie said. "That man has the bluest eyes I've ever seen. They're hypnotic."

"Like a snake," Marianne said. "You gotta watch out for him too. Or so I've heard."

"Nice meetin' you," Rea said, groaning as she got up from the floor. "I'd skip dinner if you hadn't run out of cookies."

"It was nice meeting all of you too," Anna said. "Thanks again for your help."

Marianne started down the stairs with the others, then turned and came back, as though she had forgotten something. "Did Gayle show you around?" she asked.

"She didn't show me where to find the restroom." Anna hoped Marianne would offer to accompany her to the cafeteria.

"Whatever you do, don't use the first shower stall," Marianne lectured, leading the way down the hall. "Unless you don't mind athlete's foot. And if you like to shower at night, either go early or wait till real late, or you'll be taking a cold one."

The restroom smelled moldy, the walls were dingy gray, the tiny sinks appeared to be coming loose from the wall.

"I take mine right after classes, when it's not so crowded," Marianne went on. "There's something about this place ... Sometimes I think I'm trying to wash it off." She studied Anna's expression and slapped her hand over her mouth. "I shouldn't've said that!" she mourned. "I want you to like it!"

"What did you mean, now that it's been said?" Anna pressed.

"Not the kids. They're great. *Most* of them. It's the women.

They fight and gossip all the time. And I do too. Gossip. Did you know that gossip is a sin?"

"Speaking it and listening to it," Anna agreed.

"I never thought of that, about *listening* to it. Great. Now I've got something *else* to worry about. You ever think about stuff like that? Spiritual stuff?"

"All the time."

"I've been praying for a Christian friend," Marianne said with excitement.

"I'll try hard to be an answer to that prayer," Anna vowed.

"Great! I gotta warn you though, some of the others will give you a hard time if you start talkin' about religion."

"I'm all the more glad to know I can talk to you then," Anna said sincerely. She reached over and gave Marianne's hand a squeeze. "You're an unexpected blessing."

"Thanks," Marianne said with embarrassment. "You know where the cafeteria is? My first night, I wandered around for an hour, trying to figure out how to get into the building. There's only one door we can use after five o'clock, especially on weekends. And you gotta have your badge."

"Badge?" Anna said with a frown.

"Gayle didn't take you to get your picture ID?" She looked pleased. "I'm sure she's already gone to dinner. We'll have to call Dr. Grant."

"I don't want to bother him!" Anna protested. "Won't he be at dinner too?"

"That's okay. I can page him." Marianne wore a happy smile as she pulled her cell phone from her pocket.

Following her down the stairs a few minutes later, Anna wondered if Marianne would be shocked to hear about Dr. Grant's behavior while he was absent from Casey's. She longed to confide in her new Christian friend, but she was not one to go back on her word.

Inside the guards' shack, two uniformed men were unloading boxes of equipment, leaving little space for guests. Anna leaned against the counter, and wondered how she should greet Michael. She didn't want to do anything that would give away their secret.

"Why didn't Gayle take care of this?" Michael asked, as soon as he entered the room. He wasn't smiling.

"I dunno," Marianne shrugged. "I was gonna look for her, but I was afraid they'd stop serving dinner."

Michael checked his watch. "They *will* stop serving soon. You'd better go and get something to eat."

"What about … I mean, Anna hasn't had dinner either." Marianne's cheeks were flushed with color.

"I'll see to it that she gets something when we're done," Michael promised, ushering Marianne out the door. "Go ahead," he instructed the guards.

"I'm sorry to have interrupted your dinner," Anna told him, though it was hardly her fault. "Couldn't you go, now that you've given approval for my pass?"

"You'll need to fill out some cards," he said, ignoring her question. "If you don't have the information on hand, you can stop by with it tomorrow."

She accepted a sheaf of index cards from one of the men and bent her head over the counter. She filled in the blanks as quickly as she could, wishing Marianne had called Gayle, rather than the administrator. She slid the cards back to the officer, making it a point to avoid Michael's eyes.

The gun that was strapped to the guard's shoulder was within reach, and the sight of it, up close, gave Anna pause. *What am I doing here?* she wondered. She was suddenly homesick, and frightened of the ten weeks ahead.

"I need a picture," the guard said, lifting a digital camera from under the counter. "Don't smile."

Anna found it easy to comply. The device flashed in her face and she was momentarily blinded.

"Have you had anything to eat besides leftover pancakes?" Michael asked, while the guard sliced her photo into a neat square and pasted it beside her name.

Anna looked at him with surprise. Why would he ask a question that suggested they had shared breakfast, after going to such measures to ensure no one found out?

He took the laminated badge from the guard and clipped it to her collar. "Let's go find some dinner," he said, resting his hand on her shoulder.

Anna thought she should pull away, but found herself leaning toward him instead. "I don't understand," she said, as soon as they were alone on the sidewalk. "You said you didn't want anyone to know we were together outside of work, but …"

"But everyone does seem to know," he interrupted. "Where's your coat?"

"It's … in my room."

He laughed. "I hope we're not going to work from the same script every time we meet."

"Normally, I'm very sensible," she said with embarrassment.

"I'm sure you are." His tone was serious, but he was still smiling. "Then it wasn't you who spread the story?"

"I haven't been here long enough to spread a story," Anna said indignantly. "Anyway, I gave you my word and I've kept it." *Barely*, she reminded herself.

"I'll have a word with Tina on Monday. She might have mentioned that you were still here when she left."

"I doubt if she did," Anna said. "Some of the women were talking at the dorm, saying she's very closemouthed about you."

He seemed pleased by this. "A lot of classroom windows look out on the visitor's parking lot. I guess anyone could've seen us leave together, though they're all supposed to be gone by five o'clock."

"I'm not sure what to say, if anyone asks." She stole a glance at his face, impressed anew by his good looks.

He shrugged, but offered no suggestions.

Anna stepped into the building while he held the door. She thought she could probably find the way to the food by using her nose. "Will the cafeteria still be open?"

"I think I can convince them to feed us." He led her past the staircase and around a corner. "I take it you found Gayle?"

"Yes, I did," Anna said, hoping he wouldn't ask too many questions. "I was tickled when I saw my apartment. It's more than I expected."

"You do have a tendency to look on the bright side," he said, leaving her to wonder whether it was compliment or criticism. "I don't know what was on tonight's menu." He opened a glass paneled door revealing a large cafeteria, mostly deserted. "If worse comes to worse, I guess you could make do with peanut butter crackers out of the vending machine."

Anna smiled at his memory while she canvassed the dining area for her new friends. Only Marianne remained, and she was in the process of dumping the debris from her tray.

They came into the kitchen and one of the cooks eyed them with a wary expression. "New employee," Michael explained. "Her badge was overlooked until a few minutes ago, and neither of us have had any dinner. Can you rustle something up?"

He was a commanding presence, and he was everyone's boss.

"Sure," the cook said, glaring at Anna.

"Where did she put you?" he asked, turning back to Anna. "Next to the kitchen, or beside Doris?"

Anna averted her eyes. "I didn't have much chance to get my bearings." She told herself it wasn't a lie.

"When you enter the building, do you turn right?" He stopped and frowned. "She didn't put you on the first floor, did she."

"Why did you tell her I had a disability?" Anna demanded with confusion.

"I didn't tell her any such thing. I only said she should put you on the first floor. It seems there's an epidemic of dishonesty on this campus."

"I didn't lie!" she protested.

"About that … Shall I ask whether we have oysters on hand, knowing how much you'd enjoy them?"

Anna felt her face grow warm. "If you knew I didn't like them, why did you try to make me eat them?"

"Why didn't you just say you didn't care for them?"

"I was being polite."

"Skip polite, if it means being dishonest," he said with annoyance. "I'd far rather have my feelings hurt than believe something that isn't true."

Anna couldn't imagine that he would have his feelings hurt over anything. "Given the fact that …"

He held up his hand to stop her. "Let us make an agreement right now. While I may not be able to answer all your questions, I will never lie to you. I'd like your promise that you will always be honest with me too."

Anna tried to move away, but her back was against the wall. "I always try to be honest with everyone," she stammered.

He looked disappointed, which made Anna feel ashamed.

"Anyway, why did you want me on the first floor? You were at my house; you know my bedroom is on the second floor. Stairs are obviously not a problem for me."

He smiled and looked around. "That would make nice grist for the rumor mill." He sighed and folded one of his hands over the other. "I don't have to justify the decisions I make, but for the record, I didn't want you to get involved with the group that lives on third."

"How did you know I'm on third?"

"Because Marianne isn't the type to come downstairs and introduce herself."

The cook carried out a tray laden with food, and Michael lifted it from her hands and thanked her. He nodded his head at Anna and she followed him across the dining area. Ignoring the friendly waves of faculty members, he went to a closed door and gestured for Anna to step inside. It was a small room with a table and two chairs, positioned against a glass wall.

"Is it one-way glass?" she asked with fascination.

"It serves many purposes," he explained, removing his suit coat and draping it over his chair. "No one knows for sure whether I'm in here. What do you think? Is that dishonest?"

She knew he didn't expect an answer. "I didn't mean to lie to you, about Gayle *or* the oysters. I didn't think …" She sat down and pressed her hands over her face. She tried to recall another time in her life when she had been this exhausted. Perhaps when Paul lay dying …

"So you're where?" he asked, as if unaware that she was upset. "Next to Marianne? On the east side?" He unwrapped two sandwiches and slid one in front of her.

"I'm not good with a compass, but I know I'm next to Marianne. Room 307." She squirted mayonnaise over roast beef, lettuce and tomato. "Gayle seemed stressed."

"I'm sure she was. She made herself an office on the first floor, and she doesn't want to give it up."

"Doris started showing me around before Gayle came in.

69

Maybe Gayle thought …"

He waited for her to finish, long after it was apparent that she didn't intend to. "Don't you believe adults should be accountable?"

She did believe that. "It's just that … I don't want to make enemies before I've even started."

"You'd rather have me for an enemy than one of the women?"

"Of course not!" She studied his expression with a worried frown. "Did you see the cook? When you asked her to get us some dinner?"

"Did she make faces at me behind my back?"

"She gave *me* a dirty look. If you say something to Gayle about this, she'll blame *me*."

He shrugged, as though it couldn't be helped.

Anna sighed. "There's some kind of feud going on at the dorm. I'm not sure what it's about."

He chewed for a long time, staring into her eyes. Then he swallowed and took a drink of milk. "It's been going on for years. It's not your job to fix it."

She ducked her head and opened a bag of chips. Kiss or no kiss, she had no illusions about what their relationship was going to be.

"Paula get back to school okay?" he asked.

The change in subject felt like a reprieve. "I haven't talked to her yet."

"Do you want a piece of cake?"

"Yes, thank you, since it's chocolate."

He handed her the biggest piece. "What about Andy?"

"He's probably still on the road. I'm going to call them both tonight, if a landline is available."

"The jack should be near your desk." He dug in his pocket and pulled out a business card, handing it across the table. In the lower right hand corner, his office and pager numbers were listed. "I wrote my home landline and cell number on the back."

"I won't call unless it's an emergency," she promised. She turned her head and stared into the dining room. "What should I do on Monday?"

"I'd like you in my office at 8:00 sharp."

70

"I'm normally on time for things," she said defensively. "You saw that there were no signs." She had asked him to point them out on the way back to Casey's.

"You probably won't need a sign to find your way to my office," he teased.

She forced a smile. It was hard to keep up with his frequent change of mood.

He finished his cake and deposited all his trash on the tray. Then he folded his hands on the table and looked into her eyes. "Cindy Wilson and Melody Murphy are guilty only of being young and naïve. The women on third have some sort of grudge against them, though I can't imagine why."

The twins, Anna thought, recalling that they were accused of malicious behavior.

"Whether or not Bruce Carlisle is a threat, I can't say," he went on. "I've had complaints, but nothing concrete enough to terminate his employment."

It seemed that Dr. Grant had been standing outside her room, listening to the entire conversation. "Does Brian Mason really have blue eyes that hypnotize?" she asked, hoping he would be amused.

"They haven't had that particular effect on me," he replied, rising and picking up the tray.

Anna wished she hadn't taken his counsel so lightly. She jumped up and discarded the remains of her dessert.

"I'll set you up in a study corral on Monday, so you can do research on pet therapy," he said, holding the door for her. "And I'll make an appointment with Helen Mansfield, the woman who runs the animal shelter in Briarton."

Anna nodded, rather than speak and risk making him angry again. She stood back while he dumped the tray, then walked beside him as they retraced their steps to the exit.

"I'll do some checking as to what credits you would need for an Associate's in Psychology. If you're not qualified, we may have to bring in one of the other counselors on an advisory basis."

"Will they resent being left out if you don't involve them?"

He shook his head. "I don't ask those sorts of questions. I

decide what's best for Casey's and if anyone has a different idea, they're welcome to make an appointment to discuss it."

"Where is this going to happen? I mean ... Where will the animals be kept?"

"I've got something in mind, but I haven't made a final decision. I'll show you the area when I do."

"Is it inside or outside?"

He looked down at her with a smile. "Are you wondering whether I'm going to make you spend your days in the doghouse?"

She laughed. "I think I'll manage that all on my own, thank you very much!"

He laughed too, then gave her shoulder a gentle squeeze. "I won't ask you to move to the first floor of the dorm if you don't want to. I hope we won't both regret that decision."

"I've never been one to get into trouble." She wondered what the women would say if they saw Dr. Grant escorting her to the dorm. "You don't have to walk me all the way."

"If I didn't want to, I wouldn't." Just beyond the guardhouse, he stopped, crossing his arms and tucking his hands out of sight. "Go on," he said. "I'll watch you from here."

She wanted to tell him that he didn't need to watch her at all, since the distance was short, and she could hardly be in danger. When she looked into his face though, she knew it would be the wrong thing to say. "Thank you," she said instead. "For all of it."

"You're welcome for all of it. Good night."

She lifted her hand and hurried up the sidewalk. The only real danger at Casey's, she thought, was protecting her heart from the handsome administrator.

Long after the women's dormitory had gone dark, Michael stood at his window, staring at the building where Anna would reside for the next ten weeks. He wondered if he had made a mistake in persuading her to accept the job.

She wasn't qualified as a counselor, and she was afraid of animals. If pressed, he would have a hard time justifying his decision to Casey's board. Given the rumors that were circulating around the campus, they were likely to hear of his unusual behavior and ask questions. They would accept his explanation, because he had never given them cause to doubt his word. Nor had he ever breached the morals clause in the standard Casey's contract ...

He hadn't done anything wrong in taking Anna Brown to dinner, he told himself. Or in spending the night at her home, given their chaperones. He had the right to spend his weekends away from the campus, even if he rarely exercised it.

But what of the vow he had made? It had been a vow for life, not for a specified number of years. There was no one to hold him to it. In fact, no one else was aware of the words he had spoken, the promise he had made.

It might be a moot point, he told himself, mentally reviewing the time he had spent with Anna. There simply wasn't any evidence that she was interested in him, other than as an employer. She had asked only a few personal questions about his life, obviously in an effort to be polite. Even after he assured her that the job was hers, she hadn't become any friendlier.

It appeared that she had some feelings for him, after they found themselves marooned on the side of the highway. She had seemed legitimately concerned that he would stray from the car and be unable to find his way back in the snow. She had even reached for his hand, which had touched his heart. But was she concerned for him, or only for her own welfare?

He had deserved most of the diatribe she delivered during their walk to the park. When he decided he must draw the line, he had expected anything *but* a torrent of tears with an apology for her rudeness. He hadn't meant to kiss her. If he had given it a few seconds of consideration, he would have backed away when she began to cry.

At least she hadn't *pushed* him away. In fact, she had raised up on her toes and slipped her arms more tightly around him as she kissed him back.

What did it mean, he wondered.

He was a man, he thought like a man, and he was no better off than any other man when it came to understanding women. But something told him Anna Brown wasn't like most women anyway. He didn't think she was impressed by the trappings of wealth. In fact, she had seemed put off by the luxury of his club. She had not apologized for the shabby furnishings in her home, and he suspected she wouldn't, regardless of who came to call. She was different than any woman he had ever met.

Michael sighed and turned away from the window. He could hardly ask her out on a date, given his self-imposed rule against fraternizing. Even if he did, where could he take her? Anywhere near Casey's, he risked being seen and the rumor mill would grind still harder. Even if he was willing to take her back to his club, he felt certain she would refuse to go.

He hadn't always had a fondness for expensive restaurants and gourmet dining. As a teenager, he had rebelled against his parents and their wealthy lifestyle. Michael criticized his mother when she bragged about her crystal and silver and diamonds. He refused to ride in his father's Mercedes, and he had never used the family membership at the country club. *You'll outgrow that disdain*, his father had predicted.

And now he must admit that his father was right, that he had succumbed. Somewhere along the way, he had grown used to his creature comforts and turned into a snob. He had actually expected Anna to be impressed by his club, because it sounded as if she had been poor most of her life.

"Anna," he said aloud. It seemed she had kept him from falling off a cliff, while he hadn't even realized he was in danger.

♥ Chapter 5 ♥

Anna typed the words "pet therapy" and allowed the search engine to do its job. She had arrived at Michael's office at 7:30, to be on the safe side. He invited her to take a seat on the blue plaid couch, complimented her red suit, offered her a cup of coffee, and asked whether she was settling in at the dorm. He seemed to be in a much better humor today. Perhaps he had gotten a good night's sleep.

She clicked on the first site, and read an article about a prison in Washington State. The results of their experiment were impressive − mixing pets with prisoners. It was favorable for both, with no apparent negative side effects.

She read another article, and then another. Her enthusiasm mounted with each word. This wasn't just another form of entertainment for the lucky children who were sentenced to Casey's. It was a solution, a remedy.

She chose a few articles that went into more detail and printed them, so that she would have something to show Michael for her morning's work. They hadn't talked about his expectations, so she wasn't sure what results he hoped to see. She was grateful that she had learned to do research via the computer while she was in college, so she didn't have to ask for help.

She heard the low rumble of voices and assumed the students were arriving. How she wished she could have a *real* job at Casey's, teaching American History! She would work hard to prove herself and maybe he would consider her if he had an opening the following year.

It looked as if every prison that tried the program published positive results. The crime didn't seem to matter – men and women, rapists and murderers, all were likely to benefit from caring for a dog or a cat.

Once trained, the dogs went on to provide invaluable services to a variety of people in need. They not only made life easier for people with disabilities, they sometimes saved lives. A select few were even able to give warning if their companion was about to have a seizure. She was growing more and more excited about becoming involved in a program that was doing such positive work.

At ten o'clock, she took a break, stretching and rubbing the back of her neck. She had a fair pile of articles ready for the administrator to read, but she still wasn't sure if this was the sort of information he wanted her to compile. While she was debating what to do next, he came through the door.

"How's it going?" Michael asked. He sat down in one of the other chairs and wheeled it closer to the study corral where she was working.

"I'm not certain what kind of information you wanted me to look for," Anna admitted. "But I've certainly become a fan of the program."

Michael folded his hands and made a steeple of his thumbs. "That's great," he said warmly. "To be honest, I don't know enough on the subject to give you direction. I did happen across an article this morning, in one of my online journals. Apparently some inmates have become Animal Hygienists when they reenter society, and their recidivism rate is zero."

Anna gave him a blank look. "I hate to admit it, but … I have no idea what that word means."

"I'm sorry," he apologized. "The inmates didn't return to a life of crime. You'll become more familiar with prison vernacular as time goes by."

"You're very kind," Anna said gratefully.

He shrugged off the compliment. "Have you come across details as to how we initiate the program? What sort of requirements there might be, for the institution and the people involved in implementing it? I'm sure there are a lot of legal restrictions we'll need to be aware of."

"I haven't seen anything like that, but I wasn't looking for it either. I'll refine my search."

"It may not come up with a Google search. I might have to make an official request."

Anna folded her hands neatly in her lap. "Is there anything else you'd like me to specifically look for?"

"You're doing fine if you're becoming enthused," Michael told her. "I made an appointment to meet with Helen Mansfield at the shelter this afternoon. If you can meet me in my office at 12:15, that should give us more than enough time."

"The moment of reckoning," Anna tried to joke. She moistened her lips with the tip of her tongue.

"Don't be nervous," Michael said, reaching over to pat her clenched hands. "I don't expect you to turn into a dog lover after one visit."

She forced a smile. "What if I can't … What if I'm still not comfortable with it after three or four visits?"

"Let's not borrow trouble." He fingered the sleeve of her jacket. "You might want to change clothes before we go."

"Why?" she asked. "Are dogs like bulls and don't like red?"

He laughed. "It's spring. Every dog you touch is going to shed all over that pretty suit."

Anna swallowed hard. "I kind of thought maybe I could just watch the first time."

Michael shook his head. "We need to know whether you're going to be able to overcome your fear. Don't you think it's best that we find out before we proceed any further?"

Anna knew he was right. "You wouldn't have to go along. I could report back to you afterwards. I promise to be honest." She was going to be extra nervous if he was there watching.

"I *want* to go. I'll lend you moral support."

"Do *you* like dogs?" she asked timidly.

"Yes I do. We always had a dog when I was growing up, though they were never allowed in the house." Michael stood up, so Anna did too. "You might want to go to the cafeteria a little early, so you'll have plenty of time to change and be back by 12:15. The line starts getting pretty long around 11:30."

"Okay," she said, clutching her hands behind her back.

Michael touched his fingers to her cheek. "Quit worrying," he scolded gently. "It's all going to work out."

She smiled up at him, but his words didn't raise her confidence level.

As soon as Michael had gone, Anna settled at the computer again, but she didn't resume her search. If only she had warmed to her friends' pets when she was a child! If pressed, she had obediently patted their heads, then quickly withdrawn her hand from biting range. She had listened to people talk to their pets as they did to small children, but she knew such a thing would never come natural to her. Hopefully, Helen Mansfield would be a nice person who could give her some pointers.

If only Michael wasn't going along ...

Anna went back to work, searching for any sort of instructions as to how a pet therapy program might be started. She made note of addresses and phone numbers and web sites, printing neatly and legibly. At 11:30, she signed off the pc and headed to the cafeteria.

Her new friends spotted her and invited her to sit at their table. Though they tried to include her in the conversation, she had little idea who or what they were talking about. A few minutes before twelve, she returned her tray and hurried from the building.

Entering the otherwise empty dormitory gave her an eerie feeling. She quickly changed into blue jeans and a sweatshirt, and traded her good coat for a warm jacket. Then she ran down the hall to brush her teeth and refasten her bun. When she returned, the door to her room was standing open, though she was certain she had latched it. She hesitated, suffering the impression that someone had entered her apartment. Finally, she pushed the door with the toe of her tennis shoe, careful not to make a sound.

There were two young women at her desk, rooting through the boxes she hadn't unpacked. Unaware of her presence, they were sharing what they found. None of their comments were complimentary.

Anna tried to recall whether she had packed anything

personal, other than pictures of her kids. Not that it mattered. Even if she had only brought a pile of old newspapers, the two women had no right to go through her things.

If she confronted them, she would be late arriving at Michael's office. Should she go and simply tell him what she had seen? What if these were the "twins?" He might assume she had joined the third floor troublemakers in persecuting the two women he was so fond of.

She shoved her toothbrush into her pocket and moved quietly down the stairs. She would never again leave her door unlocked, even for a moment.

♥ ♥ ♥

"Looks like you're not going to be petting any dogs," she commented, since Michael was still clad in his dark suit. They walked together down the stairs, past the security guards, and along the sidewalk to his car.

"I've got meetings beginning at four o'clock, lasting into the evening." He opened the car door for her, then went around to the driver's side. "I'm sure it will *look* as if I was playing with the animals, whether I do or not," he said when he got in. "I'm bound to be covered with hair."

"Scotch tape," Anna advised. "Wrap it the wrong away around your fingers. It makes a great clothes brush."

"How would you know that, never having had a pet?" He backed the Corvette from his designated parking place and headed up the hill.

"I'm one of those people who has a lot of mostly useless trivia stored in their head. I can recite a recipe for homemade mayonnaise and tell you how to remove a new car sticker, in spite of the fact that I'm not likely to ever use either piece of information."

"Think of it as a form of mission work," he said with a chuckle. "That clothes brush tip will come in handy this afternoon."

Anna was pleased. "Do you know the woman who runs the shelter?"

"We're well acquainted. She's been to Casey's more than once to pick up a stray." He turned his head briefly, to smile at her. "Helen is very taken with the idea of pet therapy. She's the one who has to euthanize the animals if she can't find them a home."

"What a horrible job."

"Indeed. She's likely to hug you when we arrive, though I warned her that you're not an animal lover by nature."

"Well, maybe I will be, by the end of the day," Anna said optimistically.

Helen met them at the door and took their coats. Then she picked up a puppy from an open kennel and thrust it into Anna's arms.

Anna almost dropped it as it squirmed with excitement. When she finally found a way to hold it securely, she peered up at Michael and saw that he was pleased. "I want it," she said, delighted as the puppy washed her chin with its pink tongue. "May I have it?"

"No," Michael laughed. "No puppies or kittens. We're in the market for adult dogs only."

"No cats?" Helen said with disappointment.

Michael shook his head. "I've pitched it to the board as mostly an outdoor project. Not many cats are willing to walk on a leash."

Helen regretfully agreed. "Are you ready to come into the kennel?" she asked Anna.

Anna handed the puppy back, aware that Michael wouldn't want her to waste time. "Is there anything in particular I shouldn't do?"

"Someone brought me a stray this morning. I put it into a kennel and haven't messed with it at all."

"I think Anna would rather ..." Michael began to object.

Helen lifted her hand to stop him. "I thought she could watch how I work with an animal that's not familiar with me or the shelter. After that, I've got some friendly dogs picked out for her to handle."

"Sorry," Michael said. "I should have known you would think it through."

Helen smiled at him over her shoulder, then led the way to the rear of the building.

Anna could see that Michael and Helen had a good rapport and she wondered whether the blond was attracted to him. She didn't imagine there were very many women who *wouldn't* find the tall, dark-haired man something like their favorite daydream.

She paused a moment to peer through the windows into the rooms that lined the hallway. One held cats – most of them were sleeping on the shelves fastened to the walls at various heights. Another held small dogs in stainless steel kennels and she wondered why they couldn't begin there.

At the end of a hallway, they entered an area divided into cubicles with chain-link fencing. Bowls of food and water were attached to the wall and a rubber mat provided a place to sleep. The dogs in these cages were not small and Anna's heart began to beat hard and fast.

Without hesitation, Helen lifted the latch on one of the gates and went into the enclosed area. She stooped down, held out her hand and spoke in soft, soothing tones to a large brown dog, cowering in a corner.

"That makes me think of some of our kids, when they first arrive at Casey's," Michael said, resting his hands on Anna's shoulders.

Our kids. He had included her, as though she belonged. Anna looked up at him and smiled. He met her eyes and suddenly, she was reminded of that moment at the park, when she realized he was going to kiss her. She quickly turned away.

The dog took a step towards Helen, its tail beginning to wag. Helen continued to encourage it with her voice and eventually, the dog came close enough to sniff her fingers. Helen turned her palm down and the dog sniffed some more. Finally, she began to scratch the top of its head, then to pet it. She brought her other hand up too, and scratched behind its ears, always talking to it in the same happy voice one might use with a small child.

"She definitely has a way with animals," Anna whispered.

Michael leaned down, so that she could feel his breath, warm against her ear. "You may turn out to have a way with them too. You've never had an opportunity to find out."

It was true, she thought with burgeoning hope. Whether or not she had been inclined to make friends with other people's pets,

81

she could have an undiscovered knack for it.

Helen stood up and the dog came to her feet, gazing up at her with soulful eyes. She bent down to pet it again.

"Looks like you may have to take that one home," Anna said.

Helen rolled her eyes. "I already have five dogs and six cats." She came out of the kennel and fastened the gate. "I thought you could try working with that shaggy mutt on the end. He's very friendly. In fact, he might be a little *too* friendly."

Anna bit her lip, nervous in spite of Helen's promises. She went to the cage and talked to the dog through the fencing, wondering if she had the courage to actually go through the gate.

"Come on," Michael said, lifting the latch. "I'll go with you."

Anna didn't allow herself to hesitate. She slipped through the opening and started to stoop down, but the dog didn't wait for polite gestures. It ran to her and stood on its hind feet, planting its paws on her shoulders.

Anna lost her balance, but Michael was quick to catch her and hold her steady.

"You *are* friendly," Anna laughed, scratching the dog's ears, as she had seen Helen do. It had long, wiry grey hair on its eyebrows and muzzle and ears, and black satiny fur everywhere else. "Do you have a name?"

"Charlie," Helen said, from the walkway outside the cage.

When the dog tired of Anna, it jumped on Michael and he took a turn to pet it. Anna slapped her thighs to call it back and Michael quickly left the kennel to watch beside Helen.

"He'll respond to commands," Helen told Anna. "Give it a try."

"Sit," Anna said firmly, surprised when Charlie sat. "Good dog!" she said, running her hand over his head and down his neck. "What else can you do?"

"He'll shake your hand, and roll over."

"How could someone spend all the time training him, then give him up?" Anna said, gazing into Charlie's sad eyes as she stooped down to pet him some more.

"It's the way he jumps on people," Helen explained. "They tried everything, even some punishments I wouldn't recommend, like stomping on his toes. They weren't able to break him of it and I haven't been able to either. Want to meet some of our other guests? I know you don't have much time."

Anna was reluctant to leave Charlie, who continued to wag his tail and gaze at her with devotion. She felt as if they had bonded, but she doubted whether they had a future together. She patted his head once more, then darted from the pen.

At Helen's urging, she entered the next cage and petted a shepherd mix who seemed bored by the attention. Next there was a lab mix, and then one Helen called a "Heinz 57." Anna found she was actually enjoying herself.

Michael lifted his sleeve to check his watch. "I need to head back," he told Helen. "Anna could come again tomorrow, if that works for you. What do you think, Anna?"

"That sounds fine," Anna said, turning to Helen. "Maybe you can show me how to groom them and feed them. Whatever I'm going to need to know."

Helen handed them their coats, but as Anna put hers on, her toothbrush fell to the floor.

"Did you think you were going to learn how to brush their teeth?" Helen joked.

Anna laughed, but she hoped Michael wouldn't ask why she was carrying her toothbrush in her coat pocket. She picked it up and dropped it in the trash, and imagined brushing her teeth with her finger tonight.

"I can't believe the time flew by so fast," Anna said, once they were back in the car, headed to Casey's. "Did you think it went well? I thought so. Much better than I expected. I loved that first dog. Charlie? I don't think it was just that he was first either. I know it will sound silly, but it was like we already knew each other. You're laughing," she accused Michael with good nature.

"I'm not," he said, trying to hide his smile.

"Andy and Paula will be shocked when I tell them how much I enjoyed it. And probably a little angry. They'll say, 'See, we could've had a pet all those years if you just would've listened!' "

"That would be Paula, right?"

"Andy too. He always wanted a dog in the worst way." She turned in the seat, so she could look at him. "Did Paula make a bad impression on you?"

"On the contrary, she made a very good impression. Whatever problems she may have given you while young, she seems to have matured into an admirable person. I liked her. I liked them both."

"And they both liked you," Anna admitted, recalling the Saturday night phone conversations with her children. They had both expressed approval and affection for her new boss.

"Only because I manipulated them," Michael teased.

"I really am sorry for saying that," Anna said with embarrassment. "I don't think I've ever in my life behaved worse to anyone. I was so scared. Terrified. I was looking for an excuse to back out of it."

"Not scared of me," he said, glancing at her.

"No, not at all," she assured him. "Scared to go away from home. Scared to work with animals. Scared to fail."

"You know what they say about fear – it's the opposite of faith."

"I know," Anna agreed. "But when I'm right in the middle of it, I can't think straight enough to pray my way out of it. Anyway, I'm sorry I took it out on you."

Michael reached for her hand. "We've both apologized enough. Let's try to forget all of that and start fresh."

"Thank you," Anna said with relief. "Will we call it a second chance?"

"*Another* chance," he reminded her. He squeezed her hand, then pulled away to shift gears. "Did you like Helen?"

"I did. She was very nice."

"The two of you have a lot in common. She single-parented her children too."

"Is she also a widow?"

He shook his head. "Divorced."

"I wonder if one is any harder than the other."

"I think it must be harder to see a marriage end if it was a happy one, like yours."

Anna swallowed hard and turned her head to look out the window. She tried to convince herself that an omission of information wasn't the same as lying. In either case, she wasn't willing to correct his assumption.

"The kids said your husband died of cancer?"

"He had lung cancer, though he never smoked."

"I imagine it was a difficult time for all three of you."

"Andy hardly remembers him, and Paula barely knew him." Anna didn't want to talk about Paul.

"What did he do for a living?"

"He was a psychologist at the city prison."

"Really?" Michael said with obvious surprise. "I would have expected you to mention it."

"Why? It has nothing to do with my credentials."

"Does it have something to do with why you wanted to work at Casey's?"

"No," Anna said firmly. "How many children does Helen have?"

He didn't answer right away. "Three," he finally said. "All boys, I think."

"If she has a way with children like she does with animals, I'm sure her kids will turn out great."

"Am I to assume you're comfortable enough with the situation to forge ahead?" Michael kept turning his head to look at her.

"Definitely! Oh look, now there are signs!" She pointed to the side of the road.

"Thanks to you," Michael admitted. "I hate to admit I didn't notice they were missing." He turned off the highway and shifted into first gear on the steep hill. "I'm sorry I doubted you when you said there weren't any signs."

"No more apologies," Anna reminded him. "Thanks for taking me today. And for going into the cage with me when I suffered that last minute panic."

Michael pulled into his parking space and shut off the engine. "You're welcome. I enjoyed it. If you want to spend the whole day there tomorrow, it's fine."

"I think it's a good way to be certain I'm going to be able to do it. By the end of the day I'll either be sold on the idea, or I'll pack up and go home."

He held up his finger and shook his head. "Do *not* go home. Come and see me and we'll talk."

Anna had only been kidding, but his response made her feel

good.

"Do you think you'll be able to find your way back to the shelter on your own?" he asked.

"I don't normally have trouble following directions," Anna told him, climbing out of the car.

"If you do get lost, find a pay phone and call me."

"I won't get lost," she said firmly. "But if I do, I'll call you."

He laughed and waved and hurried into the building.

♥ Chapter 6 ♥

"So tell me about your job," Marianne said eagerly, settling on one end of Anna's couch. "Working with dogs! It sounds so cool!"

"It didn't sound that way to me at first," Anna said. She pushed her shoes off and lifted her socked feet to the coffee table. "I've never had a pet and I've always been scared of animals."

"Then why did you apply for the position?"

Anna had the unhappy feeling that she wasn't meant to discuss the circumstances. "Ask me how many places I applied before I came to Casey's. I was desperate."

"I heard Dr. Grant took you to the shelter today," Marianne said.

"Word travels fast on this campus," Anna commented drolly. She wondered if every conversation would eventually turn into a discussion about Michael. "I got lost coming to Casey's the first time, so I think he was afraid I wouldn't be able to find my way there. Or back."

"I can imagine what Helen thought about *that*," Marianne said dramatically.

"Do you know her?" Anna asked with surprise.

"A little. She wants to work at Casey's, but she doesn't have a degree, so she just hangs around on the campus whenever she can come up with an excuse. I don't know why she doesn't apply for a job in the cafeteria or somethin'. It would probably pay as much as the shelter."

"I got the impression that she loves working with animals."

"Oh yeah, she does. She mostly wanted to be the one to do the thing you're doing. But Grant is way more important to her than any job. She's got a major thing for him, in case you didn't notice. She's actually kind of possessive, even if I doubt he ever gave her reason to be. I'd watch out, if I were you."

"Watch out?" Anna raised her eyebrows.

"You wouldn't want to say anything against him when you're talking to her," Marianne explained.

"I wouldn't say anything against him anyway. What makes you think I would?"

Marianne laughed self-consciously. "What I was trying to say without saying it is Helen might be jealous of you. See, he doesn't do things like that."

"Like what?"

"Giving you a ride to the shelter. He doesn't give people rides. And he doesn't eat dinner in his private dining room with new teachers."

Anna wanted to protest, but she couldn't think of anything to say. While it was flattering to think that Michael was giving her special treatment, she could see that it was going to cause friction with some of the other women.

"That day, when you came for your interview?" Marianne sat forward on the couch. "What happened after he sent everybody else home?"

Anna rubbed her fingertips over her temples, wondering how to answer without breaking her promise to Michael.

"Your car was parked on the lot by the admin building all night. A couple people saw it. And somebody said Grant was out of town."

"I'm sure that's enough to make a lot of people jump to false conclusions," Anna said, averting her eyes.

Marianne sighed. "You really didn't know him before you came and applied for the job?"

"No," Anna said. "I didn't meet him until the day I came for an interview."

"I think you're tryin' to say it's none of my business."

Marianne looked dejected. "Sorry."

"I'm sorry too," Anna said. "Now I have something to ask you. I had to come back to the dorm after lunch, to change clothes before I went to the shelter, and there were two women in my room, going through my stuff."

Marianne crossed her arms and frowned. "What did they look like?"

"They were fairly young. Not yet thirty, I think."

"Brown hair?"

"Yes, but I didn't get a very good look at them."

"Cindy and Melody," Marianne guessed with disgust.

"How'd they get in?" Anna asked, wringing her hands.

"You musta left your door unlocked."

Anna filled her cheeks with air. "Maybe I did. I just ran down the hall to brush my teeth."

"What did they say?"

Anna put her feet on the floor and clasped her hands between her knees. "I didn't confront them. I just left."

"Smart move. If you *had* said anything, they'd make up some story and tell Grant and you'd be the one who got in trouble. Well, that's if it were *me*. It seems like you have a different relationship with him than the rest of us do, so maybe he'd listen to you."

Anna sat back and contemplated the situation. "You do like Dr. Grant, don't you?"

"Pretty much. I think he's really dedicated and mostly nice."

"And fair?"

Marianne raised one shoulder. "Usually."

"Do you think he realizes he's showing partiality to the twins?"

"I dunno," Marianne said. "I don't really know him. Nobody does. Some people think he's a tyrant. They'd like to see him get replaced."

"But you don't feel that way?"

Marianne shrugged. "I don't always agree with his decisions, but I think he probably has a good excuse for making them." She grew quiet for a moment. "When I first came to Casey's, I Googled him, but I couldn't find much information. He's been here a long time. Like fifteen years? So you'd think there would be a lot of articles and stuff about him."

"Maybe he's not good about granting interviews. I think he's just a very private person. I can respect that because I'm something of a private person myself."

"I don't have anything to be private about," Marianne sighed.

"I don't either," Anna admitted with a laugh. "I think it's more that I'm self-conscious. Once I get to know someone, I don't worry about it anymore."

"I hope we're gonna get to know each other that well," Marianne said wistfully.

"I'm sure we will, if I get to come back next year."

"I'd put in a good word for you but ... I don't think my opinion counts for much."

"It does with me," Anna assured her.

Marianne looked pleased. She stood up and stretched. "Gotta go. Papers to grade − oh golly what fun."

Anna thought it *did* sound like fun. "And I need to unpack the rest of my stuff and get organized."

Once Marianne had gone, Anna set to work. It didn't take long to distribute paper and pens into the desk, and arrange her clothing in the small closet and dresser. Then she went to the window and stared up at the stars and realized she hadn't really prayed since leaving St. Louis.

"I'm sorry," she whispered. "It's not that I forgot about You, it's just that ..." But the truth was, she *had* forgotten Him. She hadn't asked for His blessing on her trip to the animal shelter, nor had she thanked Him after it went well. She mulled this over, chastising herself. She was convinced that He must be angry with her, even if she no longer believed He got angry with His children for their mistakes. She was the one who suffered when she didn't keep God first in her life. She wondered how many times she would need to learn that lesson before it sank in for good.

She vowed to do better in the coming days, then changed into her pajamas and hurried down the hall to the restroom, toothpaste in hand. She would ask Helen where to find a drugstore and purchase a new toothbrush on her way home from the shelter tomorrow.

Home from the shelter? She had lived at Casey's less than a week, but it already felt like home! She was still smiling when she slipped between the sheets and fell fast asleep.

"Did you know Michael before you applied at Casey's?" Helen asked.

Anna barely kept from smiling. "No, we'd never met before."

Helen took a bite of her sandwich. She had invited Anna to join her at a nearby deli for dinner since there had been little opportunity to chat while they were working with the animals.

"You're not married?" Helen asked.

Anna shook her head. "My husband passed away."

"I'm sorry," Helen said with a sober expression.

"Thanks. It was a long time ago."

"I've been on my own for a long time too. You have kids?"

"A boy and a girl, both in college."

"I've got three boys. Not too many men want to get involved with a woman who's got three kids and no child support. I guess you got social security for your kids, didn't you?"

Anna hesitated. "Yes, until they were eighteen. It helped."

"I'm sure it did. I've only got one left at home, and he'll graduate in May. You mind if I ask a personal question?"

Anna wished she was the sort of person to say, "Yes, I would mind." She smiled instead.

"Is there something going on between you and Dr. Grant?"

"Do you mean are we dating?" Anna shook her head 'no.' They weren't dating, so why did it seem like a lie?

"I thought I should warn you. Like most men, he does have a dark side."

"A dark side?" Anna said with surprise. "Are you speaking from personal experience?"

"I'd rather not go into detail."

Anna used her fork to pick up the chicken salad that had escaped from her croissant. What if her first impression of Michael had been correct? What if he *did* make a habit of luring women to his private club for something other than dinner?

"Did you know this program was my idea?" Helen asked.

"I think Dr. Grant mentioned that."

"I had actually hoped to be the one to set it up and run it." Helen met Anna's eyes without smiling.

Anna took a drink of her tea. "Maybe he didn't realize you felt that way?"

"He knew. I told him and he doesn't forget anything. He's got that sort of brain, you know. What do they call it? Photographic memory?"

Anna raised her shoulders, to say she wasn't sure. "He mentioned that he wanted someone who wasn't an animal lover."

Helen laughed, but it was obvious that she wasn't amused. "Don't feel bad. If it hadn't been you, it would've been someone else. Anybody but me."

"He has only the nicest things to say about you," Anna said with sympathy.

"Does he?" Helen dropped the remains of her sandwich to her plate and pushed it away. "He was nice to me after I got divorced. I was in a financial mess and didn't figure I could keep working at the shelter because the pay was so lousy. Michael went to the city council and talked them into giving me a decent salary and benefits. And he gave me a check for a couple thousand bucks. He said someone had taken up a collection, but I doubt it. I think it came out of his own pocket."

"Then what makes you say he's got a dark side?" The more Helen said, the more it seemed she only hoped to scare Anna off.

"I guess he's like anybody. Sometimes good, sometimes not." She took a deep breath and pushed her blond hair away from her face. "So, when are you coming back?"

"I'm not sure. It's up to Dr. Grant, not me."

"Call me when you find out, will you?"

They both stood and placed their dishes and trash on the tray.

"Thanks for everything," Anna said, feeling as though she'd done something wrong.

"Look, it's nothing, okay?" Helen dumped everything into the trash can and set the tray on top. "I just never saw him act like that before, the way he was with you."

"I don't know what you mean. The way he was with me?"

"Maybe it was my imagination," Helen said, watching her carefully. "It seemed like he acted so protective. Driving you here, going into the kennel with you ..."

Anna didn't know what to say. "I think he had some concerns whether I'd be able to overcome my fear and work with the animals."

"That's exactly why it doesn't make sense. Why would he hire someone who's afraid of dogs?"

Anna shrugged. "Far be it from me to explain his behavior. I have a hard enough time trying to figure out my own."

Helen studied her for a moment, then waved her hand in the air. "If I don't pick up, leave a message. I'm there all the time, but I like a little notice when someone is coming."

"I'll do that," Anna promised, and hurried off to her car. She couldn't help replaying the conversation in her mind as she drove away. Maybe she should've tried to say something comforting to Helen, but what?

She had forgotten to ask for directions to a drug store, so she headed towards Briarton, gazing around with interest. It seemed typical of a small town, with houses of various sizes standing side by side, interspersed with the occasional small business. She wondered if Michael lived in Briarton, in one of the homes she had passed. She had assumed he lived on Casey's campus, but perhaps he relished time away from the school.

As she neared the highway, Anna spied a Walgreens and turned onto the parking lot. Once inside the store, she wandered the aisles, picking out a few items that would dress up her living space. A poster with kittens and puppies bore an appropriate caption: *Making New Friends*. Bright yellow flowers stitched on a blue pillow went into the cart next. She couldn't resist the snack aisle, then added a case of bottled water. She almost forgot to look for a toothbrush.

Anna was surprised when she checked her watch and it was after eight o'clock. She hurried to the check-out, but by time she returned to Casey's, it was nearly nine. She was hiding the snacks in the box beneath her bed when the phone rang.

"Anna?" Michael said, a note of concern obvious in his voice.

"I wondered what happened to you."

"Was I supposed to come to the office when I got back?" she asked with a sinking feeling.

"No, I just assumed you'd return on time for dinner."

"Did you think I got lost?" She giggled. "Helen and I went out for a sandwich and then I stopped to pick up a few things at Walgreens."

"Did you have a productive day?"

"I learned a lot. Some of it was enjoyable, some was not. Playing with the dogs was good. Cleaning kennels was not good."

"You'll be passing that job on to the students," Michael promised. "You didn't sneak a puppy into the dorm, did you?"

"No, but you didn't say anything about kittens."

He laughed. "You'd better be kidding! Come over to the office in the morning and we'll figure out what comes next. Eight o'clock, okay?"

"Yes, that's fine," Anna said, already planning to arrive at 7:30. She hung up and hugged her new pillow.

♥ Chapter 7 ♥

Anna spent the morning making telephone calls to government offices and correctional centers that already had a pet therapy program in place. She had printed a lot of information and separated it into folders. Michael provided a drawer in one of the filing cabinets across from Tina's desk.

Anna liked working in the waiting room, chatting with Tina and interacting with Michael whenever he emerged from his office. When Tina mentioned that she would be getting married in August, Anna wondered if she could fill in during her absence. It would be wonderful to see Michael throughout the day, and feel she was really helping him. She laughed at herself – hadn't she spent eight years earning a degree so she could *stop* being a secretary?

"Dr. Grant had a dog, when I first started working for him," Tina told her. "It was a golden retriever, I think. He took it around with him, everywhere he went. The kids would all pet it and play with it."

"What happened?" Anna asked, trying to imagine the reserved administrator whistling for his dog.

"He had to have it put down. Old age, I guess."

"Wonder why he didn't get another one," Anna said thoughtfully.

Tina shrugged. "When you have kids, you expect they'll outlive you, but when you get a pet, it's pretty certain you're going to have to watch it die."

Anna thought about Charlie, the sweet dog at the shelter. Though she hadn't spent a lot of time with him, it would upset her if he had to be put to sleep. "Do you think he's the sort of person who would have a difficult time with that?"

Tina met her eyes. "He's very tender hearted. I know you're going to hear a lot of negative stuff, if you haven't already, so I wanted to throw in my two cents worth."

Anna smiled at her. "I'm sure your opinion is worth more than all of theirs added together."

♥ ♥ ♥

Michael told Anna to meet him at the front door on Thursday morning. He had tentative plans about where the kennels would be located, but wanted her opinion before he made a final decision. He also planned to give her a tour of the campus.

He began upstairs, walking slowly down the hallways, naming the subject and the teacher as they passed classrooms that were in session. The campus was clean and nicely furnished, and Anna found it easy to make positive comments. She was disappointed when she asked if she could see where the students lived.

"I've found it's best to keep the student dorms off limits to anyone who doesn't serve a purpose there," Michael said apologetically. "I know it must sound silly, but all rules are the result of some problem that arose before the rule was made."

He showed her the gym and a workout room, the swimming pool and indoor tennis court. The tour ended in the basement, at the end of a long hallway.

"I need you to exercise your imagination," Michael said, unlocking a door and leading her into a large area that was being used for storage. "This is where we're going to house the animals."

Anna looked around with a mixture of excitement and disappointment. The area had a lot of potential, but it was so far away from everything else, including the administrator's office.

"What's wrong?" Michael asked.

"Nothing!" she said brightly.

He hesitated, then stepped closer and took both of her hands. "I thought we had an agreement about being honest with one another." He tilted his head to one side and looked into her eyes.

She drew a deep breath. "I'm sorry. It's perfect, just somewhat isolated."

He squeezed her hands and released them. "I wish I could put you closer to the classrooms, but there are too many complications. Barking dogs, unpleasant odors … And you'll need easy access to the outdoors."

"I understand," Anna said. "I'm sure I'll feel comfortable with it in no time."

"I'll probably post a security guard in the area whenever the students are going to be with you. Will that help?"

"I'm not scared," Anna assured him. "I'm definitely not scared of the students."

"You need to be careful with them, Anna. They're not all like the group you met in my office that day."

"What's the worst crime any of them committed?" Anna asked. She guessed he would say breaking and entering.

"It depends on your outlook. Rape, assault, involuntary manslaughter … Some very serious offences."

Anna hoped she didn't look shocked.

"We'll put the kennels along this wall," he said, turning away. "Since there's a drain handy, the students will be able to hose them down."

He unlocked the back door with a key and she followed him outside. There was a large grassy area, shaded by mature trees. Anna liked being outside, so this was a definite plus. She gazed up at the building and tried to get her bearings.

"Is that your office?" she asked, gesturing to the window.

"It is. I hope you won't feel self-conscious?"

"Not at all. It will give me an added sense of wellbeing."

He looked pleased by this remark. "I'm going to have fencing installed, so we don't have dogs running all over the campus. And I'm going to hire an AHT, possibly two."

"What's an AHT?"

"Animal Health Technician. They'll take the brunt of the responsibility for the animals and free you up to work with the students. It will save asking Helen to come every time there's a problem."

Anna bit her lip. "Did you know she wanted this job?"

"Yes, she mentioned it several times." He paused, as though giving Anna the opportunity to pursue the topic.

She decided it was best to change the subject. "One thing that really bothers me ... They say it takes eight to ten months to thoroughly train a service dog. Won't the kids be attached to them by then? Won't it be hard to give them up?"

"The kids are meant to return to society and resume their lives, in as short an interval as possible. Our objective for the animals will be the same − teach them to serve a useful purpose, then send them out into the world to do it."

"That makes sense," Anna said, though she still thought it would be difficult. "What about Charlie?"

"Charlie? Your first canine friend?"

"Yes," she said. "Will he be part of the program?"

Michael hesitated. "Helen seemed to think he was incorrigible."

"Could we try?" Anna said hopefully.

Michael laughed. "This is what I get after one day at the shelter? Will you plead with me to keep *all* the dogs, after they're trained?"

"I won't, I promise," Anna said. "Well, I don't promise, but I'll try not to."

He kept smiling. "I'll talk to Helen about Charlie."

"I'm worried she's going to put him to sleep, because of the way he jumps on people."

"I'll call her as soon as I get back to my office, okay?"

Anna bobbed her head with satisfaction. "Will I need to take classes to learn how to teach the kids to train the dogs?"

"I don't think that will be necessary since you're going to have the AHTs to assist you. I've got several interviews scheduled, and all of the applicants have had experience with some kind of rescue program. Would you like to sit in?"

"That would be great," Anna agreed. "I'm sure I could learn a lot from them."

He led her back into the building and rested his hands on her shoulders for a moment. "I'm going to hire outside help to do the painting and install the kennels. What color would you like the walls?"

"Yellow," Anna said, without hesitation. She stood very still, so he wouldn't think she wanted him to take his hands away. "When will they start?"

He released her and backed away. "It takes time to run background checks."

Anna made a face. "I'm afraid I'm only going to get to do the program for a couple of weeks before school lets out. Could I paint it myself?"

Michael laughed, then he seemed to realize she was serious. "That reminds me of an important rule I haven't mentioned: never roam the building without a partner. An *adult* partner. And the school is off limits after five and before seven, unless you're with me."

"Does that mean I can't paint?"

"Let me think about it."

"That's better than 'no,' " Anna decided. "I work cheap and I could start tomorrow."

He laughed again. "How am I supposed to refuse an offer like that?"

Michael sent Anna back to Briarton on Friday, since there wasn't much she could accomplish before Monday. She hoped he didn't notice that her enthusiasm for visiting the shelter had waned.

Helen greeted her in a businesslike manner and ushered her into the small office where she kept records. She invited Anna to sit down, then sat at the desk, facing her. "It's going to be difficult for us to work together if you won't be honest with me," she said without smiling. "I told you that I have friends at Casey's, didn't I? Didn't you think I would hear about you and Michael?"

Anna warned herself to proceed cautiously. "I'm not sure what you heard," she said.

Helen's eyes narrowed. "I heard that the two of you spent the night together, the day you supposedly came for an interview."

"I beg your pardon!" Anna said, jumping up from the chair. She didn't even try to conceal her anger. "I sincerely hope you didn't mean that the way it sounded!"

Helen was already holding up both hands and a rosy blush was creeping over her neck.

"I don't know anything about your relationship with Dr. Grant," Anna went on. "But if you feel he has failed to keep a commitment to you, or stepped out of bounds in some way, you need to take that up with him. I am here to learn to handle the dogs. If you prefer not to be the one to teach me, then say so and I'll ask Dr. Grant to find someone else." Anna felt certain that her own face was equally red, but from anger, not embarrassment.

"I apologize," Helen said. "Obviously my source was misinformed."

"Your *source*?"

"Bad word choice. It was just a casual conversation between friends and she mentioned that you and Michael ..."

"I'm not interested in hearing anymore petty gossip," Anna interrupted. "What did you plan for me to do today?"

"Please sit down," Helen pleaded. "I'm sorry I made you so mad. I'm not much of a diplomat when I've got something on my mind."

"It's time for me to be working, not chatting," Anna insisted. "Would you like me to begin cleaning the kennels?"

Helen drew a tissue from a box on her desk and pressed it to her eyes. "If you go back and tell Michael what I said ..."

Anna walked out of the office and hurried into the room where the larger dogs were kept. She slipped into Charlie's kennel and when he stood on his hind legs to lick her chin, she welcomed the attention. "What a mess I've gotten myself into," she confided to the dog. "It looks as if we did something wrong, but he's asked me not to explain." She understood, at that moment, why dogs were considered good therapists. Charlie couldn't speak a word of judgment against her, nor could he repeat the things she said. What was more, he didn't seem to care whether or not she had done something to earn the disapproval of her peers. "Thanks," she whispered in his ear. "You're a great friend, Charlie. And right about now, it feels like you're the only real friend I've got."

By the time Helen came looking for Anna, half the kennels were clean. The two women worked together, but there was no friendly conversation. By the end of the day, Anna's shoulders were stiff with tension and she couldn't wait to return to Casey's.

"Please, please, *please* do not tell Michael that we argued," Helen said, as Anna put on her jacket and prepared to leave.

Anna wasn't willing to make such a promise. "I'll let you know the timetable as it is made known to me," she said. "Have a nice weekend."

"Thanks, you too," Helen said somberly.

Anna was tempted to ease her old car over the speed limit, but she wouldn't want Dr. Grant to hear that she had gotten a speeding ticket. It was just before six when she parked in front of the dorm, and she wondered if Marianne and the others had already eaten their dinner.

A crowd of women stood milling about at the top of the stairs.

"About time!" Sally said, when she spied Anna approaching. "We've been waiting for you, so we could thank you."

"For what?" Anna asked with bewilderment.

"Providing us with an excuse to party," Sally hooted. "You survived your first week at Casey's!"

Anna had no desire to party, but she wasn't willing to offend her new friends. As the others went to fetch jackets, she unlocked her door and invited Marianne inside. "Let's invite everyone," she suggested. "Gayle, Cindy, Melody ..."

"Bad idea," Marianne objected crossly. "Very bad idea."

"Good will has to begin somewhere!" Anna said, disappointed by Marianne's reluctance.

"She wants to invite Gayle and the twins," Marianne told Sally when she joined them.

"Go ahead," Sally said. "It'll be a quick study why we don't get along."

Angelo's was a pizza parlor with a live band. It was crowded and noisy and filled with cigarette smoke. Though Gayle declined the invitation, the "twins" accepted, then huddled in a booth, whispering like grade school conspirators. Susie drank too much and got sick. Sally drank too much and got angry when Rea snatched her keys.

"How come you don't drink?" Marianne asked during the ride back to the dorm. "Are you an alcoholic or somethin'?"

"My husband's job required that we attend a lot of social events, trying to get grant money and contributions," Anna recalled. "I usually drank a glass of wine, to try to fit in. Then one night, I couldn't drink because I was taking antibiotics. When I saw how people behaved ..."

"I usually drink a lot more than I did tonight," Marianne confessed. "I wonder if I ever behave really stupid."

"What are you doing tomorrow?" Anna changed the subject. "Want to go shopping?"

"Sure!" Marianne said. "Want to go out for breakfast first?"

"I love eating breakfast out. Where's a good place?"

"Wake me up around eight and I'll show you."

"It's a deal," Anna said happily.

Marianne suggested a buffet on the other side of Briarton, that she claimed was well worth the long drive.

They made four trips to the food bar before they were sated, and shared their histories over a final cup of coffee.

"I had this friend, Stella," Marianne said sadly. "She was for causes. I wanted to get married and have a bunch of kids and Stella wanted to save the world."

Anna reached across the table to pat her hand.

"She was a much better person than me, so how come she died and I'm still around?" Marianne wiped her eyes with her napkin. "I never found a husband so I decided I oughta carry on her work. Who was your hero?"

"My hero?" Anna repeated, wondering how to answer.

"I figured it was your husband. Somebody said you're divorced, but you wear a wedding ring so I figure he died."

"He did," Anna said, reluctant to paint Paul as a hero, though some might think he deserved the honor. "He worked as a psychologist at a prison."

"Oh, wowser!" Marianne said, pressing her hands over her mouth. "Whatever you do, don't turn around!"

"Why?" Anna asked, aching to do just that.

"Dr. Grant," Marianne whispered. "With a woman! Some gorgeous redhead!"

"Is she his wife?" Anna asked, fearful that he had lied about his marital status.

"He's not married. Go figure ..."

Anna couldn't resist. She turned her head and immediately caught sight of Michael and his companion. "Let's leave," she said, sliding down in the booth. "Quick, before he sees us."

"Too late," Marianne said. "He's coming over."

Michael didn't look happy. "Ladies," he said politely. "What are you doing so far from home?"

"Eating," Marianne stated the obvious.

"Well, you made a good choice if you're exceptionally hungry. I hear there was a celebration last night," he said, meeting Anna's eyes.

Anna glanced at Marianne and shrugged her shoulders. "We went out for pizza."

"I heard some of the ladies imbibed in more than pizza," he suggested, turning his eyes on Marianne.

"So we had a couple of drinks," she said. "What's wrong with that?"

"I didn't drink alcohol. Just soda," Anna was quick to explain.

"Some situations are not what they appear to be," Michael said. "I'm meeting a colleague for breakfast, because we needed to discuss a few matters that are coming due on Monday morning."

Marianne and Anna only looked at each other, uncertain what to say.

"I'm glad your first week finished up well enough to merit a celebration," Michael told Anna, resting his hand on her shoulder for a moment. "Enjoy your day."

The moment he walked off, Marianne nudged Anna under the table. "He's got a thing for you!" she said with excitement.

"Grant's got a thing for you!"

"He does not!" Anna protested.

"'Scuse me, but I've been at Casey's for six years and I know what I know. Grant's got a thing for you!"

"He was with another woman," Anna reminded her.

"A colleague."

"Oh, sure. Even I'm not *that* naïve."

"Situations aren't always like they seem? That was his way of tellin' you that there's nothin' goin' on."

"Of course he's going to deny it," Anna said wearily. "He doesn't want us to spread rumors, especially if she's married."

"He wouldn't go out with a married woman," Marianne said firmly. "He's not that kind of guy. He's a good person, even if he is a little near-sighted sometimes. And he's interested in you. Very interested. He didn't even care if I picked up on it."

Anna touched her napkin to her eyes, uncertain why they had filled with tears. She would hate it if Michael looked at their table and saw her crying.

"He touched you!" Marianne went on. "He doesn't touch anybody! Look, if you don't want to confide in me, that's your right, but don't lie to me, okay?"

Anna felt miserable. There it was again, someone asking for a promise that sounded so simple on the surface, but by keeping one promise, she broke another. "I ate too much. I need to get up and move around," she evaded the issue. "Are you ready to go?"

"We can go out the back door if you want, so he doesn't see you cryin'."

"I'm not crying," Anna insisted.

♥ Chapter 8 ♥

Though Michael hadn't given Anna instructions for the following week, she arrived at his office at 7:30 on Monday morning. She wondered if Michael would mention seeing her at the buffet. Maybe he would say more about the beautiful redheaded woman, explaining what sort of colleague she was.

Tina was busy pulling files, so she told Anna to knock on his door.

Michael opened it immediately. "I was about to call you, to set up our schedule for the week," he said. He had removed his coat and loosened his tie.

Anna wondered just how early he started every morning. "Are you one of those men who wear a tie while they watch TV in the evening?"

"I probably would, if I ever sat and watched TV," he said with good humor. "A suit commands more respect than a T-shirt, whether or not it should."

"Being tall also helps."

He chuckled as he adjusted his tie and put on his coat. "Is that why you were wearing those four inch heels when you came to apply for the job?"

"They weren't four inches!" Anna protested. "I'm sure I couldn't walk in four inch heels! It is a problem though, being short. I remember once when some bullies were harassing Andy and I called the police. They kept asking Andy where his mother was, ignoring me altogether."

"Was Andy taller than you by then?"

"He was taller than me in the fifth grade," Anna admitted.
"Are you unusually tall for your family?"

"My father and brother are taller than I am. What about your
family? Are they all short?"

"No," Anna sighed. "Just me."

Michael chuckled and squeezed the back of her neck. "I think
you're perfect exactly as you are."

"Thanks," she said, recalling the claims Marianne had made
after they saw Michael at the buffet. Was it possible that he did
have special feelings for her? Maybe the woman with red hair
really *was* just a colleague …

"Have a seat," he said, gesturing at the couch. "Would you like
a cup of coffee?"

"That would be nice," Anna said, though the additional
caffeine would make her jittery.

He filled two mugs and handed her one as he sat down. "Don't
spill it on your pretty dress. Is it new?"

"It is. I bought it on Saturday," she hinted.

Michael merely nodded. "How are things going? Any
problems?"

She thought of Helen. "Nothing that bears mentioning. Are
you going to allow me to paint?"

He sat back against the cushions and sighed. "If you can find
someone who'll help you, you may paint as much of the wall as
you can reach from the floor. No ladder."

"Insurance concerns?"

He nodded.

"I thought you had a nest of vipers to handle those pesky law
suits," she teased.

He laughed. "I should never have said that to you. I'm sorry."

"No more apologies," she reminded him. "I'll ask Marianne to
help."

"Except that Marianne has classes during the day."

Anna made a face. "What about after school? We'd have a
couple of hours."

"All right," he gave in.

"May we begin today?"

He tapped his fingers on his knee. "I'll try to find time to run into Briarton and pick up some paint this morning. Yellow, right?"

She wanted to ask if she could go along, until she thought of all the windows that looked out at his parking space. "What would you like for me to do today?" she asked instead.

"You don't want to go back to the shelter?" He sipped his coffee as he waited for an answer.

"Not today." She forced a tone of nonchalance. "I could work on a list of organizations that need service dogs. It sounds as if each one has their own set of requirements, depending on what sort of handicaps they're dealing with."

"You might have them send us a brochure for our files."

"Okay," she agreed. "Now, don't feel that you're under any pressure to get the paint today." She was grinning and she knew her eyes were twinkling.

Michael laughed and stood up. "Let me check my schedule. If Tina can rearrange my appointments, would you like to ride along and pick out the color yourself?"

"I'd love to," Anna said with delight, forgetting any concerns about being seen from the windows.

"Have you talked with Andy and Paula? How are things going for them?" Michael asked, as soon as they were underway.

Anna turned in the seat, so she could look at him as they traveled. "Andy's got a serious girlfriend. First one since high school."

"Are you the kind of mom who won't think any girl is good enough for her son?"

"If he loves her, I'm sure I will too."

"What about Paula? Is she serious about anyone?"

Anna laughed. "Paula is *always* serious about some guy, but it's a different guy each week."

"And what about their mother? How often does she get serious about some guy?"

Anna looked through the windshield, debating whether to answer. "I haven't been serious about anyone since I became a widow."

"Is that because you haven't given anyone a chance?" he asked softly.

She gave the question careful consideration. "I was optimistic at first, but as it turns out, I'm a very poor judge of character."

He didn't say anything, but he glanced at her several times.

Anna sighed noisily. "My friends used to fix me up and I met a few men through my church. It just never worked out." She lifted her hands and let them drop.

"So you stopped dating and resigned yourself to remaining single?"

"I don't think I made a conscious decision. I just … never fell in love." She didn't dare look in his direction.

He reached over and found her hand, lacing his fingers with hers. "Are you thinking of a bright yellow or something muted?"

She slumped with relief. "Bright yellow with sky-blue trim?"

"How about blue on bottom and yellow on top?"

"Good idea," Anna said happily. "Blue won't show paw prints as easily."

"I appreciate your willingness to be flexible."

"I appreciate you allowing me any input at all."

He squeezed her hand. "I find myself wanting to ask your opinion about all sorts of things."

Anna tried not to smile. He had paid her a high compliment and she knew it.

Michael had an important appointment at eleven o'clock, so Anna didn't spend much time considering the various shades of blue and yellow. She handed him the samples and asked for his opinion, pleased when he agreed with her choices. They read the label together, to be certain it wouldn't be harmful to the animals. Then they wandered around the store, while the paint was being mixed.

"Did you decide if you're going to ask one of the counselors to oversee the pet training program?" Anna asked.

"I've talked with Shirley Jackson about it. She wasn't thrilled to add anything to her schedule, but she's the sort of person who will change her attitude when the time comes. I asked her to drop by and introduce herself this afternoon, at 4:30. Don't forget you'll need to be out of the building by five."

"I hope Marianne is willing to help."

"Who could say 'no' to you?"

She looked up at him and saw that he was sincere.

Anna didn't find a chance to ask Marianne until the lunch hour.

"Sure!" Marianne agreed. "I'm sloppy with a paint brush, but I'm good with a rag."

They agreed to meet at the front door around 3:30, giving Marianne time to go to the dorm and change clothes first.

Anna settled on the front step at 3:25, hoping to enjoy the beautiful weather while she waited.

"Anna Brown?" one of the security guards summoned her. "Marianne Faraday says to tell you she'll be late and you should go on down and start without her."

Anna remembered Michael's warning about traveling with a partner. He hadn't said she couldn't *be* downstairs alone, just that she couldn't *go there* on her own. Maybe the rule only applied to traveling the hallways.

"Would you have time to walk me down there?" she asked the guard.

"Sure," he said. "Let me make a note in the log and inform my partner where I'm going."

Anna followed him back inside, then asked if he knew where the dog kennels were to be located.

"Yes ma'am. Dr. Grant is good about keeping us informed so we don't accidentally shoot any innocent parties."

Anna gazed at him with horror-filled eyes, until he laughed.

"I had you figured for gullible," he said with a chuckle. "My name's Russell, in case you didn't already know."

"I'm not likely to forget it," Anna said, following him down the stairs.

He turned back when they reached the door, after wishing

Anna luck with her project. She thanked him and immediately set to work.

Though Michael had expressly forbidden her to climb a ladder, there were two of them leaning against the wall. He had apparently changed his mind, she mused happily. She would work with yellow, and leave the blue for Marianne. Humming to herself, she painted a broad yellow stripe, as high as she could reach, then stepped back and considered the color. She couldn't recall whether it would darken or lighten as it dried, but in either case, she would be well satisfied.

The concrete blocks made a natural line that was easy to follow and she soon completed as much as she could reach from the floor. Excited about her progress, she set up one of the ladders and climbed to the third rung. She worked on either side, then stepped one rung higher. She hoped she could finish one wall, in case Michael came to check on her progress. He would surely be impressed.

"Hello there," a male voice said behind her. "Where'd you come from?"

Anna turned her head and found a good looking man in his forties, wearing a suit and tie.

"Where's the rest of your crew?" he asked. "You need some help getting down from there?"

He reached up and grasped Anna's waist before she could object. Even after her feet were planted solidly on the floor, his hands lingered at her hips.

She wrenched free and backed away, wishing Marianne would choose that moment to arrive.

"Are you down here by yourself?" the man said. "Maybe nobody told you about the buddy system?"

"I was escorted down by one of the security guards."

"Oh, so she *can* talk," he said with exaggerated surprise. "Are you a new maintenance person?"

"No," Anna said. "I'm a ..." She wasn't sure what her title was. "I'm doing the pet therapy. I'm not sure that's what it will be called, but I'll be working with the kids and the dogs."

"Pet therapy?"

"It's an exciting new project," Anna said. "The kids will take care of dogs brought in by the humane society. They'll be training them as service dogs for people who are disabled."

He shook his head. "I'm the head counselor at Casey's. I would've been consulted before a program like that got started."

Anna didn't know what to say. She shrugged her shoulders, to plead innocence.

"So if you're going to run this new program, why are you painting?"

"The painters couldn't get to it for a while, so I offered."

"And Grant went along with that?" he said with obvious skepticism. "Did he give you permission to use a ladder?"

Anna suddenly feared that climbing the ladder had been a mistake. "I think I may have misunderstood," she admitted, putting the paint can down and carefully balancing the brush on top. "I'd better go upstairs and check, just to be sure."

"What's your name?"

"Anna Brown. What's yours?"

He smiled, showing even white teeth. "How are you going to get upstairs without an escort, Miss Brown?"

Once again, she wished for a cell phone. How easy it would be to resolve this if she could call Tina and ask what Dr. Grant would have her do! "Would you be willing to escort me?"

He came closer and grabbed her wrist. "I'll escort you right upstairs to the security guards," he said in a stern voice. "I don't know what kind of game you're playing, but I've been around too long to fall for it."

Anna winced and tried to pull free, but he had a vice-like grip. "There's no need to use physical force," she said, hoping he couldn't hear the fear in her voice. "If you want to take me to the security guards, I'll go with you. If you have a cell phone, you could call Dr. Grant, or Tina. They can verify my identity."

He pulled her closer, twisting her wrist until she feared it would snap. "I don't want to get you in trouble, honey. I'd just hate to see you get hurt down here, miles away from everybody. You could probably scream and no one would even hear you."

Anna understood what he was trying to say. She tried to remember the tricks she had been taught, to defend herself from a bully, even while she prayed she wouldn't need to use them.

The man leaned down, until their faces were inches apart. "I'm gonna let you go this time, but next time I catch you alone, I won't go so easy on you. Am I making myself clear?"

"Yes," she said, gritting her teeth to withstand the pain.

"You wanna do something to show your appreciation?"

Before Anna could respond, he turned her loose. "Now go on back where you're supposed to be, and I'll forget I ever saw you," he said, wagging his finger.

Anna didn't want to leave without putting the lid on the paint can and washing the brush, but she wasn't willing to spend another minute in this man's presence. Giving him wide berth, she darted through the door and ran to the stairs. Now she *knew* she was breaking the rules, and could only hope she didn't run into Michael. How would she explain what she had done? She had been caught alone, on the ladder. He had trusted her and she had let him down.

As soon as she reached the dorm, she went to the restroom and ran cold water over her wrist, hoping to keep it from bruising. She wanted to know who the man was, and how much power he had. She would be careful to avoid him in the future, and he would *never* catch her alone again.

She returned to her room and paced nervously in the small area. She didn't know how to contact Marianne and tell her what had happened. She could only hope she would either call soon, or return to the dorm. It was nearly four thirty, leaving little time to return to the school, close up the paint cans and clean the brush. She had planned to wipe up any paint spatters from the cement floor too …

When the phone rang, she snatched it up with relief. But it wasn't Marianne, it was Michael.

"Did something happen?" he asked. "I went down to see how you were doing and it looked as if you left in a hurry for some reason."

"A misunderstanding," Anna said nervously.

"Did you also misunderstand about the ladder? Obviously you couldn't reach that high without one."

"When I found them propped against the wall, I thought you must have changed your mind." She hoped she could finish the

112

conversation without bursting into tears. "I'm so sorry."

"What's wrong, Anna? I can hear that something has upset you."

"I'm upset that I disappointed you by not following directions," she said, hoping to fool him.

"All right," he said calmly. "I've found someone to help you tomorrow. Report in at the office around eight o'clock."

"I'll be there. Thank you. I'm sorry." She hung up and blinked hard to keep from crying. Any of the other women might pop in on her at any moment, and she didn't want to explain her tears. If only Marianne would return! She would know who the man was, once Anna described him. She would be able to give Anna advice on what to do.

She went to the window and stared across the lawn at the stone house. Somewhere on the campus there were apartments, for those who were willing to pay. She wished she had been able to rent one so she could be assured of privacy and solitude now.

Someone knocked on the door and she ran to open it, praying it would be Marianne.

It was Michael.

He came in and closed the door behind him, then studied her with an expression of concern. "What happened, Anna?"

She lifted her chin, uncertain why she was unwilling to tell him. "Is there a rule book? Things like traveling in pairs … Is there a book that lists all those rules so I can be certain to abide by them?"

He was silent for a long moment. "New teachers usually receive a guide when they go through orientation. I'll give you a copy of everything tomorrow."

She reached up and tucked a few loose tendrils of hair into her bun. "I'll ask Marianne to go over it with me, so I don't break any more rules."

"What rules do you think you may have broken?"

She crossed her arms and stared up at the ceiling. "Am I allowed to be alone in my area so long as I don't walk through the halls alone?"

"I don't want you alone anywhere in the building," he said firmly.

"Does that rule apply to everyone, or just me?"

"It applies to everyone," he said emphatically.

"Except you?

"And the security guards."

"No one else?"

He shook his head. "No exceptions."

Whoever the man was, he had been breaking the rule too!

"Marianne got held up," she explained.

"So you went on your own?"

"A security guard escorted me down there." She knew that didn't excuse *her* mistakes. "Russell."

"Did he realize you were going to be on your own?" Michael asked, resting his hands on his hips.

"I'm sure he didn't. He only took me to the door."

"What happened to your wrist?"

She pulled her sleeve down to conceal it, still reluctant to tell him the truth.

Michael took her hand and ran his fingers lightly over the red marks. "Who did this?" he demanded. "You *must* tell me. It isn't something we can negotiate."

"It was a misunderstanding," she pleaded.

"With who?"

She pulled her hand away. "Please, can't you let it go this one time?"

"Was it a student?"

"I haven't spoken to even one child since that first day in your office."

"I can't imagine Russell would ..."

"No!" Anna stopped him. "Russell was a perfect gentleman."

Michael waited patiently.

"It won't ever happen again; I give you my word! I'll never go anywhere alone after this. I promise I won't."

The door swung open and Marianne hurried into the room, stopping short when she spied Michael. "Oops!" she said, making a face. "Sorry! I shoulda knocked. I'll come back later."

"I was just going," Michael told her. "I'll see you in the morning, Anna?"

Anna forced a smile. "Eight o'clock sharp," she said brightly.

114

♥ ♥ ♥

"Who's the head counselor?" Anna asked, debating whether to tell Marianne what happened.

Marianne sank onto the couch and stretched her legs out. "I don't think there is a head counselor. Why? What happened?"

Anna sniffed and went to the desk for a tissue. "Some guy came into my area and claimed he was the head counselor. He didn't believe me about the pet therapy. He said they would've had to check with him before they started a program like that."

Marianne laughed. "Dr. Grant doesn't have to check with *anybody* before he does something. Just the board. What did he look like?"

Anna described him, and Marianne seemed certain it was Bruce Carlisle.

"A woman counselor was supposed to come at 4:30," Anna remembered. "Shirley. Maybe she persuaded Bruce to take her place and he showed up early."

"She wouldn't do that without Dr. Grant's permission. See, he's bein' real lenient with you, so you don't get how he really is. If he told Shirley to be there at 4:30, she better either be there or call and tell him why she can't. It wouldn't be up to her to say somebody else could go in her place, or at a different time. And Bruce ... I think he's on probation for something."

Anna sat down beside her friend. "He was scary," she said in a soft voice. "He grabbed me and wouldn't turn loose." She held up her arm, so Marianne could see her wrist.

Marianne sat forward to take a closer look. "He's toast," she said with certainty.

"He said he was going to take me to the security guards, but when I agreed that was best, he refused to do it." Anna paused to take a breath and try to stifle her tears. "He wouldn't give me his name and ... He wouldn't let go of me!"

"Is that why Dr. Grant was over here?" Marianne asked eagerly. "Gettin' the details?"

"I didn't tell him. I don't know why, but I didn't."

Marianne was stunned. "You *gotta* tell him," she said sternly.

115

"No way he's gonna put up with anybody being manhandled like that. He is totally opposed to violence, no matter what the circumstances. He says there's no way we can teach the kids not to resort to violence if we do it ourselves."

"It was so strange," Anna said, sniffling and touching the tissue to her nose. "I have no idea why I wouldn't tell him. It wasn't as if I had any desire to protect Bruce."

"This isn't the first time Bruce has done something like this. Except it's usually a different kind of touching." Marianne sat back on the couch again. "I feel like it's my fault. If I woulda been there, none of it would've happened. I figured downstairs would be just like upstairs, with plenty of security."

"Russell must have thought there were other people there, getting the area ready for the dogs."

"Yeah. He wouldn't break a rule if you paid him."

"I wanted to do everything right. I didn't want to cause trouble for anybody."

"You're not the one who caused the trouble," Marianne pointed out.

"I should've asked more questions. I should've asked Russell if it was okay to be down there alone. Do you think there's a chance Dr. Grant will fire me?"

"Fire you?" Marianne was quiet for a moment. "Actually, if you were anybody else, he probably *would* fire you. Not for being down there alone, for refusing to tell him who hurt you. That's the kind of thing he's really strict about. He says secrets have been the downfall of a lot of good institutions."

Anna was filled with regret. She didn't understand why, even now, she was reluctant to tell Michael what had happened. What if Bruce did the same sort of thing to a student? Michael *needed* to know the truth!

"I'm afraid he'll think I can't defend myself," she admitted reluctantly. Something like this might prevent him hiring her back the following year. "He'll think I wouldn't be able to handle the students. Just because I'm short, people underestimate me all the time."

"I wondered about that myself," Marianne said guiltily. "You prob'ly don't weigh a hundred pounds."

"Yes I do, but that has nothing to do with it. How often do you use physical strength to subdue the students? Didn't you just say it's forbidden?"

"Yeah, but I threaten them sometimes. Being overweight, I tell them I'll sit on them if they don't shape up. They laugh and then they shape up."

"And I could tell them that I'll send them to the office if they don't shape up. It's the same thing."

Marianne tipped her head left to right. "Maybe."

Anna took a deep breath and let it out slowly. "I don't want to go crying to the administrator every time somebody gives me a hard time."

"This was more than a hard time," Marianne protested.

"I see that now."

"Then you ought to call Dr. Grant and tell him it was Bruce."

"He'll think you talked me into it."

"What's the matter with that? I could use the brownie points."

"I want him to understand *why* I wouldn't tell him."

"So tell him why."

"I will. In the morning." She blew her nose and decided she felt better. "The worst of it was, I didn't put the lid back on the can or wash out my brush or wipe up the paint on the floor."

Marianne laughed. "That was *not* the worst of it!"

Anna didn't see the humor in it.

♥ Chapter 9 ♥

Anna arrived in the administration offices at 7:45 the next morning. She wore a sweatshirt and clutched the end of the sleeve in her fingers, to hide the ugly purple bruises on her wrist.

As soon as Tina spied Anna, she picked up the phone. "I'm supposed to have security take you straight downstairs," she explained. "Let me get one of the guards."

"Are you sure?" Anna asked anxiously. She didn't want to repeat yesterday's mistake.

Tina handed her a note in the administrator's writing. She was following directions to the letter, just as Anna intended to do from now on.

Russell stuck his head in the door a moment later. "Morning, Mrs. Brown. You ready to get to work?"

Anna sighed with relief. She was afraid she had caused the security guard to be fired.

"I messed up yesterday," she told him as they walked along. "I misunderstood the rules and thought it was okay to be alone once I got to my area."

"Nobody's meant to be alone inside the school, other than between the front door and the admin offices. Dr. Grant doesn't even like security to be on our own, though there's no avoiding it sometimes."

When they arrived at the pet therapy area, Russell held the door for her.

119

When Anna stepped into the room, her eyes widened with surprise. Michael was on the ladder, dressed in worn blue jeans and a T-shirt. He had almost finished applying the yellow paint to the two longest walls.

"Always nice to know you've got another career option," Russell teased the administrator, before he winked at Anna and departed.

Michael came down the ladder and set his paint can on the floor. "Are you happy with the color?"

Anna couldn't get over the difference in his demeanor when he wasn't wearing a suit and tie. Though he didn't seem any smaller, he was somehow more approachable. "I was worried I had gotten him in trouble," she said, gesturing at the door.

"Russell's been at Casey's longer than I have. He wrongly assumed there was somebody down here waiting for you, but the brunt of the blame for what happened rests with me. I don't think I made it clear that I didn't want you down here alone." He reached into his pocket and pulled out a cell phone. "I want you to start carrying this. My cell is number 1 on speed dial. I have caller ID and call waiting, so I'll take your call immediately, any time, night or day."

"That's not necessary," Anna said softly. "I give you my word I won't …"

"Anna," he interrupted. "Put the phone in your pocket and promise me that you will have it on your person at all times when you are in the building."

She took the phone and looked it over, then tucked it into the pocket of her jeans. "Does everyone get a phone?"

"No. I added you to my personal account." He waved his hand around the room. "These are special circumstances." He caught her hand and pushed her sleeve back, exposing the bruise that encircled her wrist like a bracelet.

"I want to explain," she said, gazing into his eyes.

"I've already got a pretty good idea what happened."

"I meant … I want to explain why I wouldn't tell you."

Michael tilted his head to one side. "Because you were afraid I would think you couldn't handle yourself?"

"Yes," she said, moistening her upper lip with the tip of her tongue. "Something like that."

"Men are stronger than women. It's a fact of life. If you and I were the same size, I would still be able to overpower you."

Anna realized he was right. "Maybe I should take karate lessons," she said with frustration.

He laughed, and Anna felt a surge of relief.

"Do you want me to tell you now?" she offered.

"I want you to tell me whether you're pleased with the color."

She didn't understand why he no longer wanted to know the identity of the man who had bruised her wrist. "I'm more than pleased," she said, clasping her hands behind her back. "It's like sunshine. But why are *you* doing it? In order to have accomplished this much, you must have started while it was still dark outside. I thought you said you found someone to help."

"*I* was the someone."

She smiled at him. "Does this mean I'm not fired?"

"Of course not. None of it was your fault."

"Marianne said …"

"That I was likely to fire you?"

"Both of us. Him and me. She said you don't tolerate anyone using physical force."

"There are exceptions."

Anna waited for him to elaborate, but he didn't. "She also said that you don't like secrets."

"Some kinds of secrets are okay." He studied his hands, front and back, before grasping her shoulders and pulling her into his arms.

Anna pressed her hands to his chest, then quickly slipped them around his waist. She rested her cheek over his heart and for the first time since Bruce let her go, she felt safe.

"I'm sorry I wasn't here to protect you," Michael said quietly.

Anna drew back to look up at him, her eyes filled with tears. Then she stretched up on her toes and met his lips with hers as he bent to kiss her. She forgot everything else as she became conscious of his scent, the feel of his mouth on hers, the span of his fingers across her back as his hands dropped to her waist. She sensed that he would pull away … and then he did.

"Hey," he said, pretending to be aggrieved. "I thought I was here to help, not do the whole job by myself." He released her and stepped back, gesturing at the paint cans waiting in the corner.

Anna had not yet recovered from the kiss. She crossed her arms and averted her eyes, hoping he didn't know how his touch affected her.

He seemed to realize she didn't want to undergo his scrutiny. He retrieved the paint can and brush and climbed up the ladder again.

Anna watched the play of his muscles as he dipped the brush and spread the paint over the concrete blocks. He looked equally good in a suit or in blue jeans. He looked fit and strong and so handsome! She couldn't believe he had just kissed her. Perhaps he hoped it would erase her sour memories of the day before.

She began to feel self-conscious in the silence. She scurried to the corner and pried the lid off a can of blue paint. "How long before we can actually get some dogs and start the program?" she asked, stirring carefully with a wooden stick.

Michael laughed. "She cuts him no slack," he narrated with drama. "The kennels will be installed tomorrow. They'll have to pour fresh concrete, so you won't be able to do anything down here for a day or two. I'm going to interview a couple of the AHTs in the morning, and I'd like you to sit in. You could visit the shelter in the afternoon and choose a couple of dogs. Ask Helen not to adopt them out and tell her she'll be compensated. That ought to get you started."

"Do you think I'm ready to take that step?" she asked, applying the first stroke of blue paint.

"I hope so, because I promised we would take Charlie off her hands right away."

"Oh, thank you!" Anna said happily. "I'm sure I can eventually train him not to jump up like that." She stopped talking as she carefully painted the blue beside the yellow. "How's that look?" she asked, standing back to study it.

"Terrific. You're turning this area into a cheerful spot." He dipped his brush and filled in the last corner, near the ceiling. "This kind of project has to move at its own pace. You'll have people on hand who know about animals. You'll have me on the other end of your phone, in case there's an issue with a student … or anyone else. As for the rest, we'll learn as we go."

"First I have to learn how to use the phone," Anna said. She put her paint brush down and removed it from her pocket. "Andy and Paula showed me theirs but I didn't pay a lot of attention."

"Maybe we ought to set aside a day to go over the rules, practice with the phone, and look for a sale on tires."

"A sale on tires?"

"I don't like to think of you driving with so little tread. I'm surprised it passed inspection."

Anna made a face. "You and Andy. Next you'll be warning me that the poor old thing doesn't have many miles left."

"I'm sure Andy is right. Why haven't you replaced it?"

"It was my first car. I guess I got emotionally attached."

"Did you buy it yourself, when you were a teenager?"

Anna watched as he descended the ladder again. "I didn't learn to drive until after I was married."

He glanced at her over his shoulder. "You must have married very young."

"Right out of high school. I was only seventeen."

"The same age as a lot of our students." Michael moved the ladder to an unpainted section of wall and made sure it was sturdy. "I guess getting rid of the car would feel like an insult to your husband's memory."

"Not at all," Anna said quickly. "It hasn't got anything to do with Paul. It represented freedom. For the first time in my life, I could take myself wherever I wanted to go. I didn't have to ask someone, or wait until it was convenient for Paul. And it was small, like me. We bonded and now it's hard to send her off to the junk yard."

He climbed the ladder and looked down at her with a pensive expression. "There's something therapeutic about rescuing things. Cars, dogs, people … I think we have that in common."

Anna smiled. "Is that why you're letting me try this job? Because you want to rescue me?"

He dipped the paintbrush and faced the wall. "Maybe I'm hoping *you'll* rescue *me*. You can set your phone to vibrate or to ring," he went on quickly, without giving her a chance to comment. "To answer a call, press the picture of the telephone."

Anna wanted to ask what he meant. She wanted to know what it would take to rescue him so she could be sure to do it right. She wanted to know what he needed to be rescued *from*.

"It seems like you're no longer interested in what happened yesterday," she said. "Do you already know who it was?" Maybe Marianne had returned to her room and called the administrator.

"I think so, but it doesn't matter since there wasn't a witness. His word against yours."

Anna thought about that for a while. She wondered if it had anything to do with the rule about traveling in pairs.

"I believe *you*, of course," Michael added. "But if he denied the accusation, we couldn't prove anything. The cameras will be installed tomorrow, which should deter that kind of behavior in the future."

"I'm sorry I broke the rule."

"It wasn't your fault, but hopefully you understand now, about the buddy rule."

"I do," she said, grateful for his patience.

Anna's arms were aching by the end of the day, but when she looked at the brightly colored walls, she decided it was worth it. Michael had gone long ago, to change clothes and resume his regular duties. Before he left, he summoned a woman from maintenance to help clean up and keep Anna from being alone.

As soon as Anna finished painting, she propped the door open and went to the janitor's closet across the hall. She straddled a mop bucket while she washed the brushes, rather than stand with her back to the door. She would not allow Bruce Carlisle to catch her off guard again.

She was getting ready to lock up when a well-dressed woman came looking for her. "I wasn't there the day you had your interview," she said, extending her hand. "My name is Loretta Boswick. I'm the president of Casey's board."

"My hands are messy." Anna held them up for her to see.

"Then we'll save the handshake for another time," Loretta said agreeably. "Why don't you show me what you've done? Dr. Grant says you have a lot of exciting ideas for the program."

Anna couldn't think of any exciting ideas she had suggested, but she ushered Loretta inside.

"I like it," Loretta said with approval. "It's very cheery, even if the dogs aren't likely to notice. Can you explain how things are to be arranged?"

Anna pointed out where the kennels would go, as well as the deep sink where they would bathe the dogs, and the table where they would groom them. "And I'll have a small office in here," she said, gesturing to a cubbyhole with a door that locked. "We'll track the dogs after they leave Casey's so we'll be able to say whether or not the program is a success."

"I don't know if Dr. Grant told you, but this was my idea," Loretta said. "I've got a soft spot for abandoned animals."

Anna thought of Helen's claim, that it was all *her* idea. She smiled and nodded.

"Did you know Dr. Grant before coming to Casey's?" Loretta asked.

"No, we had never met before." Anna decided she would tell Michael how many people had asked her that question. She wondered if he would be amused.

"No one will penalize you for taking advantage, dear, if that's what you're worried about. I can see why Michael wanted to lure you to Casey's."

Anna wasn't sure how to respond to that. "It's almost five o'clock," she said. "I don't want to break any rules, being down here after five."

"I'm sure there would be an exception if you were with me, but I think we're done here anyway. Unless there's something you'd like to ask me or tell me?"

"I imagine I'll have dozens of questions next week, once we actually have animals on campus. But for now, I can't think of a thing."

As they walked upstairs together, Loretta spoke of John Casey, the man who had founded the school. "He might have been a senator, if he hadn't suffered so many tragedies," Loretta said. "I imagine you already know the story?"

"I'm ashamed to say I didn't ask about the school's namesake."

"Perhaps you'll have the honor of meeting him at the graduation ceremonies," Loretta suggested. "It was nice meeting you, Anna. I'm sure we'll be seeing one another again."

Anna exited the building and hurried across the lawn to the dorm. She was anxious to take a shower, and she was hungry.

Doris was coming down the stairs as Anna started up. "I was looking for you," she said. "Gayle wants to see you in her office."

Anna cringed. She hoped Gayle hadn't discovered the snack box beneath her bed. "Do you think she'd mind if I took a shower first? To wash off the paint?"

Doris eyed her with a doubtful expression. "She doesn't have any authority over you," she whispered. "But she does have Grant's ear and he usually gives her what she wants."

Anna hesitated, then gave in and went to knock on the door. She would apologize to Gayle, if she'd been caught with food in her room. And then she'd have to apologize again to Michael, after promising that she would do her best to mind the rules.

"Come in," Gayle called. When she looked up and saw that it was Anna, her expression turned grim. "Close the door, please."

Anna complied, then stood in front of the desk where Gayle was seated.

"I understand that Dr. Grant visited you in your room yesterday. I'd like to know what he needed to see you about."

Ann had no intention of sharing that information. "It didn't concern the dorm," she said politely.

"Anytime Dr. Grant visits this building, it concerns *me*," Gayle said. "If you won't tell me, I'll ask him."

"I asked if you knew Michael Grant before coming to work at Casey's. You denied it."

"Because it's true. We hadn't met before I came for an interview."

"That seems very unlikely."

"I'd have no reason to lie." Anna cautioned herself to keep her temper in check.

"Are you in some sort of trouble?" Gayle asked.

"Not to my knowledge." Anna didn't want to make an enemy of Gayle, but she didn't like being cross-examined when she had done nothing wrong.

Gayle folded her hands on the desk top. "I warned you about becoming involved with the wrong crowd, yet you've chosen to ignore my advice. If Dr. Grant should ask for my opinion, I won't hesitate to tell him that you've been keeping company with the wrong people."

Anna bit her lip, to keep from saying something she was sure to regret.

"You may go," Gayle said. "But don't think I'm going to drop the subject. I will pursue it with Dr. Grant."

Anna turned to leave, but Gayle called her back. "Do you know how long I've been at Casey's?"

"I'm sorry ... No, I don't."

"Almost fourteen years. That's how long I've known Michael Grant."

"I imagine the two of you are good friends by now."

"We are *very* good friends. Many women have tried to come between us, but none have succeeded."

"I have no wish to come between you," Anna said.

"It wouldn't matter if you did. That's what I'm telling you."

Anna couldn't think of anything to say that wouldn't further irritate Gayle. "May I go now?" she asked.

Gayle waved her hand at the door.

Anna trudged up the stairs with a heavy heart. Did being friends with Michael mean she must be enemies with everyone else? She wondered what he would say if she shared the conversation she'd just had with Gayle.

She let herself into her room and barely resisted the urge to stretch out on the couch. If she fell asleep, she was likely to miss dinner and she didn't want to drive into Briarton later, looking for something to eat. She gathered clean clothes and hurried down the hall to the showers, hoping the hot water would ease the ache in her shoulders.

There wasn't much hot water, making it difficult to remove the paint from her hands and face and hair. She hurried into her clothes and stopped to knock on Marianne's door. When there was no answer, she checked her watch. She had less than ten minutes before they would stop serving dinner.

The cafeteria was almost empty and so were most of the steam tables. Anna filled her plate with watery cabbage and the remains of a chicken thigh, adding two slices of bread and a large piece of chocolate cake. It wasn't much of a dinner, but at least she wouldn't go hungry.

She settled at a table, wishing she had brought something to read. She couldn't help thinking about Michael, mentally reliving the kiss, calling back the things he had said. What did he mean – *Maybe I'm hoping you'll rescue me?* Rescue him from what, or who? Surely he didn't want to be rescued from Casey's.

She glanced at his private dining area, though she felt certain he wasn't behind the one-way glass. According to Marianne, he rarely ate dinner in the cafeteria. Anna wondered if he ate at home, and whether he liked to cook. Did he do his own laundry and iron his own shirts?

Suddenly she remembered her cell phone. She had left it in the pocket of her jeans when she tossed them in the clothes basket in the closet. How could she have forgotten it! She began to eat faster, anxious to return to her room and retrieve it. What if Michael had tried to call? He might think she had run into Bruce again, and suffered a worse fate this time.

Just then, the door to his private dining area opened and he emerged with the same beautiful redhead had been with him at the buffet!

Anna wished she could disappear. She drew back behind a column and slid low in her chair, hoping they would exit without noticing her.

Michael visited the trash can with their tray, then returned to the woman and put his hand on her shoulder.

Anna wished Marianne was there to see how wrong she was about Michael Grant! How could she have believed that the handsome administrator would ever be interested in someone as plain and dull as Anna Brown. Tears welled up in her eyes, and she blinked hard to keep them from spilling over. When Michael kissed the tall woman's cheek, she covered her mouth to stifle a sob of misery.

The woman disappeared out the door that exited onto the parking lot. Michael pulled something from his pocket and studied it as he made his way toward the hallway that led upstairs to his office. It was easy to guess that it was his cell phone, but Anna no longer wondered if he would be calling her.

She gazed around the cafeteria, wondering who else had seen Michael kiss the woman with red hair. Other than the staff in the kitchen, she was the only one present now. She didn't begrudge him a relationship with another woman − he had no obligation to her, after all. But to kiss *her* in the morning and then kiss another woman in the evening spoke volumes about what sort of person he was. For all she knew, he had kissed two or three other women in between.

Better she learned the truth now, *before* she fell in love with him. She carried her tray to the trash can and threw away the remains of her dinner, taking deep breaths to try to postpone her tears. She had no right to be angry, but one didn't need to earn the right to be hurt.

Michael had calculated which window was Anna's and he was watching when she turned off her light at ten o'clock. He wondered if her muscles ached as much as his did. He had almost texted her to ask, but talked himself out of it. He hadn't urged her to call anytime she felt like talking, but he had hoped she might.

There were so many things he would like to know! He wanted to hear all about her childhood, her family, her hobbies. Did she like to sew, or knit? Did she enjoy hiking or biking or camping? It seemed she kept her deceased husband on such a pedestal, she couldn't even talk about him. She ignored his hints and refused to answer questions about her marriage. He had done some research, after she mentioned that Paul Brown was a counselor at a St. Louis prison. Copies of some of his papers were for sale, though the proceeds didn't go to Anna. How was he to compete with a dead hero?

He shouldn't have kissed her today. He should have remained

on the ladder and restricted the conversation to the pet therapy program. He shouldn't even have helped with the painting! As he was telling himself he could not, he *must* not, he got up and put on old clothes.

There was no doubt in his mind whether she had wanted to be kissed. While he was trying to resist the temptation, she raised up on her toes and made it impossible. He hadn't wanted the kiss to end, and he sensed that she hadn't either. Afterwards, she had looked stunned.

Was she falling in love with him? He hoped she was, even while he hoped she wasn't.

How was he to resolve this? He could not go back on his word and live with his conscience, yet he couldn't send Anna away. And if she remained on the campus, how was he to resist seeing her whenever the opportunity arose? She was going to be an asset to the school, of that he was certain. But how was he to welcome her into his world without welcoming her into his heart?

He turned from the window and went to the kitchen, seeking solace. His vices were innocent – he took a carton of ice cream from the freezer and dished up a large bowl. He crossed the living room and went into his office, choosing a CD to fit his mood – a lone piano playing old movie themes. He turned on the pc and began to read over a request for a grant. He wouldn't turn the computer off until two a.m., and he would be up again by six. His life was his job and his job was his life. Since he lost Tucker, he had nothing else. Why don't you get another dog, Jasmine had asked a few hours ago. He told her it was too much trouble, but the truth was, he didn't think he could put another animal down, no matter how much it was suffering.

He finished his ice cream and pulled his phone from his pocket. Briefly, he considered sending Anna a text that simply said "Good night." But he only laid the phone beside the pc and began to type.

Anna tossed and turned until 3 a.m. before she got up and went to the window. Even during the worst situations, when there seemed no solution and no escape, Anna believed a Christian should enjoy inner peace. That meant she ought to be able to sleep under any circumstances, knowing she was held in the arms of Almighty God. Since she *wasn't* able to sleep, it followed that she must have strayed out of God's will. Perhaps she wasn't meant to come to Casey's. Or maybe it was just that she wasn't meant to fall in love with Casey's administrator. She must pray for guidance and allow God to show her how to return to the right path.

It had taken her eight years to earn her degree. God had provided the means, and He had provided people to watch over her children while she attended classes. He had kept her awake so she could finish her homework, even when she had to get up a few hours later and go to work. She had earned a degree so that she could be a teacher. Perhaps she had made a mistake when she accepted a job as a ... She still wasn't sure what her title was. Dog trainer?

Why had she accepted the job? Because she was desperate, after applying at so many schools? Or because Michael had taken her to dinner, wooing her until she gave in ... Why should he put forth such an effort to convince her to come to work at Casey's? Her qualifications were nothing special. She had no experience. And it wasn't as if she were young and beautiful.

Something had happened between them, the moment they met. Anna had felt it and she thought Michael had too. She wasn't sure what to call it. Love at first sight sounded like high school. Anyway, it hadn't felt romantic so much as spiritual. As if God's hand hovered over them, delivering a special blessing.

What if Michael hadn't felt any such thing? What if he had only become confused because of the way she behaved? All that nonsense in the car about Brigadoon and second chances ... He must have thought she was daffy. He had even guessed that she wasn't a Christian!

"I was flirting," she confessed, gazing into the sky. "I was flirting with him before I found out whether he was married." She went over the conversation in her mind and the more she recalled, the worse she felt. No wonder he had invited her to spend the night at his club! A wave of hot shame passed over her body. She wondered if he would describe her behavior the same way. He was too much of a gentleman to actually say the words, but Anna knew, in her heart that he must think them true.

Michael's appearance and position had made him seem bigger than life, like a celebrity. What if he had been a homely man, short in stature like Paul? She wouldn't have hesitated to join him for dinner, but would she have thrown herself at him? She hung her head. She would have asked a million questions, but about the school, not the man himself.

From the moment she looked into Michael's dark brown eyes, she had abandoned her principles. And then, when he merely reacted in kind, she had condemned him.

Briefly, she wondered if it had been her fault with the other men as well. Though she had pushed them away, had she simultaneously given them the message that they should keep trying? She hadn't protested when Michael kissed her. She had, in fact, stood on her tiptoes to kiss him back.

It was all a mistake, she realized now. He was her boss, nothing more. He hadn't asked her on a date, he had merely tried to complete her interview over dinner.

She pressed her hands to her face with embarrassment.

"Thank you, Lord," she prayed with conviction. "I needed you to show me where I went wrong. I misunderstood. Michael has a girlfriend and I must not try to come between them." She would behave like a professional from this moment on. She would not flirt with the administrator again. Perhaps she had brought on the trouble with Bruce Carlisle too …

She returned to her bed and crawled beneath the blankets. Starting tomorrow, she would read her Bible every day and pray without ceasing. She was resigned to living the life of a single woman. She would focus on the accomplishments of Mother Theresa and set her sights equally high.

Though she knew that her thoughts were right and true, she gained no comfort from them. She buried her face in her pillow and released the tears she had been storing up since coming to Casey's. She was so confused! She couldn't claim to be in love with Michael Grant − she hardly knew him! All the same, she couldn't bear the thought that she had lost him.

You can't lose what you never had, she told herself. But the tears she shed were those of a woman with a broken heart.

♥ Chapter 10 ♥

"He's interviewing Anita Martinez," Tina said, reading the name from the clipboard at her elbow. "For the AHT position. Dr. Grant said you're going to get some dogs next week, if the AHTs can start right away?"

Anna lifted her shoulders. "Maybe."

"Aren't you excited? I'd love to do what you're going to do. I think it's going to be the best job on campus."

"I am excited," Anna said. "It's a wonderful opportunity."

Tina leaned further over her desk and lowered her voice. "I can't believe he helped you paint! I've never known him to cancel appointments for any reason."

Anna forced a smile. "Did he say whether I'm supposed to come in?"

Tiny looked alarmed. "Did I offend you? I'm sorry! Just that everything has changed since you started. Well, not *everything*. Just Dr. Grant. I've never seen him act like this before. He's so happy!"

Anna raised her hands, as though Tina was aiming a gun in her direction. "It doesn't have anything to do with me," she protested, picturing the woman with red hair. She could see that Tina wasn't convinced. "Should I knock, or just go on in?"

"Knock first."

Anna hurried around Tina's desk and knocked on the administrator's door. She hoped she wouldn't embarrass herself by starting to cry during the interview. She had hardly stopped crying all morning.

Michael opened the door and greeted her with a smile. "Come in, come in. We were just talking about you." He introduced Anna to a young woman seated on the couch and shared a little of her background while Anna sat down. "Anita is part of a program called Rent-A-Dog. They train stray dogs to serve as companions in institutions. Why don't you tell Anna how it works," Michael suggested, settling behind his desk.

Anita turned to Anna with enthusiasm. "We start out by working with them non-stop for about a week. We take turns with the same animal, so it doesn't bond to any one person. We mess with it, tease it, do whatever might normally annoy a dog that's high-strung. If it passes that test, we start taking it just about everywhere we go."

Anna tried not to look at Michael, though she knew he was watching her. "I'm not sure I'd be good at the first stage," she said honestly. "It sounds risky."

Anita held up her hand, revealing a nasty scar. "I have been bitten," she said. "It was my own fault though. I pushed that poor dog too far."

Anna glanced at Michael and he gave her a reassuring smile.

"Anyway," Anita went on. "Next we take them to places where there will be a lot of people. Like an amusement park, or a busy airport or a baseball game. We put a sign on them that says: *Please don't touch me until my trainer says it's okay.*"

"Do people obey the sign?" Anna asked.

"Usually. We have to watch little kids. They don't bother to read the sign before they put their hands within reach. And some of them can't read yet, I guess. But it's a good test, to see how the dogs will behave. After a couple of weeks of that, we start intensive training. We teach them to walk beside a wheel chair, without getting their paws squashed, and how to summon help for someone who has fallen."

"It sounds like rewarding work."

"It is," Anita agreed. "But it's a volunteer organization and my parents decided it's time for me to find a real job."

"It certainly sounds like you've got the kind of experience

we'll need," Anna said. She hoped she wasn't stepping out of bounds by saying it.

Michael began to ask questions that were more particular in nature. Anna sat back in her chair and listened, somewhat surprised when the interview became grueling. She watched Anita squirm when she was required to explain a comment. She thought back to how easy her own interview had been, and realized that, by these standards, she hadn't really had an interview with Dr. Grant.

Occasionally, Michael asked Anna a question, or directed a comment to her specifically. She knew he was doing his best to make her feel part of the decision whether to hire Anita. She also knew that he would not bend to her opinion, if they did not agree. She kept her answers and remarks short and unemotional. She thought she was acting very professional and businesslike.

"What's wrong?" Michael asked, as soon as he ushered Anita out the door. "Did something happen?"

"No, nothing," Anna assured him. "What time is the next interview?"

"It wasn't another incident with Bruce, was it?"

"I haven't seen him since …" She realized she had just admitted Bruce was the culprit, and for some reason, it made her feel worse.

Michael frowned, then gestured at the couch. "Sit down a minute, Anna. Please."

She wanted to argue, but she went to the couch.

He sat a few feet away, and gave her a quizzical look. "Are you angry about something?"

"Not at all!" she said with surprise, but she could feel her eyes filling with tears.

Michael moved closer and reached for her hand.

She pulled it away, then covered her face and started to cry.

"Did I hurt your wrist?" he asked with concern.

She shook her head. "It's nothing you did. Not really. It's just that …"

"Just that what?" he asked patiently.

She realized she was going to have to offer some reason for her behavior. "Everyone is attacking me! They're grilling me about you. About you and me. They all think there's something going on between us."

He put his hand on her shoulder and rubbed his thumb over her collar bone. "There *is* something going on between us. We shouldn't be surprised if it's evident to people, especially those who have known me for a long time."

"They're angry with me. They resent me. It's just not working!" she wailed. "I should never have taken the job. I listened to Paula. Whenever I listen to Paula, I always regret my decisions."

"What about Andy?"

She could hear a smile in his voice and it only upset her more. "It's not fair to Helen. You knew how badly she wanted the job, but you gave it to someone else." She would say whatever came to mind, to keep from telling him the truth.

"We talked about that, didn't we? I thought you agreed that Helen isn't the right person for the job."

"Maybe I only agreed so I could have the job."

"Whether or not you took the job, I wasn't going to offer it to Helen."

"I want to go home," she sniffed. "You can hire Anita to do my job. She'd be better at it anyway."

Michael was quiet for a few moments, then he reached for her hand again. This time, she couldn't make herself pull away. What if he agreed to let her quit? An hour from now, she might be packing her car, leaving the campus. She clutched his hand tightly, wanting to savor her last moments with him.

"Will you tell me who's been giving you a hard time? Was it Marianne?"

Anna thought of Marianne, pushing her to believe things that weren't true. "It's everyone," she said. "Just about everyone."

"I will be more than happy to go from person to person and instruct them to back off," he offered.

"It would only make things worse."

Michael sighed. "My first priority is keeping you here. Tell me what you want me to do and I'll do it."

How could he make such a statement if his feelings for her weren't sincere? She turned her head, so he couldn't look into her eyes. She couldn't think straight while he was seated beside her, their fingers interlocked. "Stop treating me like ... Don't treat me any differently than anyone else. Treat me exactly as you treat Marianne."

"Pretend that I don't feel anything for you?"

Anna thought he sounded as if his feelings were hurt. She shook her head, even if she no longer knew whether she was saying "yes" or "no."

Michael pulled his hand away and got up. He went behind his desk, sat down and put a box of tissues within reach.

"Are you angry?" Anna asked. She snatched two tissues from the box and pressed them to her eyes.

"My emotions are none of your concern, Mrs. Brown. Are you going to resign or will you fulfill your contract?"

Anna was shocked by his response, until she realized that he was doing exactly what she had asked him to do. She giggled and blew her nose.

Michael smiled. "I'll keep my distance until the end of the term. I don't know whether or not it will do any good."

Anna wanted to tell him that she had changed her mind. She wanted to ask him to return to the couch and put his arms around her. She wanted him to kiss her again.

But she knew she could not abide by the sort of relationship he was offering. He had kissed her in the morning, then shared dinner with another woman, and kissed her too. And perhaps he had kissed a third woman in between.

"It's worth a try," she said shakily. "I'm sorry to be a problem."

"It's not your fault, is it?"

"I don't know. I can't think straight." She got up and went to the door, but turned to look back at him. "Thank you for understanding."

He merely nodded.

She slipped out the door, closing it firmly behind her. Then she hurried past Tina and ran to the restroom across the hall. Locked in a stall, she allowed herself to weep freely. What a fool she was! Michael Grant cared about her! She *knew* he did. Maybe the redhead really was just a colleague. She was well aware of the way professional people kissed as part of their social game playing – she had seen all sorts of things during her years as a secretary.

Why didn't I just ask him? she chastised herself with misery. She feared that she would regret this day for the rest of her life.

♥ Chapter 11 ♥

The kennels were installed and the next day, the plumber
hooked up the faucets. The tables and cabinets were delivered
early one morning, then supplies began to arrive in cartons. Anna
was kept busy fastening posters on the walls, pouring dry dog
food into plastic containers, distributing paper towels and anti-
bacterial soap. She sat in on two more interviews and told
Michael she liked each of the applicants equally well. He hired
all three, given that the dogs would require care even when
school wasn't in session.

Within the week, Helen began to bring the dogs in a specially
equipped van. Much to Anna's delight, Charlie was among them.
He seemed to remember her, and when he put his paws on her
shoulders, she scratched him vigorously and spoke to him like an
old friend. His shiny black nose twitched above his grey
whiskers, almost as though he were smiling. As the other cages
were filled, he seemed to look on with approval.

Shirley Jackson visited periodically, though she complained
that she had more responsibilities than any of the other
counselors. Just as Michael had predicted though, once the
students began coming, Shirley welcomed them with enthusiasm.

The students were noisy in their excitement, and it seemed to
make the dogs excited too. Their barking made it nearly
impossible to communicate, so the students began shouting to be
heard. Shirley and Anna began to speak in whispers, and though

they giggled, the students did the same. Gradually, the dogs quieted down and they could begin a training program.

Twelve students attended during five of the eight class periods. Anna suggested that each AHT take a group of students to a different area to work with their animals. While one group washed their dogs, then brushed and combed them, another was outside, teaching their dogs to sit and heel, or walk beside a person on crutches. Anna moved back and forth between them, getting to know the students, pleased with the happy atmosphere.

Michael visited frequently, and sometimes remained for an hour. He was friendly to everyone, but never abandoned his reserve. He didn't tease or joke around and though he smiled a lot, he seldom laughed. Anna never saw him touch anyone – student or employee. She finally began to believe what Marianne had claimed from the beginning, that he had treated her differently than anyone else at Casey's.

Once or twice, she caught him watching her, but she couldn't read his expression. Had he lost interest, because of her foolish behavior in his office that day? If she asked for an audience with him, would he again reach for her hand behind closed doors?

"I heard a rumor about the two of you," Shirley confided one afternoon. "I had hoped it was true."

Anna drew her lips into a half smile and averted her eyes.

"You do like him, don't you?" Shirley persisted. "Of course you do. Everyone does. *Almost* everyone. Put it this way – everyone who is here for the right reasons."

"He's easy to like," Anna agreed. "He couldn't be anymore dedicated to the students."

"True, but sometimes I think the issue ought to be *his* wellbeing, not theirs."

"What do you mean?" Anna asked uncertainly. She wasn't sure she wanted to discuss Michael in such a personal way.

"He has nothing else, as far as I know. Just his career. No wife, no children of his own. He's always here, at the ready for any emergency. What does he do for fun? Who cares whether he's eating properly, or getting enough rest? He has no one."

"How would we know whether he does or not?" Anna asked, hoping Shirley would have a good answer. "We're not here all the time."

"I'm here more than you are," Shirley said. "We take turns being on call and I have never been called in on a weekend or in the middle of the night, that Dr. Grant wasn't already on site. I can see it in his eyes sometimes, when he doesn't know I'm looking."

"See what?"

"He's lonely. He's desperately lonely."

Anna mulled this over for days. It only added to her regrets.

Several people had seen Anna emerge from Michael's office with reddened eyes, the day she asked him to stop giving her special treatment. Before long, Marianne reported that a new rumor had circulated around the campus.

"They think you're one of the board member's relatives. They figure he was forced to make up a job for you but when you started taking advantage, he had to lay down the law."

Anna assured Marianne that she wasn't related to anyone at the school. "I had been on the verge of tears for days and I finally lost my composure while I was in his office."

"I thought maybe it was about Bruce," Marianne said, chewing her lip.

"That was part of it. All the stress and worry built up and had to come out. I felt like an idiot."

Marianne only smiled, as if she suspected there was more to the story.

Michael hadn't teased Anna or touched her since that day. He made it a point to avoid being alone with her and there were times when he seemed to go out of his way to avoid her altogether. How she wished she could take back the foolish words she had spoken! She should have asked him about the red-haired woman, mentioning that she had seen them together in the cafeteria. She would have known the truth by the way he responded, but now it was far too late.

She loved working with the students, and she was gradually acquiring confidence when it came to the dogs. She believed the program was a success, and she felt proud of what she had accomplished. But she would gladly trade it all to turn back the clock and resume her relationship with Michael. If only she were the sort of person who could go to him and admit she had jumped to conclusions! He could probably convince her that the kiss he gave the redhead was no more than a professional gesture, completely meaningless to both parties. But in order to confront him, she would have to take an emotional risk, and she was too stubborn and proud.

The weeks passed by in a blur of activity, then the school year came to a close. Anna would depart for St. Louis on Thursday, following the graduation ceremony, and she wouldn't be returning. The other women had received their contracts, complained about the terms, and delivered them to Tina before the deadline. Anna had checked her mailbox multiple times every day, but she never found a contract. She didn't share her disappointment with anyone, averse to their pity. She felt certain she would cry all the way home.

The graduation ceremony was scheduled to begin at one o'clock. Anna entered the crowded auditorium, then stopped to search for Marianne. She spotted her in the second row of the bleachers with their friends from the third floor. She scurried across the room, unwilling to be caught in front of the stage as the program began.

"We wanted to sit at the top and act obnoxious, but Marianne said it would give her a nose bleed" Sally complained.

"Please do not draw attention to us," Rea said sternly. "Grant is threatening to split us up next year, and I do not wish to live next door to Gayle."

"Is John Casey here?" Anna asked.

"She wants to meet John Casey," Marianne told the others, shaking her head with a bewildered expression.

"Why?" Tonya asked. "He's just your typical crooked millionaire."

"Look what he did!" Anna said, sweeping her arm in an arc, indicating the campus of Casey's. "All these kids, in a school rather than a prison. Don't you think that's wonderful?"

"You think this isn't a prison?" Marianne said with scorn. "There are bars on the windows, and the guards carry guns. Don't buy into the propaganda you read in the brochures."

"It *ought* to be a prison," Susie said firmly. "They committed crimes, girl. Horrific crimes."

"That's okay," Rea said, reaching over to pat Anna's hand. "She's just being our little Polly-Anna."

The band began to play "Pomp and Circumstance" and everyone rose to their feet. Anna faced the double doors where the students were making their grand entrance, but her eyes darted around the room in search of Michael.

The pet therapy program was rated a success. Various board members had sent a note to Anna, congratulating her accomplishment. How were they to know, unless Michael had reported to them? The AHTs had been hired back for the fall semester ... but she had not.

If only she knew *why*. It couldn't be spite. Whatever else she believed about Dr. Grant, she didn't believe he would reject her as punishment. Perhaps it was a matter of lacking the right college credits. He had suggested she might take online courses, but maybe the law required that she have a full degree, and experience. There had to be a good reason, but she didn't understand why he hadn't bothered to tell her what it was.

Anna planned to slip out of the auditorium near the end of the ceremony. She had packed her car early in the morning while the other women slept. As soon as Marianne departed for the assembly, she slipped a farewell message under the door to her apartment. Marianne could tell the others that Anna Brown wasn't coming back.

Michael appeared on the stage, making his way to the microphone, adjusting the height so that he wouldn't have to bend down to speak. Anna's heart accelerated as she studied his broad shoulders, his dark hair, even his hands as he raised them to ask for silence. His eyes scanned the audience and for a brief moment, she felt them connect with hers. Then he began to speak, to address the visiting dignitaries, the graduating seniors, the student body, the faculty, the audience. If not for dozens of armed guards scattered around the room, it could be mistaken for a graduation ceremony at any high school.

Michael's comments were brief, and then he introduced the mayor of Briarton. Anna watched him move to one side of the stage and cross his arms, looking over the audience with a watchful eye. He was so tall and so dignified. His appearance was impeccable − his shirts free of wrinkles, his slacks sharply creased, his tie knotted perfectly. But Anna understood that his looks weren't the only reason so many women longed to know him better. It was his character, and his nature. He was kind and caring, and compassionate beyond measure. While he might take a stern tone at times, he never raised his voice, or said anything malicious or cruel.

As the mayor began to speak, Michael descended the stairs to the floor of the auditorium. He walked slowly along the rows of folding chairs, occasionally reaching in to shake the hand of a particular boy or girl. Anna knew the students would consider it a special honor to be singled out by Dr. Grant, especially in front of their peers.

Anna heard nothing the mayor of Briarton had to say, and she suspected there were countless women suffering the same predicament. She wondered at God's wisdom in choosing such a handsome man to rule Casey's.

He had circled the room, now he began walking along the bottom row of the bleachers, shaking hands with some of the teachers, the aides, the cafeteria workers. When he reached Anna's group, he shook Marianne's hand, even as he leaned over to speak softly into Anna's ear. "I'm working on it. Hang in there."

Anna wasn't sure what he meant. He was working on … her contract? She watched with regret as he made his way back to the stage. He hadn't given her preferential treatment. No one could suggest anything untoward because he had spoken to her. He had spoken to dozens of teachers. He hadn't even taken her hand.

But she had wanted him to! How she wished that he had asked Marianne to scoot over, so he could wedge himself between them. If only he had draped an arm across her shoulders, even while everyone at Casey's looked on. Let them gossip! She didn't care!

"What did he say?" Marianne asked with excitement.

"I don't know," Anna said. She knew what he said, but she wasn't sure what he meant.

Susie leaned down between them. "There you go," she told

Anna, pointing her finger across the auditorium.

A man had entered at the rear of the room, surrounded by three men in dark suits.

"John Casey and his bodyguards," Marianne explained as they watched the entourage head to the stage. "He's so pretentious."

"Shhh!" Rea cautioned.

Anna watched as John Casey took his seat beside Michael. To think that one man could make such a difference in the world! So what if he was rich and arrogant. He had used his gifts in the right way, according to the instructions in the Bible. He had done a good work with his wealth.

The mayor finished to polite applause and John Casey went to the microphone. His speech was short – no more than a few paragraphs. He congratulated the students, then expressed his hope that they would all "go straight." He warned them that other prisons weren't like Casey's, and that they would have only one opportunity to mend their ways in this pleasant environment.

When he finished speaking, he shook hands with Michael, then left the auditorium with the same flourish of attention he had garnered on his way in.

"See what I mean?" Marianne said with disgust.

The next speaker was a pastor from a small church outside of Briarton. There was something in his gentle manner that captured Anna's attention and she began to listen, in spite of her mind's delirium.

"Life is full of twists and turns," he said. "Sometimes it seems we've gotten so far off course, we'll never be able to find our way back. But if we believe in God's mercy, He will 'wash us whiter than snow' and supply us with a new beginning."

Anna couldn't resist watching Michael, wondering if the words reminded him of their conversations regarding second chances. As his eyes swept the bleachers, they met hers for a few seconds and he smiled.

Anna's eyes filled with tears. She had been right in the beginning – Casey's *was* like Brigadoon, that legendary village in Scotland. It had appeared suddenly in her life and given her such elation while she was a part of it. Now it was going to disappear and be gone forever.

"The success of our journey will be determined by the company we choose to keep," the minister went on. "Don't believe that you can hang out with your old friends now and then, and not be influenced by their behavior. Don't have confidence in your ability to resist peer pressure, because the desire to win the admiration of your peers will remain with you throughout your life. There is only one way to resist temptation, and that is to run in the other direction, just as fast as you can, every time it rears its ugly head."

Peer pressure. Wasn't that part of the problem? Anna had succumbed to it, just as teenagers did. *No*, she argued with herself. *You don't care what the others think. Yes you do*, she admitted. She didn't want to be ostracized by the other women. She didn't want to sit alone in the cafeteria and spend all of her evenings alone in her dormitory room. Last night, she had been part of a gathering of the third floor women. They had played games, hooting with laughter until tears ran down their cheeks. Anna hadn't gone to college as a teen, and given her strict parents, she hadn't ever belonged to a group in high school. She loved being accepted by her peers, being asked to join their outings and listen to their confidences.

She looked down at her hands, turning her diamond wedding ring around and around on her finger. Before she had come to Casey's, her life had been focused on God. She had worked hard to determine His will, reading the Bible, praying and meditating, talking with her pastor when the need arose. But for the last ten weeks, she had rarely thought about God. She certainly hadn't put Him first in her life, which was the only place He belonged. If she had stayed right with God, she would've automatically stayed right with the women of the dorm, and with Michael as well. If she was unhappy now, it wasn't fair to blame Michael, whether or not he had kissed another woman.

She had lost her focus, stopped reading her Bible and rarely remembered to pray. She hadn't attended church since she left St. Louis. What a terrible disappointment she must have been to Marianne, after claiming that spiritual growth took precedence over all else! She hadn't ministered to Marianne, or to any of the other women at Casey's. She knew Susie was depressed over the fiancé who had dumped her because of a rumor. She knew Tonya was struggling to decide how great a sacrifice to make for the sake of her aging parents. What about Cindy and Melody? She hadn't prayed an intercessory prayer for any of them!

"Let's try his church some Sunday next year," Marianne whispered, applauding with gusto.

It only deepened the ache in Anna's heart.

Michael returned to the microphone and began to read the names of students who were to receive special honors. They were seated in the front row and climbed the stairs with their heads held high. Two of Anna's students were among them. She knew she couldn't claim any credit for their success, but she wanted to believe she had helped in some small way. She wanted to believe she had made a difference to someone, even if no one remembered her name.

There was to be a faculty party following the ceremony. When some of the teachers began to leave, to help set up for it, Anna joined them. She followed along until they reached the exit nearest the women's dormitory, then she darted through the door and down the sidewalk.

"Start," she commanded her ancient Volkswagen, jamming the key in the slot as she slammed the door. The motor began to chug as Anna finally gave in to her tears.

♥ ♥ ♥

Andy and Paula arrived home ahead of their mother and were already planning their annual vacation. Anna didn't tell them she wasn't going to return to Casey's, so she had no logical excuse to mope. She pasted on a happy smile, and somehow maintained it as they departed for Table Rock Lake.

While her children slept late in the one room cabin, Anna took long walks along the shoreline, pondering the future. What excuse would she offer her family for not returning to Casey's? That she missed her home and her friends? That she was frightened of the students? If she told them she hadn't been asked to come back, Paula was likely to meddle. Anna wasn't willing to imagine what her daughter might say to Michael Grant to make

149

him change his mind.

What if she couldn't find another job? She had gained some experience for her résumé, but it wasn't in a classroom. She shook her head. There were so many schools in St. Louis, surely one of them would find a place for her. She didn't want to go back to being a secretary, where she felt as if her purpose was only to help the rich grow richer. She wanted to do a good work with her life. She wanted to serve God by helping children.

She must leave the house early every morning, before Andy or Paula got up. She would go back to some of the schools and apply again. Surely Michael would give her a decent reference, if one of the schools called him regarding her performance. If he helped her land a position, she would send him a thank you note. She would tell him to drop by, if he ever happened to be in the area. And then she would be reluctant to leave the house, in case he took her up on the offer.

One morning she settled on a large rock at the lake's edge, determined to have it out with herself. She prayed and wept and prayed and listened. Gradually, she began to understand what she didn't want to believe: leaving Casey's wasn't the source of her sadness. She would find another school, eventually, but she would *never* find another Michael. He had moved into her heart and he would remain there forever. She didn't want to apply at other schools. She wanted to return to Casey's and be with Michael. She wanted to see him, even if it was only in the administrator's capacity. She wanted to hear his voice, even if it was only to discuss the business of training dogs. She wanted to tell him that she realized what a terrible mistake she had made. So what if Gayle had tried to warn her away from him? So what if the other women resented her …

But those weren't the real reasons she had pushed him beyond arm's length. She had seen him kiss the pretty redhead, right in the middle of Casey's cafeteria. If he could openly display his affection for the woman with red hair, why did his relationship with Anna need to be kept a secret? She could think of only one excuse – so the tall, red-haired woman would never find out about Anna Brown.

She gathered pebbles and tossed them into the water, watching the ever-widening circles that resulted. She wasn't the sort of woman who could cope with a complicated relationship – hadn't her marriage to Paul taught her that? There was no question in her mind whether a love story involving Michael Grant would be complicated.

"You didn't spend all those years going to school so you could fall in love and throw your education away," Anna chastised herself.

She rose from the rock and dusted off her shorts. It was her fortieth birthday and Paula said they were going to celebrate it with humor. As Anna made her way back to the cabin, she prayed that her laughter would sound sincere.

The drive home brought them within fifty miles of Casey's campus, but Anna refused her children's pleas to make the side trip. She would love to show them around, but it couldn't be done without Michael's permission. It would be embarrassing to let them learn the truth from his lips, and worse, for Michael to find out she hadn't had courage enough to tell them herself. For her own part, she feared that seeing him would only begin the painful process of leaving him again.

"Old Faithful brought us home," she chided Andy as they pulled into the garage.

"You need a new car," he argued predictably, as he unloaded the suitcases. "And if you're not gonna buy one, I'm at least getting you a cell phone."

"No," Anna said firmly. She had left the cell phone in Michael's mailbox.

"Yes," Andy said, just as firmly.

A new car was out of the question unless she was offered a contract to some other school, but she couldn't tell him that.

Paula interrupted with the wave of an envelope retrieved from Mrs. Montgomery. "It's from Casey's. She had to sign for it," she explained, gasping when Anna yanked it from her hand.

Without a word, Anna ran upstairs and shut herself in her bedroom. She pulled out a hair pin, then hesitated. The envelope was thin, as though it contained only one sheet of paper. If it contained a contract, it would be thick enough to require extra postage. What if it contained an official rejection letter?

151

Good or bad, she couldn't wait to find out. She drew a deep breath and slit the envelope with the hair pin. She found a piece of Casey's official stationery inside.

"Dear Mrs. Brown," she read aloud. "I apologize for the delay in the receipt of your physical contract, though I considered our verbal agreement legally binding. I chose to argue on your behalf for a salary commensurate with your abilities and these deliberations slowed the process. I will be happy to discuss the results of my efforts at your earliest convenience and arrange delivery of the necessary paperwork. Contracts are normally returned before June 1, so please give this matter your immediate attention.

"Due to an unexpected vacancy in the history department, I am able to offer you four classes of American History as well as one civics class for freshmen.

"You are sure to be an asset to Casey's during the years to come. I look forward to working with you again."

This was typed and initialed by Tina Peterson. At the bottom was a handwritten postscript: *I did not want you to 'settle' for Casey's. Please call upon receipt of this letter. Michael*

Anna turned the envelope over, wincing as she read the postmark. What if the offer had been withdrawn by now?

She read the letter again, more slowly. "I considered our verbal agreement legally binding," she repeated aloud. "I have no choice," she said happily. Anna looked up and caught her image in the mirror over the dresser. "You're going to get hurt," she warned her reflection, but she picked up the phone and dialed the number for Casey's without further hesitation.

♥ ♥ ♥

By noon on Friday, Anna had cleaned the house, baked a cake, and made up the guest room, just in case. She didn't expect Michael to arrive until four, but she intended to be ready by three.

She had planned to mow the grass the day before, but it had drizzled from morning till night. If the lawn mower cooperated, she thought she could mow and trim before it was time to shower and dress. She pulled the mower to the middle of the garage and pressed the little black button, though she had never understood what it was meant to do. Following Andy's strict instructions, she waited thirty seconds before pulling the cord. The engine coughed, then there was silence. She repeated this procedure twelve times before the mower finally sputtered to life.

Anna pushed it into the yard and lowered the blade. Moving slowly, she began cutting narrow strips in the wet grass.

Paula would be home by four, and could keep Michael distracted while Anna formed the yeast dough into rolls. Andy had promised to be home before five. Anna would allow the three of them to visit without her until after dinner.

It occurred to her that she hadn't asked what her salary would be. Michael must think she was a fool, or maybe he was impressed that she wasn't greedy. Should she mention the contract as soon as he arrived, so that he would know how much she appreciated his efforts on her behalf? Paul always said business should not be conducted until after a meal, so she should probably wait until he had finished his dessert.

Her foot slipped on the wet grass, giving her a scare. She had purchased cheap tennis shoes for doing yard work, but the soles were smooth and slick. Normally it wasn't a problem, because she wouldn't cut the grass when it was wet.

She mulled it over, then paused near the patio and toed off her shoes. She had a strict rule against cutting the grass in bare feet, but Andy and Paula didn't need to know she had made an exception. She concentrated on leaning forward to stare at the ground inside the handle, so that she wouldn't forget and accidentally run over her toes. She did several rows, then straightened up to rest her back.

Suddenly, two arms encircled her from behind and an attached hand switched off the mower. Terrified, Anna spun around and found herself face-to-face with Michael. He kept his hands locked on the handle of the mower, trapping Anna in the circle of his arms. "You're early," she said, trying to catch her breath.

"Which is far better than too late," he scolded. "I can't believe you're cutting the grass in bare feet!"

"I know," she said meekly. "If I caught one of the kids doing it, I would throw a fit."

"Do I have to throw a fit to make you promise you'll never do it again?"

Anna giggled.

"Am I *too* early?" he asked with a guilty expression.

Good manners prevented her from saying he was. "Of course not."

"I've missed you. Does it upset you to hear me say that?"

"No," Anna admitted. "It's nice to hear."

He made the circle of his arms a little smaller. "Did you miss me too?"

She gazed up at him, wondering what she would do if he leaned down to give her a kiss. "I *did* miss you," she said honestly. Then she ducked under his arm and stepped into the shade. "Would you like a glass of tea?" She wore old cut-offs and one of Andy's paint stained T-shirts. She was hot and sweaty and covered with bits of grass.

"No thanks." He looked around the yard. "This is a work of art."

She looked around too. The yard was laden with beautiful greenery and splashed with colorful flowers. "My husband did the landscaping. I just try to keep it the way he left it."

"What are those?" he wondered, pointing to a ground cover.

"I don't know what anything is," she admitted. "Grass," she said, pointing to the ground with her toe.

Michael laughed. "I take it you don't enjoy gardening?"

"I *do* like it. I think it's very therapeutic."

"Then why not start over? Why not replace his choices with your own?"

"I thought about putting in a bed of pansies," she said, giving it serious consideration for the first time. "They're my favorite. My mom's too. They bloom way late in the fall, at least around here. I've seen them in other people's yards."

"Pansies I would recognize. Why don't you do it?"

"Paul said they didn't fit with his theme. He was adamant about staying in theme. I took over the house," she went on, crossing her arms in a nervous gesture. "But it doesn't seem right to change the yard. I still have the last chart he drew and ..." She realized how it must sound. "The next time something dies, I *will* plant pansies," she said with conviction. "I can't just rip out living plants and throw them in the trash."

He removed his coat and handed it to her, then loosened his tie and began to roll up his sleeves.

"What are you doing?" Anna said with concern.

"I'm the one fired the gardener," he explained, going to the lawn mower and pulling the cord. It started immediately.

"You can't!" Anna protested, touching his arm. "Please!"

"Let's don't forget who's the boss," he teased with a stern look.

Anna could see that it would do no good to protest further – he was going to cut her grass. She went to the porch and watched as he pushed the mower effortlessly around the perimeter of the yard. She held his coat away from her body, lest she get it dirty, but close enough to catch his scent. How she had missed him!

He turned the corner and looked over at her.

Blushing with embarrassment, she went onto the screened porch and draped his jacket over a chair. Then she ran upstairs to shower and change clothes.

♥ ♥ ♥

"Sorry I can't offer you a glass of wine," Paula said, pouring Michael a glass of Perrier. "My mother is opposed to alcoholic beverages."

"So am I," Michael said, smiling at Anna across the table.

"But that first night …" Anna sputtered.

He shrugged. "I was trying to determine how you felt about it."

"Any chance you'll tell me why you're against drinking a glass of wine occasionally?" Paula asked.

Michael met her eyes. "Come hang around Casey's for a week or two, and listen in on some counseling sessions. When you realize how many of the students did whatever they did while they were under the influence of alcohol…"

"I can see that I'll get no support from you," Paula complained with good nature.

Anna's dinner was a success; Michael went back for seconds of everything, including dessert. Afterwards, he insisted on

155

helping with the dishes, before they all retired to the patio. Anna said little, preferring to listen as he chatted with her children. Michael knew how to draw them out, make them justify their comments, or give in to better logic.

He also knew how to deflect their questions about his personal life. It occurred to Anna that she knew almost nothing about his past.

"Well, I guess I'll turn in," Andy said, stretching his arms over his head.

"You're going to bed at nine o'clock?" Paula said with disbelief.

"They've got business to discuss," Andy reminded her. "And I've got a stack of books to read before September."

"Comic books?" she asked sarcastically. She stood and extended her hand to Michael. "Thanks for cutting the grass so I don't have to do it tomorrow."

"No problem," he smiled. "I left the trimming for you."

"Thanks a lot!" she laughed, gathering the empty glasses and disappearing into the kitchen.

"Andy," Michael said, shaking his hand too. "You're more than welcome to come hang out at Casey's if you decide to do that paper."

"I'm going to talk to my professor," Andy said with renewed enthusiasm. "Thanks for the offer."

"My pleasure," Michael said with sincerity.

Andy followed Paula and closed the door behind him, drawing the shade to offer privacy.

"Now, how will I see to sign the contract?" Anna complained, in case he thought she had coached Andy.

"There's plenty of light over the table." Michael reached for his suit coat and pulled an envelope from the inside pocket. "I got you thirty-six," he said, "since it doesn't appear that you're ever going to ask."

"Thirty-six thousand?" Anna said with disbelief.

"Dollars," he teased, obviously pleased by her reaction. "Plus an *apartment* and our wonderful cafeteria fare. It goes without saying that you shouldn't disclose the terms to anyone else."

"Of course not," Anna agreed, unfolding the papers and

looking them over. "We start August 25th?"

"A lot of people arrive early."

"Maybe I'll come early too," Anna said, certain she would. "I was wondering ... Who will take over the pet therapy program?"

Michael leaned back in his chair to study her. "I haven't found anyone yet."

"You're not considering Helen?"

He shook his head. "Helen has some personality traits that wouldn't work well at Casey's. Do you want me to elaborate?"

Anna shook her head. "You don't owe me an explanation."

"Did she give you a hard time about it?" he asked, studying her closely. "I wish you would confide in me, Anna. I won't repeat anything you tell me and I won't let it influence my decisions or affect the way I treat people."

Anna mulled it over for a moment, then she knew she had to tell him. "Helen said her sources informed her that we spent the night together." She lowered her eyes, embarrassed even to repeat the accusation. "She was pretty nasty about it."

"And how did you respond?"

"I have a bad temper when I'm pushed too far," Anna confessed.

"How well I know!" Michael teased.

Anna tried not to smile, then she giggled. "I told her that she needed to discuss it with you. I don't recall exactly what I said, but things were pretty tense between us for a while."

"Yet you feel I should consider her for the job?"

"No," Anna said without hesitation. "I just didn't want to think that I ..." She stopped and looked out into the yard, utterly confused.

"If you'd like to continue with the pet therapy project, it won't change the conditions of your contract. Same salary, same benefits."

Anna was suddenly, inexplicably, filled with joy. She didn't want to abandon the program, after working so hard to set it up. She had enjoyed the casual atmosphere where she could chat with the students about anything that interested them.

But she couldn't believe Michael wouldn't be angry with her for changing her mind, after she had repeatedly asked to be considered for a teaching position. "Are you sure?" she said.

"I want you to be happy at Casey's," he said.

She realized that telling him about the confrontation with Helen had begun a healing process. "That board member, Mrs. Boswick? She asked whether we knew one another before I came for the interview. She didn't believe me when I said we didn't. She thinks we were old friends and I cajoled you into giving me the job."

"She said something similar to me," Michael said, resting his hand over hers, rubbing his thumb across her knuckles.

Anna knew she should withdraw her hand, but she didn't.

"I don't really care what she thinks, do you?" Michael asked.

Anna remembered what the pastor said at the graduation ceremony. "Not anymore," she decided.

"Do you want to tell me about the others?" he prodded gently.

Anna thought it would feel good to tell him everything and let him sort it out. "Gayle called me down to her office."

"Her *office*," he repeated, rolling his eyes.

"She wanted to know why you had come to my room that day."

"The day Bruce cornered you in the Dog House?"

"The Dog House?" Anna repeated with a laugh.

He smiled. "What did you tell Gayle?"

"That it was nothing to do with the dorm."

"Good for you, but I'll bet she didn't take it very well."

"She felt that I was trying to come between the two of you."

"There is no *two of us*," he said with annoyance. "Anyone else?"

"Marianne, on behalf of some of the other women. And Tina. None of them said anything terrible. Well, some of them did. But not Tina or Marianne. They know that we left the campus together, in your car, the day I came for my interview. And that we didn't return until the next day. So they assume ..."

"I know what they assume," he said, enclosing her hand between both of his. "Once I realized that we couldn't return to Casey's that night ..."

"It wasn't your fault," Anna said, somewhat reluctantly. "You're not going to say anything to any of them, are you?"

158

"Not a word. But I am going to make Gayle dismantle her office; it's giving her a power complex. I've had complaints from some of the other women, so don't feel it's your fault."

He sat forward, releasing her hand and tapping the contract with his fingertips. He pulled a pen from his shirt pocket and held it out to her, watching as she signed in the designated places. When she had finished, he folded the papers and returned them to the envelope, sliding it into the inside pocket of his coat.

"There's no backing out now," he warned her with a smile. "This is a legal and binding contract. I'll stop interviewing for the Dog House and start interviewing for a history teacher. If you change your mind, let me know."

Anna was disappointed when he stood and pushed his chair under the table; she wished he would stay awhile and talk. She got up too, then watched while he reached into another pocket and held out his hand.

"My cell phone?" she said with surprise. "Why are you giving it to me now?"

"Maybe I'm hoping to hear from you," he suggested.

"Really?" Anna said with surprise.

"Really," he said. He glanced up at the windows on the back of the house. "Do you think we have an audience?"

"Paula's nose is pressed to her window for sure," she said, certain he meant to kiss her. But when he cupped her face in his hands, she turned away at the last second.

He stepped back and studied her with a puzzled look. "There's something else," he said with certainty.

"It's none of my business," Anna told him. "You haven't made a commitment to me."

"You heard a rumor?" he guessed.

"I saw you myself. I saw you kiss her."

"No," he said firmly, almost angrily. "You did *not* see me kiss another woman."

"Yes I did! The one with the red hair!"

He looked confused. "You mean at the breakfast buffet?"

"I saw you with her at Casey's. I saw you kissing her."

"Kissing her!" he said with shocked disbelief. "You did *not* see me kissing her!"

159

"You kissed her cheek. In the cafeteria. The day you helped me paint. You had kissed me that morning and ..." She could see that he was upset.

"Her name is Jasmine," he said, pulling out his wallet. He opened it and flipped through the pictures, holding one out for her to see.

Anna wanted to push it away, but she took it and held it closer to the light. There was the red-haired woman, standing beside a man who bore a resemblance to Michael.

"She's my sister-in-law."

"You said she was your colleague."

"She's my sister-in-law *and* my colleague." He leaned over her and flipped to another picture. "This is my father." He touched his fingertip to the image of an older man. "He is John Casey's personal attorney. This is my brother. He is the attorney of record for most of John Casey's businesses. This is Jasmine. She is the attorney of record for Casey's. For the school."

Anna looked back with regret. If only she had asked him about the red-haired woman! She handed him his wallet, though she would've liked to study the pictures a little longer.

"If I had said she was my sister-in-law, when I saw you at the truck stop, who knows what rumors Marianne would've started," he explained apologetically.

"She's not like that," Anna protested.

"Yes she is. I've been forced to sit down with her about it more than once."

Anna recalled the first day, when Marianne stayed back and confessed that she had a problem with gossip.

"I'm so sorry," she said sadly.

"It's not your fault. It's the circumstances."

"No, it *is* my fault," Anna disagreed. "I'm bullheaded and stubborn. Ask anyone who knows me. Ask my kids. It's because of being the youngest in a family of seven children. And short."

"Four brothers," Michael recalled.

"And all four of them love to give me a hard time about being small. They like to put their hand on my head and say, 'Go ahead, termite. Give it all you've got.' " She could see that Michael was trying not to laugh. She crossed her arms and pretended to glare at him. "Not you too," she groaned.

He grasped her shoulders and pulled her into his arms, hugging her tightly. "I knew something had happened," he said in a quiet voice. "I didn't see you in the cafeteria that night, or I would've introduced you to her."

"Now you're going to say you didn't see me because I'm short." She looked up at him and hoped he realized just how sorry she was.

He grasped her elbows and easily lifted her onto the steps, so that they were eye to eye. "Next time, will you please come to me and give me a chance to straighten things out?"

"There isn't going to be a next time," she vowed, slipping her arms around his chest. "From now on, I'll know you're innocent of any wrongdoing."

"I am not innocent. Not by any stretch of the imagination," he said seriously. "If I ever step into a confessional, I'll need to pack a lunch."

She giggled. "We're all sinners," she whispered. " 'All have sinned and fall short of the glory of God.' "

He sighed and held her close, pressing her head to his shoulder. "I can't tell you how much I missed you. It was like someone turned off the sun. When you get back, we need to spend more time together. Time on our own, away from Casey's. There are so many things I want to ask you and tell you." He leaned away and looked into her eyes. Then he put two fingers under her chin, and gave her a long, satisfying kiss. "Anna, Anna," he whispered, wrapping her securely in his arms. "I don't want to let you go, for fear you'll disappear, like Brigadoon."

"I'm not going anywhere," she promised. "Except back to Casey's, as soon as I can." She pressed her ear to his chest and listened to his heart and allowed herself to dream that one day, it would belong to her.

♥ Chapter 12 ♥

Anna dropped the last two trash bags of clothing on the floor of her apartment and turned to close the door. Then she sat down on the couch and carefully texted a message to Michael: *Here I am.* She pressed "send," then dropped the phone back into her pocket. He usually answered within a moment or two.

Anna hadn't had an easy time learning to use the features of the cell phone. She had practiced for a few days, until she could send a text message to Paula and Andy with relative ease. Then she texted Michael: *How early is too early?* In less than a minute, he texted back: *Please come yesterday.*

She slumped back on the couch, eying the boxes and suitcases and trash bags. She wasn't looking forward to putting it all away.

Someone knocked on the door and Anna hurried to open it. She hadn't heard from Marianne since the graduation ceremony, in spite of adding her St. Louis phone number to the note she had slipped beneath her door.

"Anna!" Marianne yelped, capturing her in a hug. "I was wondering when you were gonna get here! I kept wishing you'd come early!"

Anna stepped back and eyed her with a quizzical expression. "How'd you know I was coming back at all? And anyway, I *am* early!"

"I've been here for *two weeks*," Marianne complained. "I was house-sitting but the guy got a viral thing so they came back home. Dr. Grant told me you were coming back. I said I thought it was sad for Casey's that he wasn't able to hire you permanent and he said it *would've* been sad for Casey's, if that had been the case. I wanted to call you, but I lost your number. I think I stuck your note in a library book and returned it, so if you start getting weird calls from strangers … I couldn't find you in the phone book. There's a lot of A. Browns in St. Louis!"

"Two weeks," Anna said wistfully. "I wish I had known."

"Me too. Though considering all the junk that happened, you oughta be glad you weren't here." She had lowered her voice, and she turned to close the door. "Sally got in trouble with Grant. *Big* trouble."

"Oh, no!" Anna said with genuine dismay. "What did she do?"

"Nothing. I mean, she didn't start it."

"Does he know that?"

Marianne shrugged. "First he fired her, then he changed his mind and put her on probation."

"It must have been serious if he fired her," Anna said grimly, flopping down on the couch.

"It wasn't her fault. The twins junked her room."

"Junked it? What does that mean?"

Marianne sat in the arm chair, shaking her head with drama. "You know those old Beatles posters she's got? They ripped them up. They poured soda in the keyboard of her pc, and picked every flower off her African violets."

"That's terrible," Anna said, aware of how Sally took pride in her plants.

"They wrote all over her bedspread with permanent markers and it was brand new. So she got even. Who can blame her?"

"Why didn't she go to Dr. Grant and tell him what they'd done?"

"What for? He wouldn't have believed her."

It made Anna angry. "How'd they get in her room?"

"Good question. The three of them were the only ones here at the time, besides Doris. No way Sally forgot to lock her door, even if she was just going to the restroom. And you can't break into one of these rooms without a sledge hammer. If you get locked out, you gotta go get Gayle with her master key."

"Where was Gayle?" Anna asked, trying to figure it out.

"She was out of town so we can't blame her."

"What did Sally do to retaliate?" Anna asked worriedly.

Marianne made a face. "She wrote a letter to Leonard and signed it from Melody."

"Who's Leonard?"

"You know Leonard. He's Cindy's boyfriend."

"Oh, *that* Leonard." Anna wondered if Susie had helped Sally decide how to get even. "What did the letter say?"

"You don't want to know. It was pretty foul."

"Leonard showed the letter to Dr. Grant?" she guessed.

Marianne nodded. "Grant confronted Sally, she confessed, he fired her. It was awful! We were all cryin'."

"But he changed his mind?"

"She's on probation, but you know the twins are figuring how easy it'll be to get her in trouble again. And next time, she'll be gone for good. Gayle says the only reason he changed his mind is because he's short on teachers. Keeping her on probation means he can get rid of her the minute he finds somebody to take her place."

"I'm sure that's just Gayle's opinion. I doubt whether he'd confide in her about something like that."

Marianne reached over and touched Anna's arm. "Get this. Couple of days ago, he took Gayle's office away! It's like he declared war on the women's dorm."

Anna took out her phone and checked to see if Michael had answered her text message. She wasn't comfortable having this discussion, but she didn't know how to avoid it.

"Sometimes I don't get him," Marianne went on. "Like the twins. How come he always takes their side? Nobody could be dumb enough to think those two are innocent."

"They're very young. Maybe he figures they'll grow out of it," Anna said feebly.

"Did he say that to you?"

Anna shook her head. "That's just my opinion." She was going to have to be very careful not to break Michael's confidences.

"I was wondering if maybe … You can say 'no' but … Actually, we were *all* wondering whether you'd try and talk to

165

him."

"I wasn't here when it happened."

"So? You can tell him about the twins being in your room that time, going through your stuff. And how they acted when we invited them to go along to a restaurant. You said they acted like fifth graders."

"Even if I did tell him those things, it's not going to change his mind about Sally." Anna wasn't willing to jeopardize her relationship with Michael, now that things were going so well between them. "He'll only be irritated with me for getting involved."

"Is that what happened last time?"

"Last time?"

"When you came out of his office crying?"

Anna put her elbows on her knees and her hands under her chin. Here she was, back in the middle of things and school hadn't even started yet!

"I don't care what you say, I think he's got a thing for you," Marianne pouted. "Alls you gotta do is look at him when he's lookin' at you. It's obvious."

Anna sighed with depression. Michael would be disappointed in her for even listening to Sally's side of things, but she would be disappointed in herself if she didn't try to make things right. "Okay, I'll talk to him," she gave in reluctantly. "But don't get your hopes up. And don't tell the others until after I come back."

"I won't," Marianne said with excitement. "When are you gonna do it?"

"I'm supposed to check in with him as soon as I arrive," Anna said. "I think he's going to go with me to the shelter to pick out some dogs."

"That would be a perfect opportunity!"

Anna put her feet on the coffee table. Things weren't getting off to a great start.

♥ ♥ ♥

Michael had been watching for the yellow Volkswagen, and anticipating the text message that would announce Anna's arrival

166

on campus. He was working in the yard at the stone house when he spied her little yellow car, creeping up the winding road. As soon as he got her text, he went in to shower and shave and put on clean clothes. Then he texted and asked her to meet him at the guards' shack, so they could reissue her badge.

"Welcome back!" he said, as soon as she appeared.

"Thanks!" she said. "It's good to be back."

He could already tell something was bothering her. *The third floor women*, he thought with a touch of anger. He sometimes wished he could fire them all.

He said nothing while Russell went through the envelopes, seeking the one that contained Anna's badge. He waited until they were halfway up the stairs, beyond Russell's hearing. "Your friends didn't waste any time getting you involved, did they." He knew he sounded cross. "Did they really have the nerve to ask you to interfere on their behalf?"

Anna was taken aback by the harshness of his tone.

"It's not your responsibility to serve as liaison between me and those women," he said sternly. "This is exactly why I didn't want you on the third floor!"

"It's my nature to want to help," Anna said. "If you don't want to discuss it with me, fine, then we won't discuss it."

"Like the proverbial elephant in the room," he grumbled, unlocking the door to the outer office.

"Where's Tina?" Anna asked. The secretary's desk was cleared of paperwork, making it obvious that she was absent.

"She got married last week. She's on her honeymoon." He unlocked the door to his inner office, and waved her in. He had hoped to take Anna in his arms as soon as they had privacy, but it no longer seemed like a good idea. She was wearing navy shorts and a white blouse, white socks and tennis shoes. She looked like a college student. She looked beautiful.

"Sit down," he said, gesturing at the couch. "Would you like a cup of coffee?"

"Sounds great, thanks."

He had the kind of coffee maker that had a reservoir, so he quickly filled two mugs and placed them on the coffee table. Then he sat beside her.

167

"It's so quiet!" Anna said. "Isn't anyone else here today?"

Michael smiled. "Are you afraid to be alone with me?" He stretched his arm over the back of the couch.

"It's not wise, is it?"

"Because people will talk?"

"I don't care if people talk."

"You did last spring."

"Well, I don't anymore."

That pleased him. "Then why is it unwise for us to be alone?"

Anna lifted her chin. "We're attracted to one another. We're putting ourselves in the way of temptation by being alone in a private setting."

She had taken him by surprise. "You'd be tempted?" he clarified her statement.

She picked up her coffee and took a sip, then quickly set it back down. "It's hot!" she said.

He nodded. "That's the way most people like it."

She made a face. "Maybe we *should* talk about the dorm."

"We might as well get it over with," he sighed, withdrawing his arm.

"Have you asked Cindy and Melody to spy on us?" she began, without further prompting.

"Of course not," he said curtly. He hadn't *told* them to do it, but he listened to what they had to say, especially when they brought him news about Anna.

"They're constantly standing outside our rooms, eavesdropping on our conversations."

"Maybe they're hoping to be included in your perpetual parties."

Anna frowned at him. "I invited them on a couple of outings last year and all they did was sit in a corner and whisper. It seemed obvious that they had only gone so they could report back to you about what the rest of us were doing."

He folded his arms in an administrator's fashion. "Cindy was raised by an invalid mother. She was tutored at home and once she completed her GED, attended college online. She is socially backward, but that's not a crime."

"Are you familiar with Sally Carter's past?"

"Let's not turn this into a competition. I fail to see how Sally's past could justify her behavior."

Anna visibly bristled. "You just justified Cindy's behavior with her past."

"There is no comparison between Sally Carter and Cindy Wilson," he said. "Cindy is as innocent as a puppy and Sally … Did you read the letter?"

"No," Anna admitted.

"It was obviously written by someone with a disturbed mind."

"Or possibly by someone who had been so harassed, they resorted to desperate measures," Anna snapped.

He sat forward on the couch. "You've been brainwashed," he said with disappointment.

Anna crossed her arms in a tight knot. "I think *you've* been brainwashed! I live with them! I see both sides!"

He could hear that she was losing her temper, but he was close to losing his too. "You only see what those women want you to see!"

"And you only see what those *girls* want you to see!"

Michael gritted his teeth. "Technically, the whole matter is none of your concern. And if you haven't read the letter …"

"I haven't read the letter, but you haven't been a witness to Cindy and Melody's behavior."

"It wouldn't make any difference! They couldn't possibly have done anything to deserve that."

"You're wrong!"

"I am *not* wrong!"

"You *are* wrong! I can't believe you could be so narrow minded! How can you fire someone without even hearing their side of it?"

"I did *not* fire her! I told her I would be within my rights to fire her, but I didn't do it."

"You will though. As soon as you can replace her, you'll find an excuse to fire her."

He sat back and glowered at her. "Is that how you see me? Do you honestly believe I would do something so despicable?"

Anna pointedly started at something over his shoulder.

Michael clenched his jaw and waited for his temper to ease. "I spend more time listening to what goes on in that dormitory than I do arranging transfers for deserving students!" He went to the coffee pot and splashed some more coffee into his mug.

"I'm sorry," Anna said softly. "My mother used to say 'Now you've gone and made me get my Irish up.' I don't mean to question your judgment or stick my nose where it doesn't belong. Just that I think you should consider both sides before you judge."

"Look," he said, turning to face her. "Maybe Cindy is offensive to some people, but that doesn't give them the right to antagonize her. Don't you recognize the classic case of the underdog? Cindy has trouble fitting in, because she's had so little experience relating to her peers. Instead of trying to help her adjust, you choose to isolate her further."

He could see that Anna was furious. "How *dare* you include me in that ridiculous accusation! I have never done or said one unkind thing to your precious Cindy Wilson and I resent the insinuation that I have!"

"*My* precious Cindy Wilson?" he repeated. "And what kind of insinuation is that?"

"Just forget it!" Anna exploded, rising from the couch and slamming her mug on his desk, splashing hot coffee over her hand. Tears came to her eyes as she stalked to the door.

Michael put his coffee down and stood in her way. "Wait a minute," he said, grabbing hold of her arms.

"Let me go," she insisted, pulling away from him.

He lowered his hands but continued to stand in her way. "Let's back up and start over. We need to resolve this before you walk out that door." He waited for her to look up but she didn't. "Anna, listen to me. I don't care about Cindy or Sally or any of the rest of them. I care about you. About us. That's the only thing that's important to me."

"Could I please have a tissue?" she asked, touching her finger to her nose.

"Did you burn your hand?" He reached for her wrist and saw that her hand was streaked with red. Then he noticed something else – she had removed her wedding ring. She had been wearing it when she cut the grass … Had she noticed that the diamond

170

was loose, or had she taken it off because she was finally ready to move on? He cautioned himself that this wouldn't be a good time to ask. "Do you want to run cold water over that burn?"

"I just want to blow my nose," she sniffed.

He went to his desk, opened a drawer and withdrew a box of Kleenex. He held it at arm's length.

She glanced once more at the door, then came and snatched a few tissues from the box. "We'd better clean that up," she said, gesturing at the coffee she had spilled on his desk. "It'll leave a water mark."

He wiped up the coffee with a handful of Kleenex and threw them in the trash. Now let's see that hand. Maybe we ought to put something on it, so it doesn't blister."

"It's fine," Anna argued, but he had already come around the desk. He led her to the back of the room, past the conference table, to a small bathroom.

"We don't have bathrooms in our apartments, but you have one in your office?" she pouted.

He shrugged his shoulders, holding her hand under a spray of cold water. "The board doesn't want me to get very far from my desk."

She pulled her hand from under the water and scrutinized it. "I'm sorry," she said. "I didn't mean that, about you having a bathroom. I'm just in a sour mood."

"I'm the one put you in a sour mood," he appeased her. "Is this as bad as it gets?"

"You certainly got an example of my temper," she said with the hint of a smile.

It told him everything was going to be all right. "Now that I've seen you with your Irish up, I'll be more careful in the future."

Anna covered her mouth. "I can't believe I talked to you that way."

"Neither can I. If you were anyone else, you'd be on your way to the parking lot." He opened the medicine cabinet and removed a small white tube. "Let's put something on that burn."

"Don't you think adults should be accountable for their mistakes?"

"Yes I do."

"Then don't give me sympathy. It was my own fault."

"Are you willing to work through this?" he asked, squeezing a thin line of paste over the red spots and gently rubbing it in. He looked into her eyes, trying to read his own importance. "I can't take sides with your friends just because I care for you, Anna."

"I'm not asking you to. I'm only asking you to listen to both sides before you choose one."

He sighed with resignation. "Okay, tell me what happened to Sally when she was a child that's supposed to excuse her behavior," he invited, leading her back to his desk. "Do you want more coffee?"

"I don't think so." She huddled in a corner of the couch, then stood and pulled a few tissues from the box on his desk. "I hope I'm not going to need these," she said in a threatening tone.

He waved his hand so she would proceed.

"There's more to it than their unhappy childhoods, and I'm afraid you're not going to believe me, if you'll even listen."

"I *will* listen to keep it from coming between you and me. Our relationship is more important than my relationship with any of the other women, including my precious Cindy Wilson."

Anna rolled her eyes. "I care about our relationship too, but I have to answer to my conscience."

He nodded. He would nod to anything at this point, if it prevented her from fleeing.

"Remember the day you took me to the shelter? You said to change clothes, so I went back to the dorm after lunch. I ran down the hall to brush my teeth and when I came back, Cindy and Melody were in my room, going through my things."

Michael was shocked, but he knew she wasn't making it up. "What did they say? Did they give you an explanation?"

"I didn't want to be late getting to your office, so I didn't confront them. I figured there wasn't anything private or personal for them to find."

"Is that why you had a toothbrush in your pocket?"

She bobbed her chin.

"You do realize those are grounds to be fired?"

"I didn't, no. I think I burnt my tongue," she complained, touching it with her fingertips. "It's not my intention to get

172

anyone fired," she added softly.

"What else have they done?"

She took a deep breath and let it out in a noisy sigh. "They eavesdrop. They stand in the hall with their ear against the door. We've all seen them do it."

"What else?"

"Cindy called Susie's fiancé and told him Susie had been cheating."

Michael held up his hand. "I've heard this one. If you were going to pull a prank, would you use your own name?"

Anna made a face. "Cindy was upset because she thought there was something going on between Susie and Leonard."

"Susie is a very attractive woman. I seriously doubt she'd be interested in Leonard."

"She wasn't. He was the one chasing after her."

"If Cindy caused Susie and her fiancé to break up, she would only be making Susie more available to Leonard."

Anna shook her head. "I can't believe we're having this conversation! There ought to be a committee. Let them snitch on one another and the committee can sort it out."

"A committee," he repeated thoughtfully. "A grievance committee." He got up and went to the window, staring into the distance. He was hurt because Anna had jeopardized their relationship over such petty nonsense. "Is that all?"

Anna made a face. "They vandalized Sally's room. That's what preceded the letter."

He turned to look at her. "Define 'vandalized.' "

"They ruined her pc. At least, I assume it's ruined. They poured soda in the keyboard. They marked up her new comforter with permanent markers and destroyed her African violets. She's invested a lot of time in those plants. They could probably have won a prize at a county fair."

"What makes you think Cindy and Melody were responsible?"

Anna shrugged. "They were the only three in the dorm, besides Doris, and no one could ever accuse Doris of something like that. Gayle was away and no one else had come yet."

"Do you think Cindy and Melody are capable of that?" He returned to the couch and sat beside her, taking her hands in his.

For the first time, he realized that he might have been wrong about the two young women. "Don't be afraid to be honest with me."

"I think they did it," Anna said, "but I don't think they can be reprimanded without proof."

Michael remained silent for a long moment. If what Anna was telling him was true, he was guilty of a great injustice that stretched back more than a year. "Why didn't Sally call me the minute she discovered the damage? This is the first I've heard of it."

"Given the history, she assumed you would take their side."

He stood up and returned to the window. "If she had locked her door ..."

"I'm sure she did. We all do, since we've caught them snooping."

"Those doors are virtually impossible to ..."

"I know," Anna agreed.

"Gayle was away, you said?"

"Maybe she left the master key with Cindy or Melody, in case of an emergency?"

Michael felt certain she was right. Resolving all of it would take a lot of time and more patience than he could muster right now. He thrust his hands into his pockets and stared outside. "It's a beautiful day," he said wistfully.

Anna got up and joined him, gazing at the scenery. "Do you have to work all day?"

"I should," he said.

"Is there anything I could do to help? I can take dictation, or file ... I hate feeling useless when you're so busy."

"I appreciate the offer, but it would take me longer to explain what you should do than to do it myself." He watched as disappointment registered on her face. "There is one thing you *could* do though," he said, making up his mind to forget Casey's for a few hours. "I know of a person who is normally confined – would you be willing to take them out for a few hours?"

"Who?" Anna asked nervously.

"Me," he said, gratified when her face broke into a smile.

Before long, they were headed down the highway, to a small

174

town where a county fair was taking place.

"You gave me the idea," he admitted. "Maybe they'll have some prizewinning violets we can buy for Sally."

"That would mean the world to her, especially coming from you," Anna said. "I've never been to a county fair before. Are they like school picnics?"

"I guess ... Rides and games and greasy food. Will you ride the rides with me, or are you chicken?"

"Chicken? With four brothers?" She leaned back in her seat and stared at the sky – he had removed the top from his Corvette. "This car is more exciting than any carnival ride," she told him. "Do you ever put the pedal to the metal and see what she can do?"

"*She?*" he laughed. "No, I don't ever speed. What a nice headline *that* would make – Administrator of Casey's ticketed at 100 mph." He thought he would stop at a romantic overlook on the way back. In the darkness, far from Casey's he would tell her the story of his past. Like it or not, it must be done before he could try to take their relationship any further. "Are you going to tell me about Sally's unhappy childhood?" he reminded her.

"If you want me to."

"I can't be fair if I don't hear both sides, can I?"

Anna suspected he was teasing her. "She was one of nine kids. After her dad had a stroke, he lost his job and they didn't have enough income to take care of them all. They farmed them out to relatives, but none of them took Sally. She ended up in foster care."

"Oh c'mon," he said, certain she was making it up.

"Really," Anna insisted. Marianne didn't believe it either, but she found out it's true."

"Now I feel terrible!"

"Why should you? Her childhood doesn't make her any less accountable. It was wrong to write the letter, no matter what Cindy and Melody may have done. And no, I'm not switching sides. I didn't condone Sally's behavior because I condemned what the twins had done."

"The *twins*?" he said, glancing at her with a disapproving expression. "I should've guessed that Sally had a powerful motive. She had to know the letter would find its way to me." He reached across the console and took Anna's hand. "Thanks for trying to straighten it out. I wouldn't want this on my conscience."

"Thanks for giving me a fair hearing."

He laughed. "You know I didn't do any such thing. I'm sorry I gave you such a hard time."

"No more apologies," she said, sandwiching his hand between both of hers. She didn't let go until he needed to shift gears.

♥ ♥ ♥

He wanted to try every ride, leaving the Farris wheel till last. As soon as the attendant lowered the steel bar, he draped his arm around her shoulders and pulled her against his side. Around and around they went, until finally they stopped at the very top.

"What a beautiful sight!" Anna said, gazing over the countryside with appreciation.

"I was thinking the same thing," Michael said, but it was obvious he wasn't looking at the scenery. He caught her face in his hands and kissed her, gently at first, then with passion. And he went on kissing her until the car lurched and began to descend.

Anna huddled against him as she tried to catch her breath. She knew she had been right to say they must not be alone in secluded places.

They strolled the midway, lunching on hot dogs and sipping snow cones, laughing at the chant of the barkers who invited them to play games that were probably rigged. They finished the day under a large tent, where they chose some healthy African violets for Sally.

Anna gazed up at the stars as Michael drove slowly over the back roads, holding her hand whenever it was safe. She had never had a more perfect afternoon. It was nearly a miracle, given the harsh words that had been spoken beforehand. She hoped they wouldn't argue like that very often, but it was good to know that they could make up without hard feelings.

When they arrived at the women's dorm, he dimmed the lights and reached for her hand. "I hope you didn't lose the diamond," he said, rubbing his thumb over her finger.

She looked up at him and smiled. "There was nothing wrong with the ring. It just didn't belong on my finger anymore."

He traced the curve of her cheek, then reached across her to unlatch the door. "Thank you for what you did today," he said seriously.

"You mean for taking that person on an outing? The one who is normally confined?"

"That too." He chuckled. "You know what I'm talking about. It took courage to stand up to me on Sally's behalf. I respect you for trying to do the right thing."

"*Did* I do the right thing?" she asked.

"Yes you did. And from now on, you're assigned to my conscience. Whenever you see me turning a blind eye to something, call it to my attention."

"Even if it makes you angry?"

"I wasn't angry, I was jealous. Because of your affection for a group of women who bring me one problem after another."

"It's not that I ..."

He reached over and pressed his fingertips to her lips. "I wanted you to care so much about me that you wouldn't be willing to jeopardize our relationship for their sake. And I know that's not a healthy attitude."

"But it's one I understand, because it's exactly the reason I almost didn't do it." She stepped out of the car and smiled at him. "Thanks. Thanks for all of it. Thanks for a wonderful day." She slammed the door and stood waving as he drove off. Then she tipped her head back and stared into the starry night sky. "Thanks," she said again. "Thanks for a wonderful, wonderful day."

♥ Chapter 13 ♥

Anna had promised to call Marianne as soon as she was done discussing Sally's situation with Michael. She didn't remember the promise until she reached the third floor, but no one answered when she knocked on Marianne's door.

Anna retreated to her own room and sat down on the couch, where she spent a few moments remembering the highlights of the day. The bags of clothes were still piled where she had dropped them that morning, and she hadn't even bothered to hide the Tupperware containers filled with homemade cookies.

What was she going to tell Marianne? That Michael invited her to spend the day with him and in her excitement, she forgot everything else?

She pulled her phone from her pocket and sent Michael a text message, asking permission to tell Marianne where she spent the day. In less than a moment, he answered: *It's up 2 u.*

Anna got up and began to put her room in order while she rehearsed what she would say. Marianne would want details, but Anna didn't plan to tell anyone about the kiss at the top of the Farris wheel. And she wasn't going to say anything about the violets Michael had purchased for Sally either.

At ten o'clock, Anna knocked on Marianne's door again, but there was still no answer. She walked slowly around the third floor, certain the women had gathered in one room to play games and gossip. Part of her longed to be included, but another part of her understood that she could no longer join in. If she wanted to pursue a romance with Casey's administrator, it meant giving up her friendship with the third floor women who regarded him as an intimidating boss. While she was sorry, in one way, she was simultaneously relieved. Anna didn't fit in at the dorm, anymore than she had anywhere else. Though she had never been without friends, she was never completely at ease with anyone outside of her family.

Except Michael. There was something unique about their relationship. When she was with Michael, she felt as relaxed as she ever had at home. That was it – Michael felt like home. Not the home she shared with her children, or the one she had lived in as a child. It was more like the feeling she got when she stood at the window at night, staring up at the stars. It was almost a spiritual sensation, as if they belonged together. As if they were securely in God's will when they were together, and nothing could rend them asunder.

She yawned and went to the box beneath her desk, searching for a book to read. Then she put on her pajamas and took the book to bed.

♥ ♥ ♥

Anna's cell phone vibrated off the nightstand before she woke up enough to realize what it was.

"Wake up, sleepyhead," Michael said with good humor. "You're wasting a beautiful day."

Anna squinted at the clock. "It's only 8:00," she grumbled. "Technically, it's still night, isn't it?"

He laughed and that made her smile.

"I spent the past half hour with Sally and I thought you might like to be forewarned. She's probably headed for your room."

"You told her?" she moaned. "I didn't want her to know I had anything to do with it."

"Marianne told her you were planning to discuss the situation with me yesterday. I didn't really have an option."

Anna sat up and frowned at herself in the mirror. "Marianne promised she wouldn't say a word."

"I hope you didn't give *her* the number of your Swiss bank account."

Anna laughed and swung her feet out of bed. "What did Sally say?"

" 'Thank you,' at least a dozen times, which only made me feel worse. She apologized for writing the letter. She said it felt like some kind of warped justice, after what they did. I should say what *Cindy* did – calling Susie's fiancé. Did you realize he broke up with Susie because of what Cindy said?"

"Susie told me about it one night. She claims it's a blessing that she found out how shallow he is before she went through with the wedding, but ... She can't seem to move on."

"Should I ask Cindy to try to right that wrong?"

"No," Anna said. "Apparently, he's engaged to someone else now."

Michael's sigh carried through the phone.

"Are you going to talk to Cindy and Melody too?" she asked.

"In about ten minutes. Sally took pictures of her room and I'm going to ask them to reimburse her for anything they destroyed, including the pc. In return, I asked Sally to apologize to Leonard for the letter."

"Hopefully that will be the end of it," Anna said with relief. "What are you going to do with the rest of the day? Try and catch up on your paper work?"

"I was hoping to take a beautiful woman to lunch. Know where I might find one?"

"Definitely not here," she said, curling her toes as she grinned. "If you could see me now, you'd be frightened."

He chuckled. "I'm sure I wouldn't agree with that assessment, but in any case, you've got four hours to comb your hair and change out of your pajamas. I'll pick you up on the dorm parking lot at noon, okay?"

Anna didn't hesitate to agree.

She gathered her clothes and hurried down the hall to the showers. Yesterday, it had seemed like an impulse when Michael asked her to go to the fair. But today, he had called and invited her to lunch as though they were dating.

What should she say if Marianne or Gayle asked where she

181

was going?

She mulled it over while she showered. If she volunteered the information, it might sound as if she were bragging. But if anyone asked, she would tell the truth. The other women might dislike her for it, but she would rather eat alone in the cafeteria than continue to tell what seemed like lies.

She was surprised when the morning passed and Sally never came to her room. Then, when she was about to head down the stairs to meet Michael, the whole group appeared.

"Anna!" Sally said, wrapping her in a hug. "Dr. Grant said you convinced him that he needed to reevaluate the situation. Thank you! Thank you!"

"I figured you chickened out," Marianne said sheepishly.

"You're my hero," Tonya said, patting her shoulder.

"I'm not anybody's hero," Anna protested. "All I did was tell him what Marianne told me."

"Yeah, but if I had told him the exact same thing, he wouldn't have listened," Marianne said glumly. "Maybe you oughta give the rest of us lessons on how to talk to the man."

Anna lifted her wrist and saw that it was after twelve. "I'm sorry, but I've got to go. I'm meeting someone five minutes ago."

"Is the someone Dr. Grant?" Sally asked, glancing at the others.

Anna drew a deep breath. "Yes," she said.

"Are you going to get the dogs?" Rea asked.

"I don't know. Maybe."

"Is he taking you to lunch?" Marianne guessed.

"Ladies!" Tonya said sharply. "Listen to yourselves! Anna doesn't have to report to us every time she leaves the building!"

"He likes you," Sally said, watching Anna's face for a telltale sign that she was right. "He said you stood up to him, even if you had to get on a chair to do it. He doesn't ever make jokes, at least not to me." She gazed around the circle of faces, then tipped her head to one side. "I'm happy for you," she said firmly. "And for him too. I hope it works out."

"I do too," Rea said, patting Anna's shoulder. "Now go! Before he comes looking for you and gets mad at Sally for making you late!"

182

Anna pulled her door and checked to be sure it was locked. Then she raised her hand in a wave and hurried down the stairs.

"Sorry," she told Michael as she climbed into the Corvette. "They showed up as I was going out the door."

"I figured," he said. "Are you hungry?"

"Famished."

"Didn't you get any breakfast?"

"Are you spying for Gayle now?" she asked suspiciously.

"Oh no!" he said, laughing as he drove up the winding road to the gates. "Don't tell me you're hiding edibles in your room! I'll have to send in the bug patrol."

"I keep all my food tightly sealed in a box under my bed," she admitted self-righteously.

"If you had confessed last week, I'd be warning you that she'll find the box and throw everything away. But as of this morning, she no longer has a master key."

Anna covered her face. "She's bound to find out it's my fault. She'll be calling me to her office and reading me the riot act again."

He turned the car toward Briarton and Anna wondered where they were going. She hoped they wouldn't run into Helen.

"You're behind on the gossip. I made her move her stuff out of there a week ago."

"I did hear about that," Anna remembered. "And I'm sure she thinks that was my fault too."

"If they all think you've got my ear, maybe they'll treat you better."

"To my face," Anna sighed.

"Welcome to my world." He shifted gears and reached for her hand.

"Where are we going?" she asked, when he passed the Briarton exits.

"To my club. There's no snow in the forecast and they really do have good food."

Anna couldn't get her breath for a moment. He was taking her back to his club? Snow or no snow, she knew what *that* meant. He was going to get a room and this time, he would expect her to share it with him. It was her own fault! She had even admitted that she would be tempted if they found themselves alone!

"Anna?" he said. "What's wrong?"

"Nothing," she said, turning her head to gaze out the window. Maybe he only wanted to go to his club because the food was good and he knew he wouldn't run into anyone from Casey's.

"We don't have to go there, if you'd rather not."

"No, that's fine, but … It seems like a long way to go, just for lunch."

"There's something I've been wanting to talk to you about and …" He hesitated, then sighed. "I'd like to do it where we're not likely to be interrupted."

"So you were thinking of getting a room?" It felt as if her heart was in her throat.

Michael braked and downshifted. As soon as the car had slowed to a safe enough speed, he pulled onto the shoulder of the highway and stopped. He pulled up the parking brake and turned on the emergency flashers, then twisted in his seat, so he could look at her.

"Is something wrong with the car?" Anna asked, her hands pressed to her throat.

"It's a Christian club," Michael said, meeting her eyes. "Nothing like that goes on there. *Ever*. Even if I were the sort of person to take advantage of a woman in that way, they would not allow it. Is that what you thought, that first night? Is that why you got so upset?"

Anna wanted to deny it. She wanted to laugh and say, "Don't be silly!"

"Yes," she said instead. "To be honest, that *is* what I thought."

"And after all these months, your opinion of me is still so low?"

How she wished she could claim it was a misunderstanding! "I've had some bad experiences," she said, choking on her tears. "I'm afraid I've learned to judge every man by the same standard. It wasn't fair to you and I apologize."

Michael turned his head and stared out the windshield. "Is that why you stopped dating?"

She nodded, though he wasn't looking at her. "I would always warn them that I'm old-fashioned, that I believe sex should only take place between a married couple. And they would always tell me how much they appreciated my virtue. But as soon an the opportunity presented itself ..."

"Did somebody hurt you? Besides Bruce?"

She shook her head. "My brothers taught me how to defend myself."

"And were you often forced to do that?"

"No, but I thought I might have to. I would tell them 'no' and they would act as if they hadn't heard me."

"I will never try to force you to do anything you don't want to do," Michael promised. "I haven't, have I?"

"Just the oysters."

"You said you liked the first one," he reminded her. "If you had been honest ..."

"I know, I was just ... I'm sorry. It seems like I'm always having to say 'I'm sorry' to you."

"Ditto. We're both trying so hard to get this right."

"I'm afraid I'll say or do the wrong thing and mess it up completely."

"And so am I. Now ... Where would you like to eat?"

"Your club is fine." She turned in the seat to smile at him. "I would like to try the food."

"When we get there, I'll ask them to bring a copy of the bylaws, so you can see that I'm not lying."

"That won't be necessary. I believe you."

"If only you believed I was a better person than that," he said sadly.

"I do believe that. Now I do. I believed it then too. I just thought I was stupid for believing it."

"Thanks. I think," he added with the ghost of a smile.

The maître d' showed them to the same table and they sat in the same places, as if the first visit had been a rehearsal.

"What would you like?" Michael asked. "I'm sorry I didn't ask you that question last time. I was trying to impress you."

"Now you know that I'm not sophisticated enough to be

impressed," she said with a self-conscious laugh.

"I know you're too polite to refuse to eat something that doesn't appeal to you," he said seriously.

"That was only while I was trying to get you to hire me," she assured him. "Do all of the salads have anchovies?"

"None of the salads have anchovies," Michael assured her.

"Then what were those green things last time?"

"Avocado?"

"No, it wasn't avocado."

"Artichokes?"

"Ahh," she said. "I don't think I'd like them."

"You don't want to try one? We could ask that they bring them on the side."

She made a face. "For you, I'll try them. But no oysters." She put her hand on her stomach. "I swallowed them whole."

"That's what you're supposed to do."

"Then what's the point in eating them? It's worse than swallowing a pill."

Michael turned to the waiter. "No oysters," he said, obviously fighting the urge to laugh.

After their order had been taken, he sat back in his chair. "What's your dad like?" he asked.

"My dad?" she said with surprise. "He's nice. Very religious. When we were kids, he was strict, but fair."

"Is he affectionate?"

"Not very, but we all know he loves us."

Michael ran his finger around the top of his water glass. "I wish I could say the same of my dad. He planned for the three of us to have our own law firm – him, my brother and me. He still hasn't forgiven me for choosing to do something else with my life."

"Do you see him very often?"

"No. I haven't gone home for well over a year this time."

"That's sad," Anna said with sympathy. "What about your mom?"

"She'll stand with my dad, even if she thinks he's wrong."

"My mom is the same way. We'd never have a clue if she *did* think he was wrong about something."

"What was your marriage like?" Michael asked.

Anna sighed. "Could we save that conversation for another day?"

Michael looked away, but he nodded.

"We hadn't been married very long when he got sick," Anna said lamely. "I was barely twenty-four when he died."

"So you left home, had two children, and buried your husband, all before you turned twenty-five? You grew up overnight."

"I needed to do some growing up. I was very immature when I married Paul."

The waiter arrived with their salads, and the conversation turned to Casey's. Michael told her that he was going to take her suggestion and form a grievance committee at the women's dorm. Then he told her about several new programs that had been suggested, asking her opinion. Anna was flattered.

After the waiter poured a second cup of coffee, and took all their dishes away, Anna could see that Michael was nervous. She suspected he was about to talk about the private matter he had mentioned in the car and suddenly, she wasn't sure she wanted him to. What if he was about to tell her something that would come between them?

Before Michael could begin, his cell phone rang. He frowned and pulled it from his pocket. "I can't avoid it, with Tina being away," he apologized.

Anna tried not to listen, but it was obvious that there was a problem at the school.

"One of the students has gone missing," Michael said, rising from his chair and summoning the waiter. "I'm afraid I'll have to get back immediately."

Anna nearly sighed with relief.

It seemed they were both careful to speak only of neutral topics during the drive back to Casey's. Michael parked in his designated spot outside the administration building and promised to call her later. Anna felt as though she'd missed a date with the executioner.

♥ Chapter 14 ♥

The next few weeks kept Anna and Michael busy as they prepared for the start of the new school year. There were few opportunities to be alone and it was easy to avoid a serious discussion about anything other than the school. Once classes began, Michael was even busier, though he managed a trip to the basement every day. Twice, he said he needed a moment alone with Anna, and after they had closed the door to her tiny office, he kissed her soundly, and reminded her that they needed to find the time for a serious discussion.

By now, Anna was certain that she wouldn't like to hear whatever he planned to tell her. She was relieved when he didn't set a date, even while she tried to convince herself that nothing he said could change her feelings.

"This is Dawn Richards," Michael said one day, ushering a pretty blond into the Dog House. "Dawn worked on a pet project in a prison during her senior year, and she's a qualified AHT."

"That's great," Anna said, shaking her hand with enthusiasm.

"Anna oversees the project and you're to go to her with any questions or concerns," Michael said. "For example, if you should become infested with fleas, Anna will know what to do about it."

Anna wrinkled her nose at him. "Have you ever had fleas on you?" she asked Dawn.

"I have!" Randy called from behind her.

"Me too," Dawn said, giving Randy an appraising glance – they were around the same age. "It's worse than Chinese Water Torture."

Michael laughed. "Having never experienced either one, for which I am thankful, I don't have an opinion."

"The first week of school, I apparently took a few back to my dorm room and it got infested," Anna explained. "They can't reproduce from human blood, but that doesn't mean they don't enjoy a good meal wherever they find it."

Dawn laughed, even as she protested that it wasn't funny.

Anna sent her off to work with Randy, hoping they would bond and become friends.

"Aren't you concerned that they'll become a little *too* friendly and neglect their jobs?" Michael asked.

"I know how to keep them focused," Anna said. "I've got a reward system all worked out."

"What kind of rewards are you offering?" Michael asked warily.

"It has to do with who cleans the kennels," Anna explained, making him laugh.

Summer became autumn and the weather cooled. A virus went around the campus, and two of the AHTs succumbed, along with many of the students. By day's end on Friday, only two ninth graders attended class and Anna took them outside, so Dawn could catch up on her chores. Anna sat on a bench and watched the students work their dogs, while Charlie sat at her feet. Though he was otherwise well behaved, Charlie still greeted people by slapping his paws on their shoulders. Until she could break him of this habit, Charlie wasn't permitted to become a service dog. Anna was so attached to him, she secretly hoped he would never learn.

Anna turned her eyes to the window in Michael's office and imagined he was looking down at her. She patted her pocket, to be sure she had her cell phone, wondering if they might get together for dinner. She quickly searched all her pockets without finding it, trying to remember where she had used it last.

"Mrs. Brown?" one of the girls called, kneeling beside her

dog. "I think he's got a tick."

"Ewwww," the other girl said, jerking her dog's leash and backing away.

"Ouch," Anna told her.

"Huh?"

"That's what Ripley would say if he could talk. It hurts when you yank the leash."

The girl bent down and began to pet her dog, murmuring an apology.

"Is that a tick?" the student asked, pressing the hair back so Anna could see the lump.

Anna wasn't sure, and she wasn't willing to pick at it. "Why don't you take him in and let Dawn have a look." She checked her watch. "You'd better go in now anyway. The final bell's going to ring soon. I'll be right behind you."

Anna always took a quick walk around the fenced area at the end of the day, to be certain no equipment or trash had been left behind.

"Mrs. Brown?" one of the girls called from the door. Her voice had a frantic tone.

"What's wrong?" Anna ran to the door, chastising herself for dawdling.

"I don't feel so great," Dawn said, pressing both arms against her stomach.

"You look a little green around the gills," Anna acknowledged. "I'll walk you to the infirmary. Girls, put your dogs away, quickly please!" She hurried Charlie back to his kennel too, and slipped the latch in place.

Within a moment, the four females were traveling through the hallways together. The two students were delivered to a security guard at the top of the stairs, then Anna and Dawn headed towards the infirmary, passing the administrative offices on the way. Anna forgot about her cell phone until they were seated on plastic chairs, waiting for the doctor to see Dawn.

He was able to offer a diagnosis even before he took her temperature. "I'll bet you feel like you're going to upchuck, and you've got a headache."

"Am I gonna die?" Dawn asked, trying to stay upbeat.

"No, but you get to spend the night in the infirmary, so you don't pass that nasty virus on to anyone else."

As soon as Dawn was settled, Anna went looking for a security guard to escort her downstairs. When she couldn't find one, she went to Michael's office, hoping the administrator would have time to accompany her. She needed to make certain Dawn had finished her chores, then lock up and set the alarm.

Michael wasn't there, and neither was Tina.

"Tina's sick with that virus," someone told Anna. "And Dr. Grant was called away on an emergency."

Anna suffered a moment of panic. What if Michael's "emergency" was her failure to answer a call or a text? He might have thought she was in some sort of trouble and gone to the rescue. The security guards were probably out with the virus too. When Michael couldn't find anyone to check on her, he might have gone himself, leaving a waiting room filled with people. She knew she wasn't supposed to travel the hallways alone, but she decided this situation would be considered an exception to the rule.

She hurried down two flights of stairs to the basement, then ran along the hallway. It would only take her a second to grab her phone.

Dropping it into the pocket of her jeans, she promised herself not to put it anywhere *but* in her pocket from now on. She quickly checked the back door, to be sure it was locked and the alarm was set. Then she entered the kennels to check that the girls had securely fastened the gates.

Three of the dogs had managed to spill their water bowls and it would only take a moment to fill them. She checked her watch, and warned herself to hurry. The more she thought about it, the more certain she was that Michael would make no exceptions to the buddy rule. Even if she explained her reasoning, he was likely to be upset with her for taking chances. Maybe she should call him now and ask for an escort back upstairs …

"Some people never learn," a male voice drawled behind her.

Anna spun around, appalled by her bad luck. Once again, Bruce Carlisle had caught her alone.

"The AHT came down with that virus, so I had to take her to

the infirmary. Then I realized ..." She could hear the quake in her voice, and knew that he could hear it too. "I was just leaving."

"Change in plans," he warned with a wicked smile. "Now you're staying because we've got stuff to talk about."

"Like what?" Anna asked nervously.

"Like you getting me in hot water over nothing. How's that for a topic?" He reached for her, then drew his hand back, seesawing it in the air. "Don't touch her!" he warned himself. "She and her friends will lie and you're likely to go to jail just for looking at her."

"I don't know what you're talking about," Anna said, inching her way to the door. "I didn't get you in hot water. I didn't even tell Dr. Grant what happened between us last time."

"Yeah, but you did tell Marianne, the stupid cow. She told everybody I roughed you up. I haven't had a friend in this place since the day I met you."

"I'm sorry," Anna said, though she could hardly believe she was saying it.

"I've been watching for an opportunity to talk to you," Bruce said, dropping a slim book on the table. "This is my last chance and I'm not walkin' away from it."

"Then say what you have to say," Anna advised him. "Dr. Grant is on his way downstairs right now."

Bruce grinned. "No he's not. He's stuck with an office full of people and no secretary. We've got all kinds of time."

"What do you want to talk about?" Anna was scared, but she hoped he didn't realize *how* scared. She stood with her hands on her hips, trying to appear nonchalant.

"You and Grant. That's what I want to talk about. I heard a rumor that you two get together off school grounds."

"So what?" Anna was only a few steps from the door, but she feared he would lunge for her if she tried to escape.

"I figured you for a goodie good. I'm just surprised you'd mess around with a married man." He wagged his finger at her, shaking his head with disapproval.

Anna had asked Michael if he was married and he had answered that he was not. She didn't believe Michael would lie, especially about something like that.

"Gotcha!" Bruce said with obvious delight. "You didn't know, did you."

"He isn't married," Anna said with conviction.

"I didn't figure you'd believe me so I brought proof." He picked up the book and waved it in the air. "It's right here, the whole story. Even has a picture of his gorgeous wife, Jeanne Casey."

"Jeanne Casey?" Anna repeated, in spite of herself.

"John Casey's little girl. His only child. How popular do you think you're gonna be when he finds out his son-in-law is committing adultery with you?"

"We haven't committed adultery," Anna said, feeling her face grow warm. "Is she ... Does she have red hair?"

Bruce laughed. "Hard to say – the picture's in black and white. Wanna have a look?"

Anna knew she should say "no" but the temptation was more than she could resist. "I'd like to satisfy my curiosity, but you're going to hold it just out of reach, aren't you."

"You think you know me so well?" He tossed the book on the table and Anna caught it before it slid off the edge. She picked it up and flipped through to the end, then started over, turning the pages more slowly.

And there was Michael, standing with his arm around a tall, pretty woman with blond hair.

At least it wasn't red.

"May I read what it says?" she asked Bruce.

He shrugged. "Go ahead."

She read the caption first. *Dr. and Mrs. Michael Grant of John B. Casey's Institute.* Underneath the picture, a brief article explained that Jeanne Casey's father had started the school, then donated it to the state, retaining the property rights to give him some modicum of control. His son-in-law served as administrator and the couple lived on the grounds.

"This might be a very old picture," Anna pointed out. She noticed that her hands were shaking.

"That doesn't make him any less married."

"They could've gotten a divorce." She stared hard at the picture and decided Michael looked much younger. There was no sprinkle of gray hair at his temples, no lines of worry and fatigue around his eyes.

"You think John Casey's gonna let him stay on after he divorced his daughter?"

Maybe Jeanne Casey had died, like Paul. Maybe she had been killed in a car accident. But if that were the case, why hadn't Michael mentioned it? Why keep it a secret?

Anna closed the book and laid it on the table. She was sorry she had looked, sorry she hadn't told Bruce she was only interested in whatever Michael Grant chose to tell her about his past. "Why are you doing this?" she asked. "Why should you want to come between us?"

"Because I hate to see him make a fool out of another woman."

Anna tried to imagine Michael Grant breaking hearts at every opportunity. The image simply didn't fit with the man she knew.

"I know how you feel," Bruce said in a kind voice. "Would you like to go somewhere and get a cup of coffee and talk about it?"

"No," Anna said. "There's nothing to talk about."

"You need to vent, honey. I'm sure you feel like your poor little heart will never recover."

"My poor little heart is just fine," Anna said, taking a deep breath. "Thanks for your concern, but ..." Her phone began to vibrate and she pulled it from the pocket of her slacks. It was a text message from Michael: *I'll pick you up at 7.*

Before she realized what he was going to do, Bruce snatched the phone from her hand.

"Give me that!" she cried, trying to take it back.

He laughed and held it over her head, reading the message aloud. "So, the two of you have a hot date tonight, huh." He began typing a message into the phone, turning his back when Anna tried to grab it away. "*Made other plans,*" he recited. Then he pressed "send" and dropped the phone into his pocket.

Anna turned and headed for the door. She would run up the stairs and arrive in Michael's office only seconds after he read the message. He might be angry at her for going downstairs unescorted, but he would understand once she explained.

"Whoa!" Bruce said, grabbing her wrist before she could escape. "You're not goin' *anywhere*, Ms. Brown. Not until I'm done with you and that might take a while. I've been waiting for this chance a long time."

Anna was nearly paralyzed with fear. She remembered Michael's words: *even if we were the same size, I'd be able to overpower you.* She must stay calm, no matter what Bruce said or did. She stopped struggling and let her wrist go limp. Her brothers had warned her that some men thought it was more fun if a woman resisted.

Bruce released her, but moved in front of the door. "So why *didn't* you tell him about our last little get together?" He sounded as if he were merely curious.

"I should have. My wrist was black and blue."

"But you didn't, did you," Bruce said in a singsong. "Maybe because, secretly, you like things rough. Could that be it?"

Anna considered her options. She could run to the back door and push it open. The alarm would sound in three seconds, unless Bruce knew the combination. She calculated the distance and decided he would stop her before she was halfway there.

"I'm not gonna do anything," Bruce went on with a smile. "I just want you to go with me and have a cup of coffee. We'll talk, then I'll bring you back."

"I'm not going anywhere with you," Anna said.

"You're gonna do what I say you're gonna do," Bruce told her, moving around the table. He wore an ugly smile as he stretched and managed to catch her arm.

"Let me go!" Anna said, trying to wrestle free.

"No way," Bruce said, dragging her over the table, scraping her back against the edge.

"I'll report you this time!" Anna cried, making a frantic effort to free herself. "I'll get you fired!"

"Too late, honey. Today's my last day and spending time with you is my special farewell gift." He hooked one arm around her neck and pulled her off the table, then wrapped his other arm around her waist.

Anna was helpless. None of the tricks her brothers had taught her were of any use in this situation. She warned herself again to

196

stay calm. Sooner or later, he would loosen his hold and she must be prepared to grab the opportunity to escape. She must not waffle. Given a chance, she must think fast and strike with all of her might.

"This is gonna be fun," Bruce whispered near her ear. "I've been lookin' forward to it."

Anna refused to panic. She held very still, hoping he would believe she was giving up.

Grasping her shoulders, he turned her around so they were face-to-face. Anna had already formed a fist, tucking her thumb between her folded fingers. Without hesitation, she jabbed her hand at his face, aiming for his eyes.

"Ow!" he shrieked, covering his right eye as he staggered backward. "You idiot! You blinded me!"

For a few seconds, Anna worried that she might have actually damaged his eye. Then she remembered that she must run for her life.

She had hesitated too long. Bruce cupped his eye with one hand, while he clutched the neck of her shirt in the other. He twisted it, forming it into a noose as he forced her to her knees.

Anna clawed at the fabric with both hands as her windpipe threatened to collapse. There was no way to free herself, or to fight him off. Unless he let her go, she was likely to be strangled to death.

Just as she began to see bright lights dancing before her eyes, Bruce released her shirt. Anna slumped to the floor, wheezing as she struggled to fill her lungs with air. To her surprise, she could see Charlie through the legs of the table. The hair along his back stood up straight as he emitted a steady growl.

"Call him off," Bruce said. He was frozen in place, eying the dog with obvious terror.

Anna pulled herself up with the aid of the table and leaned against the wall. She drew slow, even breaths, resisting the urge to gasp.

"Call him off, I said!"

Each time Bruce tried to move, Charlie crouched, showing his teeth and snarling.

Suddenly the door swung open and Russell appeared. "What's

going on in here!" he demanded, glaring at each of them in turn.

"She poked me in the eye," Bruce told him, still shielding his eye from view. "And now she sicced that crazy mutt on me."

"Here, Charlie," Anna said hoarsely, holding out her hand. "C'mere, boy."

"Put the dog in his kennel and we'll take this upstairs," Russell ordered. "Dr. Grant can sort it out."

Anna's back stung and she still couldn't breathe properly. She moved slowly to Charlie's kennel, confused when she saw that the gate was tightly latched. She opened it and followed him in, stooping down and wrapping her arms around the dog's neck. "Thank you, Charlie," she whispered. "Good dog! Good boy!" She buried her face in his neck for a moment, then stood and backed out of the cage.

"C'mon, Mrs. Brown," Russell called from the other room.

Anna went slowly around the corner, looking for Bruce.

"You all right?" Russell said with concern. "You need to sit down a minute?"

"Where is he?" Anna asked, one hand encircling her throat.

"He took off, but that's okay. Dr. Grant will catch up with him sooner or later. You want me to get you a drink of water?"

"I'm okay," she said, grateful for his kindness.

"Then we need to head upstairs. We're short-handed on account of that nasty virus going around."

Anna walked slowly to the door, but didn't step into the hallway until he did. She watched while he used his master key to lock the door, then she walked close to his side as he climbed the stairs.

She didn't want to talk to Michael right now. She didn't want to admit how stupid she had been. She didn't want to talk to anyone. She didn't even want to look at anyone. She wanted to go back to her room and lock the door. No one could break down one of those doors, once they were locked. That's what everyone said.

"You sure you're all right?" Russell asked, as they approached the administrator's office. "Maybe you're comin' down with that virus."

"I'm okay," she said, in little more than a whisper. "Do I have to talk to Dr. Grant right now?"

"Did the man hurt you, Mrs. Brown? Because we oughta be handling this a whole different way if he hurt you."

"I'm fine, I'm not hurt," Anna insisted, though her back stung and she thought her arm might be bleeding.

"With Mr. Carlisle going off like he did, there's no need to bother Dr. Grant with it now, if you're sure you're okay."

"I'm okay," Anna said.

"Then you go on back to the dorm and I'll just file a report. If Dr. Grant has any questions, he'll get in touch with you."

"Thank you," she said, turning away before he could change his mind. She hurried down the stairs and pushed out the front door, then bent over with her hands on her knees, barely resisting the urge to vomit. How many times had her brothers lectured her about the kind of man who would force a woman? How many times had she rolled her eyes and lectured them about being overprotective because she was small?

Anna straightened up and regarded the distance to the women's dormitory – it had never seemed so far. What if Bruce was waiting for her, crouched behind one of the cars on the parking lot? She could hear her heart thundering in her ears as she started down the sidewalk. Then she broke into a run and didn't stop until she was in her own room, the door securely locked.

She looked around, and everything seemed to be in order. She opened the closet, but there was no one there. She pulled the chair away from her desk and checked beneath it. She went to her bedroom and fell on her knees and checked under the bed. Anna knew no one could squeeze beneath the couch, but she laid down and lifted the skirt, to be sure. Then she stood and looked around for other hiding places. Satisfied that there were none, she went to the window.

"Why?" she asked, staring stonily into the sky. Anna had asked the question many times in her life, and she knew better than to expect an answer.

She dug in her pockets, searching for her phone, before she remembered that Bruce hadn't given it back. She wondered what sort of text messages he might be sending the administrator.

Michael would think she had gone mad.

Suddenly Anna giggled, then she began to cry. She took the box of tissues from her nightstand and carried it to the couch. She huddled in the corner and drew up her knees, but it hurt her back to sit that way. She put her feet on the floor and leaned forward, keeping her eyes trained on the door. She began to sob harder as she relived the trauma in her mind, unable to believe what had happened, what *might* have happened if Charlie hadn't come to the rescue. Would Bruce have strangled her? Would he have held on until she passed out and then …

Anna whimpered and went to the mirror, studying the ugly red mark on her neck. Had he only meant to keep her from running away, or had he actually tried to …

She remembered the horrible feeling when her thumb nail made contact with his eye. It reminded her of wrestling the skin off a piece of raw chicken. What if she really had blinded him?

She told herself he deserved it, and far worse!

Charlie. Charlie had saved her.

She lifted her blouse and twisted, trying to see the abrasions on her back. It was red and raw looking, but there was no blood. She remembered her arm and pushed her sleeve up. The top layer of skin had been scraped away in a broad band from her wrist to her elbow and the fabric was speckled with blood. She quickly pulled the sleeve down again, and closed her eyes.

When she opened them, she saw that the woman in the mirror had aged. Anna thought she could feel crow's feet sprouting at the corners of her eyes.

She should've told Russell what really happened, but the thought of telling anyone filled her with revulsion. She didn't want to talk about it. She didn't want anyone to know.

Hadn't Michael told her that Bruce had been accused of such things before? One day he would hurt some young woman far worse than he had hurt her, and it would be partially her fault for letting him get away with it.

Today was his last day … but why? If Michael had fired him, wouldn't he have asked him to leave the campus immediately? Bruce must have quit. It meant he could go to another school and get a job and do the same thing to someone else.

She had to tell Michael. She had to tell him the truth. But how could she, since Bruce had stolen her phone?

Anna began to pace between the couch and the closet. What should she say to Michael? Should she tell him she had seen the picture, that she knew he was married?

No, she decided. She would only tell him about Bruce. Which meant confessing that she had gone downstairs alone. What a coincidence that the second time she broke the rule, Bruce had come looking for her. Would Michael believe it was a coincidence? Surely he wouldn't think she had planned to meet the man who had bruised her wrist! But if he found out that Bruce had brought a book containing a picture of him and his wife … How would she convince him that she hadn't agreed to meet Bruce downstairs so she could see it?

"He had a copy of that book," Russell told Michael. "The one with the picture of you and Jeanne."

Michael chewed his lower lip as he predicted Anna's reaction. "But you don't know what he might have said to her." It wasn't really a question.

"No sir, I don't. The book was lying there on the table. One of the dogs was out, and it appeared to be holding the man at bay. Mr. Carlisle was covering his eye. Said Mrs. Brown poked him."

"Was Anna upset?"

"She was extremely upset."

"She wasn't hurt?"

"She said she wasn't, but I'm thinking it might've been best if I had brought her straight to you."

Michael tried to imagine what Anna might be thinking. That he had lied to her? Certainly he had omitted the facts when he said he wasn't married … and then lectured her about being anything less than totally honest with him! He thought of her temper and felt certain she must be furious. What else could have prompted such a curt message – *made other plans*. He needed to think hard about what to say. Why hadn't he told her the truth in the beginning? There had been plenty of opportunities. Driving back to Casey's from St. Louis ... or the day they visited the shelter ... Why hadn't he told her while he was at her house, in the darkness on her patio?

"Thank you for letting me know," he told Russell. "I'll look in on her right away."

As soon as Russell had gone, Michael went to the waiting room and sent everyone away, asking them to reschedule their appointments on Monday. Once the door was locked, he checked his cell, hoping for another text message from Anna. *Made other plans* ... Would she give him a chance to explain or would her Irish temper let her turn her back and refuse to listen to anything he tried to say? She knew he had something difficult to talk about, after their trip to his club for lunch. She must realize Jeanne was part of what he had planned to tell her!

He headed across the lawn to his house, let himself in and went to the living room window. Gazing up at Anna's room, he could only see the reflection of the trees in the glass. Until darkness fell and she turned on a light, he wouldn't even know if she was there. By now, she might have gone to the cafeteria with her friends. Or she might have gotten in her car and headed to St. Louis for the weekend ... or perhaps for good.

He knew he would have no peace until he talked to her, even if only to hear her say she never wanted to see him again. He dialed her cell, only to be told that her number was unavailable. That meant she had either driven into a dead zone, or that she had turned off her phone.

He sat down on the couch and drummed his fingers against his knees. He could not sit here all night, wondering what she was thinking and feeling. No matter how much she might despise him now, he must see for himself that she was all right, that Bruce hadn't hurt her.

He got up and left the house, heading to the women's dormitory. He spotted her Volkswagen with an audible sigh of relief, then perused the other cars and saw that the women of the third floor were all present. If Anna was in someone else's room, he would find her. He would ask to speak to her in his most austere administrator's tone. Somehow, he would persuade her to leave the dorm with him, to go someplace where they could talk

202

with relative privacy. He would make his confession in whatever words he could find, then allow her to judge him as harshly as he deserved.

He knocked softly, then listened for movement behind the door. He waited a moment, then he knocked again. "Anna?" he called into the crack of the door. "I need to speak with you."

♥ ♥ ♥

Anna sat cross-legged on her bed, surrounded by used tissues. If she opened the door, he would see that she had been crying and he would want to know why. What would she say?

She knew she must tell him what Bruce had done, what he had apparently planned to do. But she *couldn't*. She wasn't ready. She might *never* be ready.

He knocked again, and called her name once more. If she didn't answer, would he pull out his master key and enter anyway? The thought made her scurry off the bed, though she stopped before opening the door. She crept up to it and listened, but all she could hear was absolute silence. Had he given up and gone? She didn't want him to think something had happened to her and break into her room, but she didn't want to talk to him either.

Andy had convinced her to bring the landline phone along, just in case. She went to her closet and rummaged through the boxes until she found it. Quickly, she plugged it in, then searched her purse for the card with all of Michael's phone numbers. She dialed his number at home.

His message ended and the beep sounded and she still didn't know what to say. "I'm not feeling well." It wasn't a lie. "I'll call you as soon as I'm better."

Once he read the report from Russell, he might guess that she was more upset than ill, but he could hardly break into her room and accuse her of lying.

She returned to her bed and pulled back the covers. Then she buried her face in her pillow and once more, began to cry.

♥ ♥ ♥

Michael stood in the cafeteria with his arms crossed in an administrator's posture, gazing around with a stern visage. He didn't want to talk to anyone unless they had news about Anna. He wanted to know where she was, and whether she was all right. If she wanted to postpone speaking to him, he could wait. He just needed to know that she was all right.

A crowd of women from the third floor went through the line, then sat together in a corner. They seemed as light-hearted as usual, as though nothing was amiss. If Marianne suspected something had happened to Anna, she would have approached him right away. Did that mean Anna was all right, or did it merely mean Marianne wasn't aware of what had happened?

When nearly everyone had gone, he exited out the back door and walked as far as the parking lot in front of the women's dorm. Anna's car was still there.

He didn't want to go into the dorm and knock on her door again. The other women had likely returned and might all be gathered in Anna's room. While he had every right to interrupt and insist on a private consultation, he wasn't willing to force her to talk to him. If he barged into the dorm and embarrassed her in front of her friends, it would only provoke her further and require additional apologies. He didn't want to risk the slim possibility that they could salvage the relationship, once her temper cooled.

On the other hand, what if she was badly hurt and *couldn't* answer the door? He shook his head. Russell surely would've realized if she needed emergency medical attention. He continued to outguess himself until he was incapable of making a decision.

He returned to the stone house and took off his coat and tie. He was on his way to the bedroom when he noticed that the message light on his landline phone was blinking. He draped his clothing over the back of the couch and hurried to the kitchen counter. He slid onto a stool as he pushed the button, and sighed with relief when he heard Anna's voice.

She wasn't feeling well ... Maybe she had the virus that had infected so many of the students and faculty and staff. He wished he could take her some juice, or check that she had plenty of aspirin. He went to the window and gazed across the campus to her room. One dim light burned, and he could see shadows moving across the curtain. Was she watching television? He stood there a long while – thinking, praying, rehearsing.

He would wait until tomorrow. He would call to ask how she was feeling and if she wasn't hostile, he would try to explain what she had seen in the book.

He changed clothes and went to his home office, though he knew there was little chance he'd be able to concentrate.

Anna stood at the window and prayed for comfort, but it didn't come. She didn't understand what had happened today, but one thing she *did* understand – she had brought it on herself. How many times had Michael told her he had good reason for the rules he made? He had even explained that each rule was made in answer to an incident. Why did she have to be so strong-willed?

It was pride. It had to do with being short, being the youngest, being a girl. She was always trying to prove herself, prove that she could handle worse situations than anyone else. Time after time, she had suffered the consequences of her own stubborn will.

She could apologize to Michael and promise him that she wouldn't do it again, but why should he believe her? She had made the same promise last time. He might even think there was more to it than a simple error in judgment. He might wonder if she had deliberately gone downstairs alone to meet Bruce Carlisle. And she wouldn't blame him if he did!

As if that wasn't bad enough, she had lowered herself to Bruce's standards and looked at the book. She remembered the thoughts that had filtered through her mind when Marianne said she Googled the administrator, trying to learn about his personal life. *It's none of our business*, she wanted to tell her. Michael had a right to privacy. Why then, had she looked at the book?

Why hadn't he told her he had been married? Maybe because his wife was the daughter of John Casey. Maybe because he didn't yet know her well enough to trust her with his secrets. She hadn't been willing to confide in him either. How many times had he suggested that she and Paul had enjoyed an ideal marriage? She hadn't corrected him, even though nothing could be further from the truth.

The truth. How many times had Michael stressed the importance of telling the truth? Even if they hadn't lied to one another, they had both withheld the truth.

"If he gives me another chance, I'll tell him everything," she vowed, staring up at the stars. What if he *wouldn't* give her another chance? Surely he would fire her this time. If he wanted the rest of Casey's employees to tow the line, he couldn't keep making exceptions for her.

How she had prayed to find a job after she graduated! She had gone from school to school, praying each time that *this* time, she would be hired. She had been so disheartened when no one was willing to give her a chance.

Until she came to Casey's.

Hadn't she known, that first moment, that this was where she belonged? The minute he took her hand. Even before he took her hand. The minute their eyes met ...

It wasn't the job – she finally understood that. It had nothing to do with pursuing her career. It was all about Michael. She was in love with Michael Grant and she felt certain that he was in love with her too. No matter what their pasts may have held, they were meant to spend the future together. She loved him and she would always love him. The job didn't matter anymore. What mattered was Michael. He needed her. He needed someone to watch over him, to nag him to get enough rest, so that the dark circles would disappear from beneath his eyes. He needed someone who could tempt him to leave the campus and go out and have fun. Hadn't he said it himself, when he asked her to spend the day with a person who was usually confined?

He needed her and she needed him as well. She needed to be needed. She needed to be loved and cherished. She needed to be teased about being short and complimented when she came up with a good idea.

"It's my Brigadoon, not his," she realized. Their story wasn't about a man, it was about a woman. A woman who was willing to give up everything to be with the man she loved. She thought back to their first conversation, about fate and chance and destiny and choices. It had all happened exactly as it should – getting lost so that she ran out of gas as she arrived at Casey's. The snow that forced them to St. Louis and gave them an opportunity for that first kiss. God had made His will clear from the moment they met.

But just as Michael said, their fate depended on their own choices. They could choose to accept God's perfect will or they could rebel and spend the rest of their lives living with their regrets.

There is *something going on between us. We shouldn't be surprised if it's evident to people, especially those who have known me for a long time.* Michael had embraced the relationship long ago. Hadn't he told her that he didn't normally socialize with anyone from Casey's? How many times had she asked herself why the handsome administrator had walked out on an office filled with people to summon her back into the building … Michael had chosen her last spring. All this time, he had only been waiting to see if she would choose him too.

" 'Be it unto me according to Thy word,' " she prayed. And for the first time in months, her heart was calm and her spirit was at rest. God knew what was in their hearts. He would give them both a second chance. *No*, she smiled. *Another chance.*

She was suddenly exhausted. She turned from the window and climbed into bed and fell immediately into a peaceful sleep.

At 4:00 a.m., she suddenly sat up, wide awake. Something was wrong. Was it one of her children, or was it Michael? Or had Bruce Carlisle snuck into the women's dormitory …

She must call Michael and tell him everything. She started to get up, then groaned as her back reminded her of her injuries. Moving slowly, she pushed the covers away and went around the room, turning on all the lights. She went to the door and listened, but she could only hear the sound of her own heartbeat.

She pulled on jeans and a sweatshirt and cautiously left her room. The lights in the hallway were dim, but she could see that no one was there. She scurried past the closed doors of her dorm mates, surprised to find Susie's door standing open. She was even more surprised when she went into the restroom and found Susie in the first shower stall, dressed in a white nightgown garnished with yards of delicate lace.

Anna opened her mouth to warn Susie about the athlete's foot fungus when she noticed something in Susie's hand. "What are you doing?" she said with horror, though the answer was obvious. Without thinking about it, Anna grabbed Susie's wrist, digging her thumb into Susie's palm, forcing her to drop the single-edged razor blade.

"I wasn't going to do it!" Susie sobbed. "Honest I wasn't!"

Anna wrapped her arms around the pretty blond and held on tight.

"He didn't let me explain," Susie cried. "He wouldn't take my calls. I sent him a letter and he marked it 'return to sender.' I didn't know what to do!"

"He doesn't deserve you," Anna told her.

"I could've told him about the twins, about the things they do to people. But he wouldn't let me tell him anything."

Anna didn't know whether to let Susie talk, or try to keep her from talking.

"God hates me!" Susie wailed. "Why does He hate me?"

"God doesn't hate you," Anna protested. "He loves you Susie! God loves you!"

"Then why is He letting this happen?"

"I don't know," Anna admitted unwillingly. "Sometimes we can't see the reason, but that doesn't mean He doesn't have one."

"I can't do it anymore," Susie said brokenly. "I'm so tired. I just want to go home."

"That's a good idea," Anna said, leading her away from the showers. "Should we call someone to come get you?"

"My sister will come. Would you call her for me?"

"Of course," Anna said, guiding her back to her room. She pressed her into a corner of the couch and looked around. There was an afghan at the foot of Susie's bed, so she brought it and tucked it around her.

"I'm exhausted," Susie said, pulling the afghan to her chin.

"Sometimes you have to say 'time out' and take a break," Anna consoled her.

"Time out," Susie announced loudly.

"Where's your phone?" Anna asked. "I'll call your sister for you." She hated to call someone at four-thirty in the morning, but she didn't know what else to do.

Susie yawned. "I don't know what I did with it. I think I left it in my classroom."

Anna patted her pockets, then remembered that Bruce had stolen her phone. It seemed as if the incident with Bruce had happened a lifetime ago. She went to Susie's desk and found a pad of paper and a pencil. "You want to come with me to my room? So we can call your sister?"

Susie shook her head and snuggled deeper into the couch. "I'll wait here." She recited the number, then closed her eyes.

Anna didn't think she should leave Susie alone, but she didn't want to argue with her. "I'll be right back. You stay put and wait for me, all right?"

"I'm not going anywhere," Susie promised, laying her head on the back of the couch.

Anna had only gone halfway to her own room when she heard a door slam. She turned and ran back, but the it was already locked. "Susie!" she called. "Open the door! It's Anna! Open the door!"

But she knew Susie wasn't listening. She was looking for another razor blade, or searching her apartment for some other means to put an end to her unhappiness.

"Jesus help me!" Anna prayed, running to the stairs. She needed to get Gayle to come and unlock Susie's door. She would drag her up the stairs, if she had to. There wasn't time to explain.

She reached the landing before she remembered – Gayle no longer had a master key! Michael had taken her key away because of the things Anna told him. If Susie died, it would be *her* fault!

She raced back up the stairs to her own room. The phone was on her desk, though she didn't remember digging it from the bottom of the closet. Michael's card was on the desk top, though she didn't remember removing it from her purse.

"Michael, come quick!" she pleaded, the moment he answered. "Susie's trying to kill herself. She locked the door! Hurry!"

"I'm on my way," he said.

She dropped the receiver and ran down the hall to Susie's room. "Susie!" she called. "Don't do it! Please don't do it!" *Where were all the other women? Why didn't they come and help her?* "Susie! Listen to me! God loves you, Susie! Please open the door!"

"Go away!" Susie called. "Leave me alone!"

"I'm not going away. I'm going to stand out here knocking all night. Open the door and let me in."

"No!" Susie shouted. "Just go away!"

Suddenly Michael was there. He tried to insert the key into the lock, but his hands were shaking too badly. Anna placed her hands over his, steadying them. He turned the key and there was Susie, huddled on the couch, staring at them with widened eyes.

"I wasn't going to do it," she told Michael. "Not really."

Anna sat down beside her, while Michael knelt at her feet.

"You're okay now," he said softly. "You're going to be all right."

Anna tried to remember what she had done with Susie's sister's phone number. "On my desk," she told Michael. "Her sister's number. She asked me to call her sister to come get her."

"I think we need to call an ambulance," Michael objected. He reached into his pocket for his phone, but Susie grabbed his hand.

"Please," she pleaded. "Please just let my sister come get me."

Anna could see that Michael was uncertain. "Call her sister and ask her what to do," she suggested, wiping away Susie's tears with the sleeve of her sweatshirt.

"She'll come get me," Susie said with relief, sinking back into the corner of the couch. She recited the number and Michael punched it into his phone. Then he got up and moved away, though he didn't leave the apartment.

Anna was glad. She didn't want to be left alone with Susie. What if she made another mistake? What if Susie tried it again and she couldn't stop her in time?

It was nearly an hour before Susie's sister arrived. Michael was watching for her, while Anna sat on the couch with Susie. The minute her sister appeared, it felt as if a heavy weight had been lifted from Anna's shoulders. She jumped up and hurried into the hallway.

Michael followed, as though he didn't want her out of his sight.

"I need to go and get the razor blade," Anna whispered. "I'm afraid someone will step on it and cut their foot."

"Razor blade?"

Anna was suddenly overwhelmed with the horror of what had happened. She stepped into Michael's arms and began to sob uncontrollably. She locked her arms around his waist and wept until her eyes began to burn from her tears. All the while, Michael held her close, stroking her hair with one hand, promising her that everything was going to be all right. When she finally settled down, Michael offered his handkerchief and she wiped her eyes and blew her nose. She looked up at him and smiled, then wrapped her arms around him again. She loved his scent. She wanted to ask him please to never change deodorant or cologne or whatever it was, because she loved the way he smelled. She resisted the urge to giggle at such nonsense. He would think he should call an ambulance for her.

"I was going into the restroom and she was standing in the shower stall. She had on that beautiful nightgown. I imagine someone gave it to her as a shower gift." Anna swallowed hard. "She had a razor blade and I knew what she was going to do."

"But you managed to talk her out of it," he said, smoothing her hair away from her face.

"I took it away from her. I had to."

"Anna!" he said softly. "You could've been hurt!"

She shuddered. "She said she wasn't really going to do it, but when I went to call her sister, she slammed the door. So I ran to my room and called you."

"What happened to your cell phone?"

Anna groaned. "Bruce took it. He wouldn't give it back. He's the one who sent you that message."

"*Made other plans*?"

She lifted her shoulders, unable to remember.

"He didn't hurt you, did he?"

"He *did* hurt me," Anna said, feeling her eyes well with tears again. She turned her back and lifted her sweatshirt, far enough to expose the abrasions and bruises. Then she pulled up her sleeve and showed him the scrape that was beginning to scab over. She looked up at him and saw how angry he was.

"What else did he do to you?"

"I poked him in the eye, and then … Charlie. He was choking me. He was holding my shirt. He twisted it so tight, I couldn't breathe." She traced the line on her neck as she remembered. "I don't know if he meant to do it, but he was strangling me. And then Charlie got out of his cage. I can't figure it out because the gate was latched. And then Russell came."

Michael wrapped her in his arms, but his touch was gentle, mindful of her injuries. "Russell said you weren't hurt. I didn't know …"

"I didn't *want* you to know … I wasn't thinking straight." She blotted her eyes with his handkerchief. "Please, can I keep him?"

Michael leaned back and looked into her eyes with confusion.

"Charlie. He saved my life. I think he saved my life."

"Yes," Michael said without hesitation. "We'll keep him and feed him steak every night."

Anna smiled. "I'm going to go pick up that razor blade. I'll be back in a minute, okay?"

He seemed reluctant to turn her loose.

When Anna exited the restroom, Susie and her sister were standing in the hallway, speaking quietly to Michael.

"Thanks," Susie called to Anna, then the two pretty blonds disappeared down the stairs.

Anna had the razor blade in her hand, uncertain where to dispose of it.

"Let's wrap it in paper before we throw it in the trash," Michael advised, following her to her room.

Anna folded the paper again and again, then wrapped it with tape. She dropped it in her waste can, and wiped her hands against her jeans. "Can I ask you one question?" she said. She needed to get it over with. She couldn't think of anything else until she understood why Michael hadn't told her about Jeanne Casey.

"You can ask me anything," Michael said seriously.

"You said you're not married. Are you divorced?"

He hesitated, and his expression grew pained. "I *was* married, a long time ago. My wife committed suicide."

Anna gasped, horrified that she had forced him to speak of it. "And now I did *this* to you! Drug you over here to deal with Susie. I shouldn't have called you! I should've called Gayle, but I didn't know. I should've called 911, or just waited for her sister to get here."

"No, Anna," Michael said firmly. "You did right to call me. I'm not upset because this situation brings back memories. I'm just sorry to have to tell you what kind of person I was." He held up both hands. "Don't feel sorry for me until you've heard the whole story."

Anna collapsed into her desk chair and looked up at him. She felt as though she were trapped in a nightmare that would never end.

Michael went to the door again, pushed it shut and turned the lock. When he faced her again, he looked pale and exhausted.

"It's okay," Anna consoled him. "Nothing you say will change the way I feel about you."

He held up his hand to stop her. Then he crossed the room to the window, where the sky was beginning to lighten. "My dad worked for the firm that handled John Casey's business. I had recently passed the bar and been hired. They threw a big party at a nice hotel and Jeanne came with her dad. She got drunk and made a fool of herself. I felt sorry for her. I got her a room and put her to bed. That was all it took for her to decide she was in love with me."

"Most men would've taken advantage." Anna understood why Jeanne Casey had fallen for the handsome young attorney who was also sweet and kind.

Michael dug his hands into his pockets. "Her dad made me a proposition. He offered me Casey's if I would marry his daughter.

213

She was older than me and she'd always been troubled." He glanced at Anna, then stared at something on the floor. "I can't tell you how badly I didn't want to be a defense attorney ... So I made the deal."

Anna tried to guess what had gone wrong. "It wasn't what she wanted? Jeanne?"

"She wanted *me*, but she didn't want to be here." He lifted his hand and waved it through the air. "After we were married, I found out why Casey started the school. When Jeanne was fifteen, she was caught shoplifting at a mall. She fought with the security guard and managed to unholster his gun. She fired and hit a little boy in the knee cap." Michael withdrew his hands from his pockets and laced his fingers over his chest, as though he might pray. "I found the file in the basement at the firm."

"She didn't tell you about it?"

He shook his head. "No one told me. My dad knew. He defended her. He said he *couldn't* tell me. Attorney/client privilege."

"Would it have made any difference, if you had known?" Anna asked softly.

He spread his hands, palms up. "I don't know. But this was, understandably, the last place she wanted to be. She expected her dad to make me change my mind, but John wasn't about to do anything that might induce me to ask for an annulment." He pushed his hands down into his pockets again. It seemed as if he wasn't sure what to do with them.

Anna stood up and started toward him. "Please," she said. "You don't have to tell me this now."

"Yes I do," he said. "I should've told you a long time ago."

Anna just stood there, an arm's length away, waiting.

"I don't think she meant to go through with it," Michael went on. "I think she timed it so that I would find her and save her. They were pouring the foundation for the house that day. She expected me back before dinner but things went wrong. It was late, almost dark."

"Are you the one who found her?" Anna asked in a small voice. She already knew he had lived through far worse than she had.

He nodded, and rubbed the back of his neck. "I've never forgiven myself. I traded her life for this, for a job at Casey's. So I decided … I decided that Casey's was all I would ever have. I made a vow that I would never marry again, that I would spend my life alone."

Anna went to him and this time, he didn't stop her. She put her arms around him, and she could feel how tense he was. She didn't say anything for a long while, but she prayed, silently, fervently. "Together, we saved Susie," she said, though she knew it wouldn't make any difference.

"*You* saved Susie."

"If you hadn't come so quickly …"

He leaned back, so he could look at her face. "What were you doing up at that hour of the morning?"

"I don't know. I woke up and couldn't go back to sleep."

"Because of what happened with Bruce?"

"I don't know. Because of everything."

"Now we know why Gayle didn't put you on the first floor," he said, pulling her close. "God needed you on the third floor, to save Susie."

"She said she wasn't really going to do it," Anna argued, feeling a tightness in her chest. She closed her eyes, as though she could block the image of Susie, standing in the shower stall with a razor blade in her hand. "I don't like thinking it was up to me to stop her from killing herself!" she protested tearfully.

"God chose you," Michael said softly. "It may be the reason He brought you to Casey's last spring."

Anna looked up at him while she mulled it over.

"He's been using you to save a lot of people at Casey's," Michael went on. "The students. The dogs. Sally and Susie. Me."

She sighed and laid her head on his chest.

"In the morning …" He stopped himself. "It's already morning," he said, with what sounded like surprise. He stepped back and took her hand. " I want to show you something. Will you come with me?"

"Of course I will," Anna said, and followed him into the hallway, down the stairs and out the front door of the dorm.

Dawn was breaking and the birds were out in force, chirping

and singing. Anna inhaled deeply. The air had never smelled so fresh and clean.

♥ ♥ ♥

Michael wondered if Anna was too tired to understand what he had told her. He had agreed to marry someone in order to have the job he wanted, or more accurately, to avoid the job he didn't want. He had refused to change his mind, even once he realized how legitimate Jeanne's objections were. They had done nothing but argue for days, and Jeanne had warned him, over and over, that she would not move to Casey's campus. That morning, she had thrown hot coffee in his face and promised that, if he went to Casey's to watch them pour the foundation for the house, he would regret it for the rest of his life. It had been an accurate prediction.

Would Anna wake up tomorrow and realize he was a monster? He would give her plenty of time to think it over. He wouldn't pressure her in any way. He wouldn't even ask what she was thinking or feeling.

"Where are we going?" Anna asked, as they headed towards the main gates.

"To my house. You're not afraid to be alone with me, are you?"

"I could never be afraid of you," she said. "Do you live in the stone house?"

"No one told you?"

"I didn't want to ask, for fear they'd think …" She giggled, a sound like music to his ears. "I didn't want them to think I liked you too much."

He turned the knob and stood back so she could enter first.

"Don't you lock your doors?" she said with surprise.

"Not when someone calls me in the middle of the night and tells me to hurry."

She looked around with sparkling eyes. "What a wonderful house," she said, going into the kitchen, circling the round oak table, skimming her hand along the backs of the chairs. There was a counter between the living room and kitchen and the local newspaper was neatly folded on one end. "Do you sit here to eat?"

"Sometimes." Generally, he took his food to his home office and ate while he worked.

She crossed in front of him and went down two steps into the living room, tilting her head to gaze at the massive stone fireplace. "It's beautiful," she said.

"I'm glad you like it."

"It's so open and light ... All the windows." There were high windows all around the room, capturing the light no matter what time of day. "May I see the rest?" she asked politely.

"Of course," he agreed, gesturing to the stairs. They walked up side by side and spent a moment in each of three bedrooms.

"Which one is yours?" she wondered, locking her hands behind her back as she studied the furniture and the pictures on the walls.

"None of these. It's downstairs."

"May I see it too?"

He wondered what she was thinking. Was she contemplating a future within these walls? Was it really possible that she could forgive him for what he had done to Jeanne?

He went down the stairs ahead of her, then turned into an alcove that led to the master bedroom. He waited outside the door while she went in to look around.

"You didn't take time to lock the door, but you took time to make your bed?" she said, crossing her arms and turning to hear his answer.

"I didn't actually go to bed last night. I snoozed in the recliner." He rarely slept in the bed. In fact, it had been weeks since he'd used it.

"You need to go to bed at a decent hour and get a good night's sleep," Anna lectured.

He smiled, touched by her concern. "Are you ready to see what I brought you over here to see?" He allowed a touch of impatience into his voice, though he was only teasing.

"I am," she said, following him across the living room. "Wait! What's that room?"

"My office." He leaned against the door jamb while she went

217

in to inspect it.

"Is that my hat?" she asked.

He had fitted it over a bust of Socrates, the white pompon dangling near the philosopher's nose.

"Yes. I'm sorry I never returned it."

She turned to look at him and she was smiling. "All right," she said. "I'm ready now."

He could feel his heart beat quicken. This wasn't the way he had planned to show her what he'd done. He had rehearsed his lines a dozen times, but now none of them would work. He took her hand and led her to the back door. "Close your eyes," he instructed.

Anna closed her eyes without asking why. He helped her down a couple of steps into the grass.

"Okay," he said. "You can open them now."

Anna opened her eyes and looked around. The sun was just coming up and the colors were muted in the half light. "I'm standing in your back yard, but … I'm not sure what you're showing me."

"Take your time," he said, with laughter in his voice.

Anna turned in a slow circle, until she finally realized what he wanted her to see. "Pansies. You've got pansies!" she squealed. They were planted all over the yard, around the inside of the fence, in scattered flower beds surrounding bird baths and wooden benches. "They're everywhere! I've never seen so many pansies. What an odd coincidence!"

"Anna," he said, folding his hands, making a steeple of his thumbs. "It's no coincidence."

She turned around again, and her mouth formed into an 'O'. There were hundreds of plants, all in full bloom. His back yard was a virtual sea of pansies. "You did this?" she said with awe.

"I did it for you. I've been working on it every day since I came back from St. Louis."

Anna's eyes filled with tears. "I'd love to have a picture. The kids will think I'm exaggerating. And my mother … she'll want to come and see it for herself."

He came and stood behind her, putting his arms around her shoulders, resting his chin on the top of her head. "I dug up the stuff I've planted over the years, and moved it outside the fence. I wanted to show you that ... that you'll always come first."

Anna rested her arms over his. "It's the nicest thing anyone's ever done for me," she said tearfully. "I don't know what to say."

He smiled and inhaled the scent of her shampoo. "You don't have to say another word. Your initial reaction was my reward."

"But after the way I've treated you ... How can you keep on being so nice to me?"

This time he laughed out loud. "After the way *you've* treated *me*? You saved me, Anna! You made me remember there's a whole world outside Casey's fence. You got me to go back to church. You thawed my heart. You taught me how to love again."

She turned in his arms and looked up at him. "I began to love you the first day, the moment I saw you the first time," she confessed in a whisper.

"I don't deserve your love," he said solemnly. "I'll never be good enough to deserve your love."

She shook her head with a stern expression. "None of us deserves to be loved. It's not about being good enough."

"It was a horrible thing I did, putting my career before Jeanne's happiness."

"I won't disagree. But it's not the worst thing anyone's ever done. You didn't know, did you, that she was *that* opposed to it? Before you married her, I mean?"

"I'm not sure it would've made any difference."

"Even so," Anna said. "You deserve a second chance at happiness. We all do."

"There are no second chances," he reminded her.

"*Another* chance then," she said willingly. "God is always waiting to forgive us, but we're so reluctant to forgive ourselves." She pulled away from him and went to the back steps and sat down. "I have a confession too. We'll get everything out in the open and clear the air and then we'll put it all behind us."

Michael hoped she wasn't going to confess that she'd been seeing Bruce Carlisle behind his back. He shook his head as he went and sat on the step. He thought he could forgive her anything.

Anna sighed deeply, then reached for his hand. "I don't think

I've ever mentioned this, but I have a sister, Nan, who has Down syndrome."

"Is she the one who's allergic to pets?"

Anna nodded. "I was the youngest, and very spoiled. Not with *things*, since we never had any money. But I knew how to whine and wheedle and get out of doing stuff. I was lazy."

"That's hard to believe," Michael said. "These days, you're a regular dynamo."

She glanced up at him with a grateful smile. "Thanks, but I was most definitely a lazy, spoiled brat. My sister Maureen was planning her wedding and one day she said to me, 'I'm glad you're not ambitious. It's good to know there'll always be someone to watch over Mom and Dad and Nan.' "

"How old were you?"

"Seventeen, about to graduate high school. I immediately got a picture of my future, working as a cook in the elementary school, like my mother. Coming home and playing with Nan every night. Nursing my parents when they got old and sick."

"Do you think that's what she had in mind?"

Anna lifted her shoulders to her ears. "Whether or not she meant to, she changed my future with that remark. I began to spend every minute thinking about what I was going to do to escape my fate."

"I hear what you're trying to say, but it's not the same thing as trading a marriage for the job you want."

"I'm not done," Anna warned him. She turned so she could see his face. "One of my friends wanted to become a psychologist and she heard that Paul Brown was going to give a lecture downtown. She asked me to ride along."

"So that's how the two of you met," Michael said.

"Afterwards, he stood at the door and shook hands and when it was our turn, he invited us to go and get a cup of coffee. He was very short. Not much taller than me."

"Would you rather save this story for another day?" Michael offered.

"I don't want to tell it at all, but I have to and I'd just as soon get it over with."

"All right," he agreed. "I won't interrupt again."

She drew a deep breath. "So we went for coffee and when my friend went to the restroom, Paul asked if I'd show him the city the next day. Here I was, some worthless high school kid, and here he was, some renowned psychologist, wanting to spend time with me. I took the subway and met him at the Lincoln Memorial. We did all the touristy things and then he flew home. But he called me nearly every day after that. And six weeks later, he drove to Arlington, we had a quick ceremony, and off I went to St. Louis as his bride. I wasn't even there for my sister's wedding."

Michael wasn't sure what to say. "Did you grow to love him?"

"I do now, in a Christian sort of way, but back then … I definitely did *not* love him. He was a very difficult man. He belittled me and criticized me and bossed me around like a slave. And he was far too strict with the kids, especially Andy."

"I'm sorry," Michael said, putting an arm across her shoulders. "You couldn't have deserved any of that."

"Well, I thought I did. I married Paul to keep from watching over the nicest parents who ever lived and my sweet sister Nan. I figured I deserved every bit of what Paul handed out. He was diagnosed soon after I found out I was pregnant with Paula. My life was a nightmare. There was no laughter, no joy, no love. None at all."

She sat up straight and touched her fingers to her eyes. "I didn't want to take care of anyone but myself and I ended up caring for Paul through months and months of sickness. Years really. Along with two small children. My mother wanted to come and help me … Can you imagine how *that* made me feel?"

"Anna …"

"There is only one way to live your life, and that's according to God's plan," she went on with conviction. "He doesn't bargain with us. We have to put Him first and when we do, we can handle whatever life throws our way. Even if we face a terrible fate that no one would ever wish for, so long as we're in His will, we can have joy in the midst of our adversity." She turned and met his eyes. "You're no worse than anyone else, Michael. We all make deals with the devil and then have to live with our regrets."

"Thank you," he said, though he still didn't feel that her

mistakes were as great as his own. "Are you sure you didn't make up the whole story to try and make me feel better?"

She shook her head. "You deserve another chance, Michael. You're always giving others another chance – the kids, the teachers, even the dogs. I remember something you said to me in the very beginning, when you were explaining your philosophy about the kids. You said we aren't meant to spend too much time dwelling on the past. We're meant to confess and repent and move on. You've done enough penance by now. More than enough. God forgives you and He wants you to forgive yourself."

"I know that, but …"

"No 'buts,' " Anna said firmly. "He's your Father! He doesn't want you to spend a lifetime suffering for something you didn't even mean to do. God loves you, Michael. He wants you to have some happiness now." She slipped out from under his arm and knelt on the step in front of him, resting her hands on his knees. "Listen to me, Michael Grant. I love you and I want to take care of you. It's why God sent me to Casey's. It had nothing to do with teaching history, or training dogs, or saving the children. The way I can help save the children is by saving you. You *are* Casey's. You're a hero. In heaven, the angels rejoice every time you get out of bed. Or out of the recliner, I guess I should say."

Michael was amazed by the sound of his own laughter. "I am *not* a hero," he protested. "Not by any stretch of the imagination."

"Yes you are. You're half saint. Everyone says so. I admire you completely. I adore you. I want to spend the rest of my life making sure you eat your vegetables and get enough rest. In a bed, not a recliner. I want to iron your shirts and bring you a box lunch every day and chase away all those crazy women who will do anything to get your attention."

Michael leaned back on the step and gazed at her, dumbfounded. "Are you asking me to marry you?" he said, expecting her to sputter and deny it.

"Yes," she said without hesitation. "Yes I am."

He wondered whether he had fallen asleep and this was the strangest, happiest dream he'd ever had. "Well then, the answer is 'yes.' I accept."

"Good," Anna said with satisfaction. "I'm glad we got that

settled." She leaned forward and kissed him, then she turned and sat beside him again, giggling with happiness. "I've never been so tired in my life, but I don't want to go to sleep, in case I might miss the best part."

"*This* is the best part," Michael said with emotion. "This moment, right now, is as good as it can ever get, this side of heaven."

"That's what you think," Anna promised.

The End ... for now!

Thanks for reading Another Chance. If you enjoyed it,
you might like to try the other books in
A Series of Chances:

#2 - Not By Chance
#3 - One More Chance
#4 - Take a Chance (e-book only)
#5 - A Good Chance (e-book only)
#6 - If By Chance (coming in 2016) (e-book only)

If you prefer standalone books:

Billie's Opportunity
Rescuing Ladybugs
Quicksand!
Maggie's Mondays
Miss Eden's Garden (e-book only)
Wrestling Ichabod (e-book only)

And for children - A Hole in the Fence (it's free!)